ANGELS ON TOAST

Also by Dawn Powell, available from Vintage Books

THE WICKED PAVILION

THE GOLDEN SPUR

DAWN POWELL

Angels on Toast

WITH AN INTRODUCTION BY
Gore Vidal

VINTAGE BOOKS

A Division of Random House, Inc.
New York

FIRST VINTAGE BOOKS EDITION, FEBRUARY 1990

Introduction Copyright (c) 1989 by Gore Vidal
Copyright 1938, 1940 by Dawn Powell

Library of Congress Cataloging-in-Publication Data
Powell, Dawn.
Angels on toast / Dawn Powell.—1st Vintage Books ed.
p.   cm.
"Originally published by Charles Scribner's Sons...in 1940"—T. p. verso.
ISBN 0-679-72686-1
I. Title.
PS3531.0936A83   1989
813'.52—dc 20   89-40281
                                      CIP

All the characters in this book are fictitious.

Manufactured in the United States of America
10   9   8   7   6   5   4   3   2   1

To

Max Perkins

DAWN POWELL, THE AMERICAN WRITER

Gore Vidal

Once upon a time, New York City was as delightful a place to live as to visit. There were many amenities, as they say in brochures. One was something called Broadway, where dozens of plays opened each season and thousands of people came to see them in an area which today resembles downtown Calcutta without, alas, that subcontinental city's deltine charm and intellectual rigor.

One evening back there in once upon a time (February 7, 1957, to be exact), my first play opened at the Booth Theatre. Traditionally, the playwright was invisible to the audience. One hid out in a nearby bar, listening to the sweet nasalities of Pat Boone's rendering of "Love Letters in the Sand" from a glowing jukebox. But when the curtain fell on this particular night, I went into the crowded lobby to collect someone. Overcoat collar high about my face, I moved invisibly through the crowd, or so I thought. Suddenly a voice boomed...tolled across the lobby. *"Gore!"* I stopped; everyone stopped. From the cloakroom a small, round figure, rather like a Civil War cannonball, hurtled toward me and collided. As I looked down into that familiar round face with its snub nose and shining bloodshot eyes I heard—the entire crowded lobby heard: *"How could you do this? How* could you *sell out* like this? To *Broadway!* To *commercialism!* How could you give up *The Novel?* Give up the *security?* The security of knowing that every two years there will be—like clockwork—that *five-hundred-dollar advance!*" Thirty years later, the voice still echoes in my mind, and I think fondly of its owner, our best comic novelist. "The field," I can hear Dawn Powell snarl, "is not exactly overcrowded."

On the night that *Visit to a Small Planet* opened, Dawn Powell was fifty-nine years old. She had published fourteen novels, evenly divided between accounts of her native Midwest (and how the hell to get out of there and make it to New York) and the highly comic New York novels, centered on Greenwich Village, where she lived most of her adult life. Some twenty-three years earlier the Theater Guild had produced Powell's comedy *Jig Saw* (one of *her* many unsuccessful attempts to sell out to commercialism), but there was third-act trouble, and despite Spring Byington and Ernest Truex, the play closed after forty-nine performances.

For decades Dawn Powell was always just on the verge of ceasing to be a cult and becoming a major religion. But despite the work of such dedicated cultists as Edmund Wilson and Matthew Josephson, John Dos Passos and Ernest Hemingway, Dawn Powell never became the popular writer that she ought to have been. In those days, with a bit of luck, a good writer eventually attracted voluntary readers and became popular. Today, of course, "popular" means bad writing that is widely read while good writing is that which is taught to involuntary readers. Powell failed on both counts. She needs no interpretation, and in her lifetime she should have been as widely read as, say, Hemingway or the early

Fitzgerald or the mid O'Hara or even the late, far too late, Katherine Anne Porter. But Powell was that unthinkable monster, a witty woman who felt no obligation to make a single, much less a final, down payment on Love or the Family; she saw life with a bright Petronian neutrality, and every host at life's feast was a potential Trimalchio to be sent up.

In the few interviews that Powell gave she often mentioned as her favorite novel—surprisingly for an American, much less a woman of her time and place—the *Satyricon*. This sort of thing was not acceptable then any more than it is now. Descriptions of warm, mature, heterosexual love were —and are—woman's writerly task, and the truly serious writers really, heartbreakingly, flunk the course while the pop ones pass with bright honors.

Although Powell received very little serious critical attention (to the extent that there has ever been much in our heavily moralizing culture), when she did get reviewed by a really serious person like Diana Trilling (*The Nation*, May 29, 1948), *la* Trilling warns us that the book at hand is no good because of "the discrepancy between the power of mind revealed on virtually every page of her novel [*The Locusts Have No King*] and the insignificance of the human beings upon which she directs her excellent intelligence." Trilling does acknowledge the formidable intelligence, but because Powell does not deal with morally complex people (full professors at Columbia in midjourney?), "the novel as a whole...fails to sustain the excitement promised by its best moments."

Apparently to be serious a novel must be about very serious—even solemn—people rendered in a very solemn—even serious—manner. Wit? What is that? But then we all know that power of mind and intelligence count for as little in the

American novel as they do in American life. Fortunately neither appears with sufficient regularity to distress our solemn middle-class middlebrows as they trudge ever onward to some Scarsdale of the mind, where the red light blinks and blinks at pier's end and the fields of the republic rush forward ever faster like a rug rolling up.

Powell herself occasionally betrays bewilderment at the misreading of her work. "There is so great a premium on dullness," she wrote sadly (Robert Van Gelder, *Writers and Writing*, Scribner's, 1946), "that it seems stupid to pass it up." She also remarks that it

> is considered jolly and good-humored to point out
> the oddities of the poor or of the rich. The frailties
> of millionaires or garbage collectors... Their ways
> of speech, their personal habits, the peculiarities
> of their thinking are considered fair game. I go
> outside the rules with my stuff because I can't
> help believing that the middle class is funny, too.

Finally, as the shadows lengthened across the greensward, Edmund Wilson got around to his old friend in *The New Yorker* (November 17, 1962). One reason, he tells us, that Powell has so little appeal to those Americans who read novels is that "she does nothing to stimulate feminine daydreams [sexist times!]. The woman reader can find no comfort in identifying herself with Miss Powell's heroines. The women who appear in her stories are likely to be as sordid and absurd as the men." This sexual parity was unusual. But now, closer to century's end than 1962, Powell's "sordid, absurd ladies" seem more like the comic Carol Burnett than the dread Alexis of *Dynasty* fame.

Wilson also noted Powell's originality: "Love is not Miss Powell's theme. Her real theme is the provincial in New York who has come on from the Middle West and acclimatized himself (or herself) to the city and made himself a permanent place there, without ever, however, losing his fascinated sense of an alien and anarchic society." This is very much to the (very badly written) point. Wilson finds her novels "among the most amusing being written, and in this respect quite on a level with those of Anthony Powell, Evelyn Waugh, and Muriel Spark." Wilson's review was of her last book, *The Golden Spur*; three years later she was dead of breast cancer. "Thanks a lot, Bunny," one can hear her mutter as this belated floral wreath came flying through her transom.

Summer. Sunday afternoon. Circa 1950. Dawn Powell's duplex living room at 35 East Ninth Street. The hostess presides over an elliptical aquarium filled with gin, a popular drink of the period known as the martini. In attendance Coby—just Coby to me for years, her eternal escort; he is neatly turned out in a blue blazer, rosy-faced, sleek silver hair combed straight back. Coby can talk with charm on any subject. The fact that he might be Dawn's lover has never crossed my mind. They are so old. A handsome young poet lies on the floor, literally at the feet of E.E. Cummings and his wife, Marion, who ignore him. Dawn casts an occasional maternal eye in the boy's direction, but the eye is more that of the mother of a cat or a dog apt to make a nuisance. Conversation flows. Gin flows. Marion Cummings is beautiful;

so indeed is her husband, his eyes a faded denim blue. Coby is in great form. Though often his own subject, he records not boring triumphs but improbable disasters. He is always broke, and a once distinguished wardrobe is now in the hands of those gay deceivers, his landladies. On this afternoon, at home, Dawn is demure, thoughtful. "Why," she suddenly asks, eyes on the long body beside the coffee table, "do they never have floors of their own to sleep on?"

Cummings explains that since the poet lives in Philadelphia he is too far from his own floor to sleep on it. Not long after, the young poet and I paid a call on the Cummingses. We were greeted at the door by an edgy Marion. "I'm afraid you can't come in." Behind her an unearthly high scream sounded. "Dylan Thomas just died," she explained. "Is that Mr. Cummings screaming?" asked the poet politely as the keening began on an even higher note. "No," said Marion. "That is not Mr. Cummings. That is Mrs. Thomas."

But for the moment, in my memory, the poet is forever asleep on the floor while on a balcony high up in the second story of Dawn's living room a gray, blurred figure appears and stares down at us. "Who," I ask, "is that?"

Dawn gently, lovingly, stirs the martinis, squints her eyes, says, "My husband, I think. It *is* Joe, isn't it, Coby?" She turns to Coby, who beams and waves at the gray man, who withdraws. "Of course it is," says Coby. "Looking very fit." I realize, at last, that this is a *ménage à trois* in Greenwich Village. My martini runs over.

To date the only study of Dawn Powell is a doctoral dissertation by one Judith Faye Pett (University of Iowa, 1981). Ms. Pett has gathered together a great deal of biographical material, for which one is grateful. I am happy to know, at last, that the amiable Coby's proper name was Coburn Gilman, and I am sad to learn that he survived Dawn by only two years. The husband on the balcony was Joseph Gousha, or Goushé, whom she married on November 20, 1920. He was musical; she literary, with a talent for the theater. A son was born retarded. Over the years a fortune was spent on schools and nurses. To earn the fortune, Powell did every sort of writing, from interviews in the press to stories for ladies magazines to plays that tended not to be produced to a cycle of novels about the Midwest, followed by a cycle of New York novels, where she came into her own, dragging our drab literature screaming behind her. As doyenne of the Village, she held court in the grill of the Lafayette Hotel—for elegiasts, the Lafayette was off Washington Square at University Place and Ninth Street.

Powell also runs like a thread of purest brass through Edmund Wilson's *The Thirties*: "It was closing time in the Lafayette Grill, and Coby Gilman was being swept out from under the table. Niles Spencer had been stuttering for five minutes, and Dawn Powell gave him a crack on the jaw and said, '*Nuts* is the word you're groping for.'" Also, "[Peggy Bacon] told me about Joe Gousha's attacking her one night at a party and trying to tear her clothes off....I suggested that Joe had perhaps simply thought that this was the thing to do in Dawn's set. She said, 'Yes: He thought it was a social obligation.'" Powell also said that "Dotsy's husband was very much excited because the Prince of Wales was wearing a zipper fly, a big thing in the advertising business." A footnote to this text says that Dawn Powell and Wilson carried on a correspondence in which she was Mrs. Humphrey

Ward and he "a seedy literary man named Wigmore." Later, there is a very muddled passage in which, for reasons not quite clear, James Thurber tells Dawn Powell that she does not *deserve* to be in the men's room. That may well be what it was all about.

Like most writers, Powell wrote of what she knew. Therefore, certain themes recur, while the geography does not vary from that of her actual life. As a child, she and two sisters were shunted about from one midwestern farm or small town to another by a father who was a salesman on the road (her mother died when she was six). The maternal grandmother made a great impression on her and predisposed her toward boardinghouse life (as a subject, not a residence). Indomitable old women, full of rage and good jokes, occur in both novel cycles. Powell's father remarried when she was twelve, and Dawn and her sisters went to live on the stepmother's farm. "My stepmother, one day, burned up all the stories I was writing, a form of discipline I could not endure. With thirty cents earned by picking berries I ran away, ending up in the home of a kindly aunt in Shelby, Ohio." After graduation from the local high school, she worked her way through Lake Erie College for Women in Painesville, Ohio. I once gave a commencement address there and was struck by how red-brick New England Victorian the buildings were. I also found out all that I could about their famous alumna. I collected some good stories to tell her. But by the time I got back to New York she was dead.

Powell set out to be a playwright. One play ended up as a movie while another, *Big Night*, was done by the Group Theater in 1933. But it was World War I, not the theater, that got Powell out of Ohio and to New York in 1918, as a member of the naval reserve. The war ended before her uniform arrived. Powell wrote publicity. Married. Wrote advertising copy (at the time, Goushé or Gousha was an account executive with an advertising agency). Failure in the theater and need for money at home led her to novel writing and the total security of that five-hundred-dollar advance each of us relied on for so many years.

Angels on Toast was the first of Powell's novels to become, if not world famous, *the* book for those who wanted to inhabit the higher, wittier realms of Manhattan where Truman Capote was, later and less wittily, to camp out. It is 1940. War had begun to darken the skyline. But the city's magic is undiminished for the provincial Ebie, a commercial artist whose mother is in the great line of Powell eccentrics. Ebie lives with another working woman, Honey, who "was a virgin (at least you couldn't prove she wasn't), and was as proud as punch of it. You would have thought it was something that had been in the family for generations." But Ebie and Honey need each other to talk at, and in a tavern

> where O. Henry used to go...they'd sit in the dark smoked-wood booth drinking old-fashioneds and telling each other things they certainly wished later they had never told and bragging about their families, sometimes making them hot-stuff socially back home, the next time making them romantically on the wrong side of the tracks. The family must have been on wheels back in the Middle West, whizzing back and forth across tracks at a mere word from the New York daughters.

Brooding over the novel is the downtown Hotel Ellery, where for seventeen dollars a week Ebie's mother, Mrs. Vane, lives in contented squalor.

> BAR and GRILL. It was the tavern entrance to a somewhat mediaeval looking hotel, whose time-and-soot-blackened façade was frittered with fire-escapes,...its dark oak wainscoting rising high to meet grimy black walls, its ship-windows covered with heavy pumpkin-colored chintz....Once in you were in for no mere moment.

In its remoteness, this world before television could just as easily be that of Walter Scott.

It is also satisfying that in these New York novels the city that was plays so pervasive a role. This sort of hotel, meticulously described, evokes lost time in a way that the novel's bumptious twentieth-century contemporary, early talking-movies don't.

> Another curious thing about these small, venerable, respectable hotels—there seemed no appeal here to the average customer. BAR and GRILL, for instance, appealed to seemingly genteel widows and spinsters of small incomes.... Then there were those tired flashes in the pan, the one-shot celebrities, and on the other hand there was a gayer younger group whose loyalty to the BAR and GRILL was based on the cheapness of its martinis. Over their simple dollar lunches (four martinis and a sandwich) this livelier set snickered at the older residents.

Ebie wants to take her mother away from all this so that they can live together in Connecticut. Mrs. Vane would rather die. She prefers to lecture the bar on poetry. There is also a plot: two men in business, with wives. One has an affair with Ebie. By now, Powell has mastered her own method. Essay beginnings to chapters work smartly:

> In the dead of night wives talked to their husbands, in the dark they talked and talked while the clock on the bureau ticked sleep away, and the last street cars clanged off on distant streets to remoter suburbs, where in new houses bursting with mortgages and the latest conveniences wives talked in the dark, and talked and talked.

The prose is now less easygoing than it was in the early novels, and there is a conscious tightening of the language although, to the end, Powell thought one thing was different *than* another while always proving not her mettle but *metal*. *Angels on Toast* ends with a cheerfulness worthy of Shakespeare in his *Midsummer Night's Dream* mood: everyone where he or she should be. I can think of no one else who has got so well the essence of that first war-year before we all went away to the best years of no one's life.

The Wicked Pavilion (1954) is the Café Julien is the Lafayette Hotel of real life. The title is from *The Creevey Papers* and refers to the Prince Regent's Brighton Pavilion, where the glamorous and *louche* wait upon a mad royal. From Powell's earlier books, the writer Dennis Orphen opens and closes the story in his mysterious way. He takes no real part in the plot. He is simply there, watching the not-so-magic wheel

turn as the happy island grows sad. For him, as for Powell,
the café is central to his life. Here he writes, sees friends,
observes the vanity fair. Powell has now become masterful in
her setting of scenes. The essays—preludes, overtures—are
both witty and sadly wise. She also got the number to
Eisenhower's America as she brings together in this penulti-
mate rout all sorts of figures from earlier novels, now grown
old: Okie is still a knowing man-about-town and author of
the definitive works on the painter Marius, Andy Cal-
lingham is still a world-famous novelist (based on Ernest
Hemingway), serene in his uncontagious self-love, and the
recurrent Peggy Guggenheim figure is back again as Cynthia, an art gallery dealer. One plot is young love: Rick and
Ellenora who met at the Café Julien in wartime and never got
enough of it or of each other or of "the happy island," Powell's unironic phrase for the Manhattan that she first knew.

A new variation on the Powell young woman is Jerry,
clean-cut, straightforward, and on the make. But her peculiar wholesomeness does not inspire men to give her presents; yet "the simple truth was that with her increasingly
expensive tastes she really could not afford to work. . . . As for
settling for the safety of marriage, that seemed the final defeat, synonymous in Jerry's mind with asking for the last
rites." An aristocratic lady, Elsie, tries unsuccessfully to
launch her. Elsie's brother, Wharton, and sister-in-law,
Nita, are fine comic emblems of respectable marriage. In
fact, Wharton is one of Powell's truly great and original
monsters:

> Wharton had such a terrific reputation for ef-
> ficiency that many friends swore that the reason

his nose changed colors before your very eyes was because of an elaborate Rimbaud color code, indicating varied reactions to his surroundings....Ah, what a stroke of genius it had been for him to have found Nita! How happy he had been on his honeymoon and for years afterward basking in the safety of Nita's childish innocence where his intellectual shortcomings, sexual coldness and caprices—indeed his basic ignorance—would not be discovered....He was well aware that many men of his quixotic moods preferred young boys, but he dreaded to expose his inexperience to one of his own sex, and after certain cautious experiments realized that his anemic lusts were canceled by his overpowering fear of gossip....Against the flattering background of Nita's delectable purity he blossomed forth as the all-round-He-man, the Husband who knows everything....He soon taught her that snuggling, hand-holding and similar affectionate demonstrations were kittenish and vulgar. He had read somewhere, however, that breathing into a woman's ear or scratching her at the nape of her neck drove her into complete ecstasy....In due course Nita bore him four daughters, a sort of door prize for each time he attended.

The party is given by Cynthia now, and it rather resembles Proust's last roundup: "There are people here who have been dead twenty years," someone observes, including "the bore that walks like a man." There is a sense of closing time; people settle for what they can get. "We get sick of clinging vines, he thought, but the day comes when we suspect that the vines are all that hold our rotting branches together."

In 1962 Powell published her last and perhaps most appealing novel, *The Golden Spur*. As so often was the case with Powell, the protagonist is male. In this case a young man from Silver City, Ohio, called Jonathan Jaimison. He has come to the city to find his father. Apparently twenty-six years earlier his mother, Connie, had had a brief fling with a famous man in the Village; pregnant, she came home and married a Mr. Jaimison. The book opens with a vigorous description of Wanamaker's department store being torn down. Powell is now rather exuberant about the physical destruction of her city (she wrote this last book in her midsixties, when time was doing the same to her). But there are still a few watering holes from the twenties, and one of them is The Golden Spur, where Connie mingled with the bohemians.

Jonathan stays at the Hotel De Long, which sounds like the Vanderbilt, a star of many of Powell's narratives. Jonathan, armed with Connie's cryptic diary, has a number of names that might be helpful. One is that of Claire Van Orphen, a moderately successful writer for whom Connie did some typing. Claire gives Jonathan possible leads; meanwhile, his presence has rejuvenated her. Her career is revived with the help of a professionally failed writer who studies all of Claire's ladies' magazine short stories of yesteryear; he then reverses the moral angle:

> "In the old days the career girl who supported the family was the heroine, and the idle wife was the baddie," Claire said gleefully. "And now it's the

other way around. In the soap operas, the career girl is the baddie, the wife is the goodie because she's better for *business*....Well, you were right. CBS has bought the two [stories] you fixed, and Hollywood is interested."

Powell herself was writing television plays in the age of Eisenhower and no doubt had made this astonishing discovery on her own.

Finally Cassie, Peggy Guggenheim yet again, makes her appearance, and the famous Dawn Powell party assembles for the last time. There are nice period touches. Girls from Bennington are everywhere, while Cassie herself "was forty-three—well, all right, forty-eight, if you're going to count every lost week end." She takes a fancy to Jonathan and hires him to work at her gallery. By the end of the novel, Jonathan figures out not only his paternity but his maternity and, best of all, himself.

The quest is over. Identity fixed. The party over, Jonathan heads downtown, "perhaps to 'the Spur,' where they could begin all over." On that blithe note Powell's life and lifework end, and the magic of that period is gone—except for the novels of Dawn Powell.

Grateful acknowledgment is made to the following people, who helped in the preparation of this volume: Howard Frisch, Al Silverman, Jacqueline Rice, Gore Vidal, and the staff at the Elmer Holmes Bobst Library at New York University.

ANGELS ON TOAST

ALL CHARACTERS IN THIS BOOK

ARE FICTITIOUS

I

THERE was a bottle of Robinson's B.E.B. right in Lou's bag but Jay Oliver wasn't interested.

"The hell with cooping up here in the compartment," he said. "Let's go down to the club car. I like to see people."

"I don't," said Lou. "I got things on my mind."

The porter brought the ice, glasses and soda.

"Okay," sighed Jay. "I might as well stick around a minute."

He sat down and kicked his shoes off. They lay on the floor jauntily toeing out, reddish brown, sleek, very much Jay Oliver. He crossed his stockinged feet on the seat opposite and viewed them complacently, marked the neat way the crimson clocks in the gray hose matched the herring-bone stripe in his blue suit.

"Paid four fifty for these socks," he stated briefly.

Lou took his suit coat off and hung it in the closet. He had put on about ten pounds in the last year, but there was something about a little extra weight that gave a man a certain authority, he thought. All right so long as it didn't get him in the middle and he'd have to watch it so that he didn't blow up like his old man had. One ninety was all right for five-eleven—he could carry it because of his big shoulders—but two hundred was the beginning of the end. Even this ten pounds made him a touch short of wind and made sitting around in his clothes uncomfortable. He undid his collar—he wore a separate white with his new imported colored shirts,—hung up the tie, a Sulka clover-leaf pattern, over the hanger, then sat down beside Jay's feet.

"Some shirt there, Lou," said Jay. "What'd it set you back?"

"Eighteen bucks," said Lou. "I swore I'd never wear a pink shirt but it was the goods that got me. Feel that material."

"Say!"

Jay leafed over the *American* and folded it at the sporting page so that the crouching figure of a Northwestern star, football under arm, seemed ready to whiz past Lou in a perpetual touchdown. Jay was still a little sore because Lou wouldn't wait over for the fight that night and plane out the next day, but he'd get over it. Lou hadn't told him that he had his reasons for booking the General. You don't have to tell all you know.

"If we got to take a train, why couldn't we have taken the bedroom train on the Century?" complained Jay. "Give me the New York Central any day. I took the Commodore Vanderbilt out of New York last month and slept like a baby. Not a jolt."

"Ah, you can't beat the General," said Lou. "You got to admit the Pennsylvania's got a smoother roadbed."

So far as he was concerned Jay could get out if he wanted to and let him do some thinking. Jay was all right, Jay was his best friend but a little bit of Jay went a long way. Lately, although their businesses were not the same, they seemed to be in everything together, and you can't have even a best friend knowing every damn move you make. Or was Jay his best friend? Jay was Whittleby Cotton and Whittleby Cotton was really his best friend. If Jay was

2

ever eased out there his successor would be Lou's best friend.

"What's your wife think of your opening a New York branch?" Jay asked.

"What would I be telling her for?" Lou wanted to know. "I don't go round looking for trouble."

He was still disturbed by Mary refusing to say good-bye to him. He had been jumping in and out of town at a minute's notice for years, hell, that was his business, and she had never uttered a peep until this morning. What did she know? What did she suspect?

"You just got back from New York three days ago," she had said. "We've scarcely had one evening together since I got back from my cruise. I can't understand why you can't handle these things by telephone the way other men do."

"Honey, you wouldn't understand even if I told you," he answered breezily. "I'd be wasting my time."

"I really believe," she said in a low voice and then he realized she was serious about it, "you *prefer* being away from home."

So he explained how tricky his New York contracts were and how he had to keep feeding them in person,—telegrams and telephone calls were never effective, but while he was talking she quietly rose and left the table, her coffee and the toast she had just buttered, untouched on her plate. He had always been glad Mary had been so well brought up that she wouldn't dream of making a scene; but this silent indignation could get your goat just as much as a couple of plates flying through the air. He started to go after her, then shrugged, you can't let these things get you. When he called out good-bye to her a few minutes later there was no answer from behind the closed bedroom door. The baby had been sick so he did not dare stop to say good-bye to her either, for fear she might be sleeping. Outside he looked up at the bedroom window, half-expecting Mary to be there waving good-bye, but the shade was drawn to shut out the sun,—that meant she had one of her headaches,— those headaches, he suspected, that came from controlling her feelings too well. It annoyed him now that such a little thing as his wife's unusual parting mood should cross his mind when he had so many important things to think of,— a lot more than old Jay could ever guess. There was the matter of his ex-wife showing up in Chicago, old Fran whom he'd never expected to see again. As long as she hung around town there was the danger of Mary finding out he'd been married before. He was a close-mouthed man and after he and Fran broke up, so long as she seemed unlikely ever to bob up again, he saw no necessity for going into all that business with the new friends he made in Chicago. By the time he and Mary were married it would have been senseless to bring up the matter. No reason why not, but it would be hard to explain that the sole reason for his keeping it secret was that he liked to forget the ups and downs of his life before he settled in the West. With old Fran running around Chicago, goodness knows what Mary was likely to hear. Smart man that he was he had certainly outsmarted himself in not making some deal with Fran last time he saw her to keep out of his territory. It was not like him to make such mistakes.

What really was on Mary's mind, he wondered. A little fleabite, that's all it was, but that closed silent door of hers leaped out of the page of Jay's newspaper where the touch-down hero should be. It stuck out of flying Indiana villages, diminished, it winked at him from the highball glass in his hand. Lou clenched his fist and socked the green plush cushions. He could handle anything if he only knew what it was, but he hated being tormented with these trifles he did not understand. His wife not saying good-bye to him and then Judge Harrod, his wife's uncle, cutting him, sitting back there in the club car this very minute smoking a Perfecto and reading *The Atlantic Monthly* as intently as if it was the stock closing news,—so intently that he did not see Lou's outstretched hand.

"Nuts," said Lou clearly and finished his drink.

Jay freshened up their glasses.

"Flo will tell Mary you're getting N. Y. offices," he said cheerfully. "Flo can't keep her trap shut five minutes."

Sure, Flo would tell her. That is, if Mary gave her the chance. Flo had met them at the Drake for lunch and heard them talking over the plans. Jay's main office had been in New York for years so he had plenty of suggestions, and Flo put in her oar now and then, as if she was an old New Yorker. Mary wouldn't mind not having been told the business details, she never showed much interest in the office anyway, but what would hurt her would be the fact that Lou hadn't asked her downtown for lunch when Jay had his wife down, especially when she loved eating in the Cape Cod Room as Lou well knew. Those were the things that hurt Mary, and the things that were least important to Lou. The point was that Jay took care of those little matters because he had a guilty conscience, but you couldn't explain that to Mary or she'd remember it someday when he, Lou, might have a guilty conscience himself and be fixing it up with a nice luncheon. Jay figured that if he buttered up his wife before every trip and brought her a present afterward it gave him his freedom.

"Personally, Lou, I'd take the Rockefeller Plaza office," said Jay. "It's central, and you got your address. Unless you think you'd get more prestige out of the Empire State building. Personally, I don't think you will."

Was anybody asking for advice?

"You don't need a whole floor, you know," pursued Jay. "You don't need a lot of antique furniture. All you need is a desk, a telephone and a good-looking receptionist."

"I suppose you'll pick her out," said Lou.

"I could," said Jay. "I know how to pick."

"I was thinking of a nice older type," said Lou with a straight face. "Lavender gray marcel, lorgnette, class, yes, but the mother type."

Jay gave a snort of laughter.

"Get a blonde and let me age her," he suggested. "Listen, Lou, no kidding, though, you don't need to set up a palace suite like you've got in Chicago. In New York when they see a swell suite of offices they think Chase National's just about to take over. Keep it simple."

How about letting Lou Donovan take care of his own business in his own way?

"I got my eye on a log cabin," said Lou, "unless you think I could do with one of those Hudson River coal barges."

"Indiana is a lousy state," said Jay looking out the window. "Take South Bend. Or Terre Haute. Flo wants to buy a melon farm down by Vincennes but I say if we buy any farm it'll be in Pennsylvania. That's a state."

"You going straight to the Waldorf?" asked Lou. "I got a suite reserved if you want to bunk with me."

Jay took out a pearl-handled knife and began paring his nails.

"Can't stay at the Waldorf," he said. "That's where I stay when I'm with Flo. I'll be at the Roosevelt."

"Looking for a little party?" Lou asked.

Jay shook his head.

"Ebie?" Lou asked, getting the idea finally.

Jay nodded.

"Getting on at Pittsburgh," he said.

Lou shrugged.

"Give me a hand with her if any of Flo's relations pop up, will you?" Jay asked.

Lou didn't say anything. Jay made more trouble for himself taking chances that way, saying good-bye to his wife at one station and picking up Ebie at the next. And like as not he would go into the club car any minute now and try to promote the first skirt he saw till Ebie got on. If he, Lou, was as scared of his wife as Jay was of Flo he'd give up running around, or else get out and stop making excuses. Lou used to run around but since he'd been married to Mary he kept out of trouble, still doing what he liked when he liked but in out-of-the-way sectors and on a strictly casual basis. Jay was forty, all tied up by Flo, but so afraid he'd miss something he could never enjoy what he already had. He said it was because he'd been in a t.b. sanitarium once for six years and always felt he had to make up for lost time. He couldn't say good night to a hat-check girl without getting all messed up in something, though. His friends were always fixing up Flo so she wouldn't walk out whenever she found out things. She never found out anything she didn't want to, though, she knew when to play dumb and get a booby prize of a new car or bracelet. It annoyed Lou for Jay, a pal of his, to never learn any technique, to go on that way, walking into trouble.

7

"All right, say it, you don't like the idea of Ebie," Jay said when Lou was silent.

Lou shrugged again.

"Ebie's a good egg," said Jay. "I always go back to Ebie. Don't get the idea she's a tramp just because she's an artist. Ebie's all right."

"Ebie's all right, then," said Lou. It was nothing to him what his friends did, but it irritated him to see a smart guy like old Oliver, a guy who pulled down between twenty and forty thousand a year, let any one woman get a hold on him. Ebie was a commercial artist, she hung on to her job, but how, nobody knew, because she skipped all over the country at a telegram from Jay. Jay thought she wasn't a gold-digger because she had gone to Art School and made her own clothes and asked for loans instead of out-and-out presents. You couldn't tell him anything.

"Oh, I admit she's not F.F.V. like your wife," said Jay, a little nastily just because Mary was not friendly with Lou's office connections, "but she's good-hearted. She'd give me the shirt off her back."

"I'll bet," said Lou.

"I think a hell of a lot of Ebie," said Jay. "Ebie's done a lot for me. Ebie's a darn good egg."

No sense in making him touchy.

"Ebie's all right on a party," said Lou. "You can have a good time with Ebie."

He was willing to bet money that *anybody* could have a good time with Ebie, if Jay only knew it.

"Ah, but there's more to Ebie than that," insisted Jay. "Ebie's got a deep side. Everybody sees those blonde curls and gets the idea she's a featherbrain, but I wish I had her mind. The other night we were sitting around listening to

8

'True or False,' and Ebie could answer four out of every five questions just like that. Reads everything."

"I'm surprised you don't cut loose and marry her," Lou said drily.

Jay Oliver was visibly shocked.

"Marry Ebie? Listen, you can't marry a woman that makes love as well as Ebie," he said. "You know that, Lou."

It was warmish in the little room in spite of air-condition and fans. Lou got up and propped the door open. It was one of those unexpected impulses he often had at certain moments that made him think he was born lucky, for a minute before or a minute later would have been wrong. This was the exact instant that a tall stooped man in loose gray suit was making his way down the corridor and Lou's hand was immediately outstretched.

"Well, Judge Harrod," he saluted him, "I didn't get a chance to speak to you in the club car. Why not come in and have a highball?"

The tall man shook hands without smiling. He was well over six feet and the sagging folds of flesh in his neck as well as the slow careful walk indicated that he was a man used to carrying a great deal more weight. His eyes, gray and almost accusingly penetrating, were deepset under a thick hedge of white tangled eyebrows and these with the high-bridged commanding nose and stern straight lips gave him a dignity that the wide, unmanageable ears and pure bald head bones, as openly marked as for an anatomy lesson, must have enjoyed mocking. His teeth, strong and yellow as field corn, were bared in a momentary smile, none too warm.

"You've heard of Judge Harrod," Lou waved a hand to Oliver. "My wife's uncle. This is Jay Oliver, Judge, Whittleby Cotton, you know."

9

"I see," nodded Judge Harrod gravely. "How do you do?"

Jay made a reluctant motion to rise but was waved back to ease by the Judge.

"No, I can't join you, Louis," said he. "I have some papers to attend to in my compartment. I didn't know you were going to New York. Mary didn't mention it at lunch."

So Mary had been to the Harrods' for lunch.

"I guess she and Mrs. Harrod were going to a matinee," Lou ventured easily.

"A recital," corrected the Judge. "Myra Hess was the soloist, I believe. I understand she was to be guest of honor at cocktails later at our house."

"Oh, yes," said Lou, reddening, for this was another matter that annoyed him, that Mary should be an integral part of the Harrods' social life except when he, Lou, was home. He didn't really give a damn and, of course, Mary knew how musicales, contract, and formal dinners made him squirm, but he would have liked to have all his customers see him making himself at home in the Judge's pleasant garden, large Tom Collins glass in hand, the Judge's blue ribbon Scottie sleeping trustingly at his feet, the Judge's big shot friends—governors, bank presidents, bishops, all hanging on to Lou Donovan's sound analysis of business conditions. If such pictures could have been distributed without the actual boredom of listening to an evening of musical baloney or highbrow chit-chat, Lou would have been quite happy. But after half a dozen efforts on both Mary's side and the Judge's to include Mary's husband in the Harrod social life with nothing but embarrassment on all sides, the contact dropped back to a family matter between the Harrods and their favorite niece,

Mary. Lou suspected that he was barely mentioned, even, during these family conclaves. He found he could make use of the connection conversationally without the bother of going through the actual meetings, and this suited him fine, except for the increasingly rude attitude of both Judge and Mrs. Harrod when they met him. They knew well enough that Mary was crazy about him, but they acted when they met him alone, as the Judge was acting now, as if Lou Donovan, in speaking of Mary, was presuming upon a very slight acquaintance to refer to this intimate member of the Judge's private family. The fact that he happened to be her husband did not lessen the outrage.

"Sure you won't have a quick one with us, Judge?" Jay Oliver asked hospitably. Jay knew of only one way to dissolve his faint uneasiness with either superiors or servants, and that was to get drunk with them very quickly, and it was this simple formula of his that probably accounted for the hot water he so often found himself in, because it was during these ice-breaking friendly drinks that he was most easily taken advantage of. The Judge did not respond to the friendly offer.

"Hmm, I seldom drink in the afternoon, hmm," said the Judge, and then decided to soften the rebuke with a worse one. "It seems to me unnecessary to my mental processes,—hmm, as well as to my pleasure, hmm. I daresay other men are differently constituted, and possibly depend more, hmm, on, hmm."

His sentence trailed off into a final cough.

"I'll say I depend more," laughed Jay comfortably. "I can't think without a shot first, then I can't relax without another."

Lou was embarrassed by Jay's easy assumption that his

own brain processes and the Judge's belonged in the same conversation, even though in any argument with Mary on Jay Oliver's intelligence he was always quick to say the advantage was Oliver's. Oliver's business took more brains and common sense than the Judge's, Lou always declared.

"I drink to think and think to drink," chuckled Jay.

"I see, hmm," said the Judge. "That, of course, is one way of, hmm."

His voice, earnest, unctuous, and benevolent, was a pat on the head, a well-son-are-we-sorry-now-we-smoked-the-cigarette voice, and his "hmm" was a kindly purring growl that finished off a vague sentence, punctuated a phrase, a stroking soothing lullaby to suspicion; and in sterner, more official conversations it was an official seal on the basic authority of his statement. His voice was always prepared with this apologetic butter, though if it had been unmasked and not keyed to the inferior class or age of his listeners it might have been a harsh whine of intolerance. It was as if his highly exaggerated pharynx, romping up and down his throat like a busy bell-boy, was a jack-in-the-box, and this little lurking demon, as each phrase clicked shut, sprang out with a gurgle of "Yay, bo, amen!"

"Mr. Oliver and I were discussing the opening of my New York office, Judge," Lou said, and as usual when he talked to the Judge he oiled up his own voice.

"A New York office, eh? Ah," said the Judge. "That ought to please Mary. I heard her saying just today how sorry she was to miss the fall concerts again. There's one she spoke of only this week—could it have been the Modern Music one? Something at Carnegie Hall. Too bad she wasn't able to come along with you."

"Oh Mary hears plenty of music right there at home.

We've got the finest radio, she doesn't need to miss anything," Lou assured him confidently. "Naturally on business trips like this I wouldn't have time to take her to any musical affairs. I have to be on the job every minute."

"After all, Judge, you haven't got Mrs. Harrod along, have you?" Jay put in with a guffaw, and was that the wrong tack, for the Judge did not smile.

"I see, hmm," he said. "And of course Mary's having a big dinner party Thursday, that's true. I suppose you have to rush back for that."

"Oh sure," said Lou, who had forgotten all about that party.

"Well, good day, Mr. Oliver, good day, Donovan," said the Judge.

"One of the richest men in the country," said Lou as the door closed. "He could buy out the Gold Coast if he felt like it. Has his own plane, keeps a three hundred acre estate in Maryland, pays three thousand bucks for his hunters, has a bass lake and camp in Wisconsin, Christ, he's rich. Pretty close to the White House, too. Like a father to my wife and me. They brought her up, of course."

"Looks like an old buzzard," observed Jay, yawning. "I wouldn't want him nosing around me, I can tell you, and sounding off to my wife."

That was the kind of dope Jay was; he never took in any connection outside his immediate business that might be needed in some other way.

"I don't need to worry about that," said Lou shortly. "I don't fool around, not in his precinct anyway." Then, as this sounded a little too pious, he added more amiably, "Never do anything you can't deny. That's the old Donovan motto."

"You're a smart guy, Lou," Jay said with a sigh. "You and Ebie ought to like each other more."

Now Lou was willing to go into the club car, feeling that it would give him another chance at the Judge, so they went back presently, but the Judge was not there. Instead a fellow in a threadbare greenish plaid suit got them into a conversation about the difference between English and American business methods. He was a bronzed leathery little fellow with scrappy sandy hair and bleached eyelashes, buck teeth, long humped nose, and tufts of fuzz sprouted out of his ears and nostrils. Lou could not make out from his speech whether he was a genuine limey or just wished he was.

"Take the Duke of Windsor," said the stranger. "A personal friend of mine. My name is Truesdale, here's my card, T. V. Truesdale, originally an old Nebraska family, migrating from South Carolina, and incidentally the present governor is a connection on my mother's side. For the past eighteen years, of coss, I've lived abroad, personally representing the royal families of England and Europe. My wife, of coss, is Eldorana May, the operatic singer, here's a picture of her, a clipping I just chanced to catch in *The London Times* a few days ago. Of coss I read all the foreign papers, German, French, not Russian of coss,—'wife of T. V. Truesdale,' you see the caption there."

Lou examined the clipping, yellowed, with the faded picture of a sumptuous looking brunette of at least a twenty-year ago era, checked on the caption, passed it on to Oliver, who studied it with interest.

"What do you mean you represent the royal families?" he asked.

Mr. Truesdale, who had whipped out the picture like

magic from a bulging scuffed brown briefcase, replaced it now in a large manila envelope which he handled as tenderly as if it was a valuable second mortgage.

"Did represent, did, did," he corrected in his nasal singsong voice. "Europe is to me a dead country. Look at this Spanish situation, that will spread, don't you see, there'll be no business left in Europe. That's why I'm in America once more. America's the only country. And don't think they don't know it over there. I am not a Communist, though I was at one time a member of the Socialist party, voted for Eugene Debs, believe it or not, and personally I feel that there are many things to be said for Joseph Stalin, though I can't say the same for Mr. Chamberlain. Not after what he did to my friend Windsor. One of the nicest fellows you'd hope to meet. I said to him, to Windsor, that is, I said, 'Look here, sir,' I said, 'I don't understand the way half of these Britishers talk, it's not our language at all, do they have to mumble and squeak as if their mouths were full of hot marbles?' and he said 'Truesdale,' he said, 'it's the bunk, they don't have to at all, it's purely an affectation.' "

He paid for his beer very carefully from a frayed ancient pigskin wallet, and this too he fondled as he had his briefcase, as if these were all that had been rescued of his priceless treasures when the palace was destroyed.

Oliver was having a fine time listening to the stranger, winking at Lou over each anecdote. This was the real music of the rails, some eccentric stranger popping up telling his life story, it passed the time while Indiana slid past the window, towns popped up, announced their names with a placarded station momentarily thrown on the screen, then dissolved into fields, forests, hills. The brown stranger

swept through a score of countries, his story was mounted
on the wind, it sweetened their drinks, it mingled in Lou's
mind with a picture of Mary's closed door and the house
in Winnetka.

"What was your royal racket, sir?" Lou asked.

The stranger's pale eyes moved suavely from the per-
fection of Lou's gray suit to the ravelling cuff of his own
shirt, and he looked down at this cuff now with astonished
concern.

"I must apologize for my shirt," he said. "My laundry
did not arrive as I left the coast so I was obliged to borrow
from the porter. Disgraceful looking. I hate that sort of
thing. I like the best clothes, always have, always will. Well,
as I was saying, when I was travelling in Africa I bought
for the royal family. If any member of the royal family
was about to make a tour of Africa or India or possibly
even Canada, I'd go ahead, investigate the private tastes
of all the biggies he would be likely to meet, get dossiers
on all the leading families, find out maybe that the Chief
of the Kenja tribes has a musically inclined daughter, suggest a harmonica as a gift on the royal visit. The man
before me, as I happen to know, on a previous royal tour,
suggested an accordion as a gift, a tremenjus mistake, of
coss, in the tropics, since the thing's nothing but glue, so
it fell apart in the heat of the first day, and did not create
the right international goodwill intended."

"Pretty smart," said Lou, pleased at such a complicated
job. "Look here, maybe I could use you in my business."

He ordered a drink for the man and was even more
impressed when the stranger refused, insisting on drinking
only his own beer which he paid for himself from his worn
wallet. Lou was sorry Oliver was there to hear the guy's

story as he would have liked to present him as someone
he had long sought for his staff of superspecialists.

"I may look you up sometime," said Truesdale, without
eagerness, but efficiently slipping a calling card into Lou's
hand. "You can usually get me at the Ellery, in New York,
or the Knickerbocker in Los Angeles, or the Lafayette in
Havana. I was stabbed in Havana last October. Look."

He was rolling his pants leg above the knee, showing a
scar on his knobby calf when Judge Harrod beg—hmm—
pardoned himself past them and brought Lou up short. He
went back to the compartment, leaving Jay to the stranger,
and indeed did not see Jay again till they reached Penn
Station, for Ebie had gotten on in Pittsburgh. Ebie was in
the corridor beaming when he got out in the morning, and
the three of them got together for an eye-opener, Jay,
glassy-eyed with a terrific hangover and Ebie still a little
tight from all night drinking and inclined to giggles and
squeezing both their arms. Lou was more than ready to
drop them both when they got to the station but just as
they stepped into the waiting room Jay clutched him.

"My God, Lou, look!" And there coming at them out
of the crowd was Flo Oliver, no less, laughing triumphantly,
and hanging on to some old lady who looked as if she
must be her mother.

"I caught the plane to surprise you!" Flo screamed.
"Didn't I put one over on you!"

She was upon them before either man could think what
to do about Ebie, until Lou was inspired to quietly take
Ebie's arm and say, "Well, Jay, so long. Ebie and I have
got a day ahead of us. Oh, Flo, this is Miss Vane. Jay,
you remember my speaking of Miss Vane—the artist who's
going to handle the decorating of my new office."

"I just came down to meet Mr. Donovan," babbled Ebie.

"Just like me," Flo giggled and snatched Jay's arm. "Mama and I couldn't wait to see your face when you saw me here."

"Nothing like a little surprise," Lou said. "Come on, Miss Vane. Good-bye, Flo."

He firmly manipulated Ebie away from the happy little family reunion, leaving Jay still mopping his head in a daze, still paralyzed from the shock of danger. The poor sap just stood there, not having sense enough to make the most of his miraculous escape, gaping after his loyal friend and Ebie as long as they were in sight.

"Now, what, for Christ's sake?" Ebie muttered in disgust as they got into a taxi. "Good Lord, what a squeeze that was."

"Waldorf," said Lou to the driver.

"I'm still shivering from the shock," Ebie confessed. "Honestly, you don't know what a thing like that does to you. So that's his wife."

"That's Flo, all right," said Lou. Ebie really was shivering and Lou put his arm around her shoulders. He hoped to heaven she wasn't going to start his day off with a little womanly hysteria but she soon had herself under control. Looking out through the back of the cab he was suddenly aware of a familiar figure standing by the curb waiting for a cab. It was Judge Harrod and he was looking straight at him with an expression of unveiled contempt.

II

THE stupidity of having a wife who could spring a surprise like Flo's on you! The stupidity, Lou kept repeating
to himself, of allowing yourself to be so nearly trapped by
her when a few simple precautions in advance would have
cleared everything. And above all the stupidity of permitting yourself to be rescued by a business friend who would
always have that on you!

Ebie was disgusted, too, that was the first thing she and
Lou had ever had in common. They stopped in the New
Yorker for a quick shot to brace their nerves after the shock
of seeing Flo, then rode uptown in silence since there was
only one thing to say and that was what a dope Jay Oliver
was, can't he manage anything like a grown man! The
picture of his baffled docile face looking pleadingly after
them while Flo and her mother encircled him with gay
chatter was not an impressive one, but if that was the kind
of guy Ebie fell for, all right, so Lou said nothing.

"God-damn fools," Ebie said suddenly with a bitter
laugh. "Both of them, I mean. Thanks for pulling us out
of that. God knows what Jay would have done if you hadn't
stepped in pretending I was with you."

"I'd expect the same thing from Jay in the same situation," said Lou. He was beginning to admire himself for
the instinctive good sense he had shown in saving his friend's
face. He felt a little fonder of Jay (though still a little
contemptuous) for permitting him to give this faultless
exhibition of sterling male friendship.

"Ah, he would never have done the same thing," said Ebie. "It would never have even occurred to him."

Of course it wouldn't, Lou reflected; though Ebie looked dizzy she did have sense enough to know that much.

"I'd set aside the next forty-eight hours for him," she said.

"Want to have dinner with me?" Lou asked. Ebie shrugged a might-as-well. He could stop by at her apartment that night around seven. He dropped her at Saks Fifth Avenue and went on to the Waldorf.

When he came back to the hotel that night to wash up, Jay had called twice, and Lou knew what he wanted was for him to fix things up so Ebie wouldn't be sore. There was one urgent message to call Mr. Oliver back at Jack Dempsey's place by six or Suite 26B by seven, but Lou tossed the notes in the wastebasket. If you were signing up for a New York office, seeing bankers and realtors all day—in fact taking one of the biggest steps in your business career, you certainly didn't have time to help some poor dumb-bell out of a wife-trap. Lou felt he had fixed up the front for Flo, now let Oliver do his own fixing with Ebie. He had a laugh when finally a telegram came "Please take Ebie to a show or something and explain situation to her but not to Rainbow Room or Victor Moore show."

Taking a shower Lou thought how well things had gone for him that day. He'd clinched a swell suite of offices on Fifth Avenue in the Fifties, he'd lunched with and made a good impression on one of the biggest hotel men in the country, he'd started a whale of an idea on a kind of hotel survey, and so far as he was concerned, he was J. P. Morgan. He often in the past had dated up a red-headed hostess in a near-by nightclub but tonight he felt more like bragging than he felt like sex, so the date with Ebie was okay. There was no attraction there so it made it sort of homelike. He thought they'd go down to Cella's for a steak and some old-fashioneds, maybe drop in the Plaza later for some highballs and talk. Ebie seemed to have more sense than he'd given her credit for, so it was all in all a rather cheerful prospect. He tried two ties with the newest shirt, finally picked the dark red. Going down in the elevator, he thought it would be funny if he ran into Oliver or Flo in the lobby but he'd brush them off. It was ten to seven, and Ebie's apartment was only a dozen blocks off.

The elegance and respectability of the apartment house when Lou finally reached it stumped him. First there was the Park Avenue address when he had expected some West Forties rooming house, then there was the courtesy of the doorman at mention of her name, a courtesy reserved as he well knew only for the solvent. He found himself vaguely shifting his plans for the evening to something more pretentious—Voisin's, he thought, or the Persian Room, but still he wasn't sure. Once in her apartment he was even more baffled. The fact that Ebie wasn't ready and that a quiet elderly maid had him wait impressed him as favorably as the obvious expensiveness of the apartment. There was a something or other about the place that he could not quite classify or duplicate in his own home though God knows Mary certainly had a better background than Ebie. Maybe it was all the pictures, though he had a half dozen much bigger oil paintings at home that he'd paid at least fifty or sixty dollars apiece for at Marshall Fields. There was her drawing table, easel, and desk that might have looked freakish anyplace else but in this de luxe background, with grand piano, Persian rugs, odd bits of sculpture, these artists' tools seemed a charming decoration since they had so obviously justified their use. Lou sat down and lit a cigarette, oddly pleased with this surprise about Ebie, and still puzzling over the quality in the place he couldn't name. Maybe it was the casualness without disorder of the gadgets lying around, or the aura of good address which gratified his senses like a specially fine cognac, and he kept rolling it over on his tongue in the same sensuous way,— Park Avenue duplex, must be at least four thousand, and for the first time he felt a little jealous of Jay. It made him look at Ebie more closely when she came down from the balcony bedroom. To tell the truth he'd never had a good unprejudiced look at Ebie.

Of course lots of women look better in their own places. Once in a while you get a stunner who knocks them cold in a restaurant but back in her own living room takes on the second-rate lifelessness of her own handpicked ordinary background. Still the majority of women come out better in their own homes, so it wasn't really so surprising that Ebie should look quite dignified, and unusually pretty, coming down the staircase to music, for the radio was playing a Paul Whiteman recording of "Afraid to Dream" as sumptuously soft as the white bear rug in front of the great fireplace. Ebie was a girl who changed at every appearance from pretty to chic to naïve to plain tart, but this was a good night, the socko from Oliver had challenged her. Her hair was reddish gold tonight—Lou dimly recalled it as platinum at one time—and instead of the cutie-pie curls it was arranged in two plaits around her head so that her small naughty face with knowing hazel eyes looked not the least tartish. She wore a long-sleeved brownish-gold dinner dress and the amber jewelry on that with her hair and coloring was something that struck an odd new chord in Lou, something that didn't seem to stem from Ebie herself but from some new force Lou had never struck before.

"I know I'm too dressed up, Lou," she said guiltily, "but that's what I always do when I'm mad."

"You're still mad at Jay?" Lou asked.

"Raging," she said positively and this for some reason struck Lou as extraordinarily amusing for he roared with laughter.

"He's such a fool," she said plaintively, "he never plants anything right."

"He was lucky this time," said Lou.

"Oh, he's always lucky," said Ebie. "Jay always comes out all right except it's always somebody else that has to wangle him out. I'm crazy about Jay, of course, but I do despise a fool. If he wasn't such a natural born genius in business I'd have been through with him ages ago, but he isn't a fool in everything, thank God."

"Jay's a good business man," agreed Lou.

"He ought to save his money, though," said Ebie. "I try to tell him that."

Lou wondered just how much of the grandeur of Ebie's place was due to Jay Oliver's money. Jay would be fool enough to think he had to pay for an apartment, buy the works, when all any intelligent guy needed to do in these cases was to buy dinners and birthday presents. Ebie poured out two highballs.

"Nice place, this," Lou said. "I guess there's some good money in commercial art."

Ebie shrugged.

"I could make more if it wasn't for Jay," she sighed. "I throw up any assignment when he's in town. I'm a fool, you don't need to tell me."

23

"He don't appreciate it," Lou said. "I doubt if Jay knows what you do for him."

Ebie looked gloomily into her glass.

"I'm always a sap," she said. "I'm a sap for all my friends. I'm a sap for that louse that handles my stuff, too, Rosenbaum. He says to me, 'Do me a favor, Ebie, put up a friend of mine for a few days will you, you got a big place.' So for six weeks I put up his friend. It looks to me like I've got her for life."

"So it's a woman," Lou said.

Ebie tried to look insulted.

"I don't let any men stay here," she said haughtily. "No, this friend of Rosenbaum's is a foreigner. She doesn't want to go back because of war. Rosenbaum can't have her at his house on account of his wife. I'm always being a sucker for somebody."

"German?" asked Lou.

"A little of everything," said Ebie. "White Russian, mostly, I guess. You'll meet her if you stick around. She's always here. Trina's all right, only why is it always me that's got to be the goat?"

"You only got yourself to blame, girlie," said Lou. "Same as Jay. You can't blame anybody else for trouble when you walk right up and shake hands with it."

"I wish I had somebody like you to talk good horse sense to me once in a while, Lou," Ebie said. "As you say Jay's as bad as I am."

It was a surprise to find how really intelligent Ebie was. They had a few highballs and by the time they got out of the apartment it was too late to take in a show so they went over to Leon and Eddie's and ate a steak watching the floor show. They didn't talk about Jay after a while except to wonder where he went and whether Flo was smart enough to catch on. Ebie didn't see why Jay didn't send his wife to Mexico for the fall and Florida for winter like other men did. Then you knew where they were and could relax.

"A fellow doesn't need to do anything that drastic," said Lou, smiling. "A little common sense is all anybody needs."

Ebie was bitter about all of Jay's weaknesses now but Lou didn't say anything because of Jay being his best friend. There was plenty he could complain of but a pal was a pal. Ebie was a good sport, Lou had to admit it. She didn't try to put on a big show of being as smart as a man, the way Flo was always doing, and she didn't put on an act of being a pure young thing before she met Jay. She was on the level, told him about a couple of other affairs she'd had and then she asked him if he'd ever been mixed up with anybody. He was on the verge of telling her about his secret first marriage and about Francie popping up now to hound him, but pulled himself together in time.

"Men don't discuss those things, girlie," he said.

For some reason that made Ebie rather sore.

"Oh, they don't, don't they?" she said. "Then why are they always asking me about things like that? All right, I wish I hadn't confessed anything to you now if you're going to turn into a gentleman."

Lou tried to kid her out of her sulks because he did like her, especially after the apartment had shown him she was no tramp as he had once thought. He took her over to La Conga where they danced, something she said Jay didn't care about but she did. They bumped into a man just leaving the place with a trim-figured little woman who smiled at Ebie.

"My house guest," Ebie whispered to Lou. "The Kameray woman. She's with Rosenbaum."

"Not a bad figure," Lou said looking after the undulating movements of Mrs. Kameray's hips appreciatively.

Ebie turned out to be a good dancer and they danced and drank till the place closed. It had been the best evening Lou had had in New York for years,—friendly, restful, altogether what he needed. He said so to Ebie in the cab.

"I'll bet we had a better time than Jay," she said, her face darkening. "I damn well hope so anyway."

"Listen, don't be so hard on Jay," Lou laughed. "You can't be that mean to a fellow's pal. Have a heart."

He put his arm around her. The sun was shining in her bed-room window when he woke up.

III

"But why Maryland?" Jay Oliver wanted to know. He had been summoned to the Waldorf by a phone call from Lou with the insinuation that there might be a nice bit of business waiting there for him. Lou had had luncheon on the roof with Rosenbaum, the advertising and promotion wizard, and then taken him to his suite for completing their deal with Rosenbaum's multi-millionaire backer. The project involved a big order from Whittleby Cotton so Lou was glad to do his friend Oliver a favor. Unfortunately Jay had the shakes so badly from his last night's celebration that he didn't half-appreciate this piece of luck and in fact didn't seem to be able to get anything through his head.

"What's the matter with Maryland?" Rosenbaum asked.

"I don't say anything's the matter with Maryland—I just wonder why Maryland," Jay feebly explained. "You got Virginia—the Carolinas—take Virginia Beach. Ever stay at the Cavalier there? If you want swank, I mean."

"Oh, take another bromo and forget it," Lou called curtly from the serving pantry. "What the hell's biting you today, Jay?"

He came out of the pantry with a bowl of ice-cubes and set it down on the low table before the sofa, where Jay was sitting. Through the windows, curtained in heavy pink toile de Jouy, the afternoon sky seemed marvellously blue, with bubbling clouds stiffly whipped, looking as if the great chef Oscar himself had shot them out with a pastry-gun.

This serene vista seemed to be no comfort to Jay Oliver for he stared out gloomily.

"I hate this damn town," he said. "No offense to you, Rosenbaum. I realize it's your home town."

Rosenbaum shrugged.

"We New Yorkers don't care what anybody says. Maybe we don't have civic pride like other cities. Maybe we're just smug. Anyway go ahead and hate it."

"I don't like Maryland, either," said Jay. "I put in the worst week of my life at the Lord Baltimore one summer. A dame had put detectives on me."

"Will you get over that grouch?" Lou exclaimed. "Maryland or California, what the devil do you care? You're in. It's the sweetest contract you've seen in many a moon, old boy."

"I just don't seem to get the idea," Jay said. "I know it's a big deal or Rosenbaum here wouldn't be in it."

"Call him Syd," said Lou. "We're all friends here."

"If you don't mind I'm going to call him Rosenbaum," said Jay. "I mean if we're going to be personal friends. I always call my personal friends by their last names—first names are just for business purposes."

Jay was getting into one of his nasty moods, as usual at the wrong time and with the wrong people. It was a mystery to Lou how Jay could do the business he did when he was so careless with his contacts. Lou was especially nice to Rosenbaum now to make up for his friend's rudeness. He started to fill his glass but Rosenbaum put a warning hand over the top of it. Drinking was the one feature of business that he heartily disliked. He was a big loose-limbed man with pale gray protuberant eyes, gnarled heavy features, loose mouth and curly graying brown hair. His big shoulders and build made him appear athletic which was far from the truth, just as the humorous curve of his lips and the alert twinkle in his eye libelled his somber brooding nature. If he resented Jay's irritability he did not· show it.

"Mr. Oliver missed the Major's explanation," he said.

"Call me Jay," Jay said.

"The property we're dealing with is that big stretch of woodland along the Chesapeake that the Van Duzers started to develop in 1928 then lost to the Chemical Bank. Well, the Chemical Bank is the Major. What we're doing now is building it up into one of the most exclusive resorts in the country. Stables, fox-hunting, health baths, thirty beautiful manors serviced by one great hotel or club."

"You say you can rent these houses for a week-end or a month," Jay said.

"We want your finest goods, Jay," Lou said. "The Major's crest on all the linen."

"Everybody is the Major's guest, you see," said Rosenbaum.

"Be a millionaire for a week-end, see, that's the idea," said Lou, genially. He clapped Jay on the back for he was in a fine mood. The very air of the room seemed charmingly alive with little floating dollar signs and fat little ciphers, commas, more ciphers, all winging around happily, waiting for a mere scratch of the pen to call them into action. The Major's conversation had left this agreeable effect, and although Lou had put in three hard days in the City to say nothing of his nights, and had, right up to the noon conference today, been worn out with nerves and other complications, the final settling of the proposition had left him miraculously refreshed. Like the

colored porter on the Pullman, too tired to do anything till
the five dollar bill galvanized him into a perfect frenzy of
efficiency. "Thought you were tired, George," Lou had
teased him. "Nothin' rests me like money, suh," George
had grinned back.

"Sounds like a big job," Jay admitted.

"There's a fortune in it for all of us," said Rosenbaum.
"If you knew the Major like I do you'd know he's a
cautious bastard. He won't put a nickel into anything unless
he's going to get fifty back."

"I suppose we'll have to put a lot of time from now on
sticking around Baltimore," Jay said. "Baltimore or Washington. You can have them both."

"Don't kid yourself, this place is one of the best locations
in the country," said Lou. "Look. Catch a plane at two-
thirty—you're in Baltimore at 4:15. Car meets you and
takes you straight to Castles-in-the-Woods. You meet the
richest men in the country. The cream of society. You're
the Major's personal guest. Don't tell me that isn't good
stuff."

Rosenbaum went to the table and opened up his brief-
case, fumbling in it for photographs which he silently passed
to Jay.

"We're going to modernize the whole place," said Lou.
"Wait till the natives see what we make of that state."

The pictures reminded Lou that he had not showed
Rosenbaum the photographs of his house in Winnetka, so
he went in the bedroom and brought back the snapshots
of the place, the picture of the kid playing with her poodle
in the backyard, and the snapshot of Mary in her sable
coat standing beside the Packard.

"My wife," he said.

Rosenbaum glanced politely at the pictures, made appropriately flattering comments.

"I'll bet Mary's sore you're not home for that dinner she's giving tonight," Jay observed.

Lou looked at his watch.

"I'd better call her," he said. He had gotten over his disturbance over her strange behavior at parting and in the exultation of his unexpected good fortune today remembered only how proud he was of his high-bred wife and the excellent way their marriage was conducted. He remembered he had not told Rosenbaum about his wife's connections yet, though he had mentioned them casually to the Major. Both their wives were from the Lucerne convent, then a year at the Boston Conservatory, the Major's father-in-law was a judge, Lou's uncle-in-law was a judge. These little coincidences had been mentioned casually by Lou, that was all, but they had helped. No less a private authority than the recent train acquaintance, Mr. Truesdale himself, had furnished Lou with these little personality tidbits about the Major, at eleven o'clock that very morning, by telephone.

"Speaking of Maryland," said Lou, "did I tell you my wife's uncle has a big show-place down there, not far from your spot? Judge Minor B. Harrod."

"Oh, yes," said Rosenbaum, impressed. "I know of him, of course. Your wife a Harrod?"

"Mary Harrod, she was," said Lou, "Boston originally. Are you married, Rosenbaum? I'd like Mary to meet Mrs. Rosenbaum."

Rosenbaum smoked a cigar impassively.

"If they meet it will not be in the Castles-in-the-Woods," he observed, sardonically. "Part of my job is to protect the guests from non-Aryan intruders."

31

"Well, if you're ever in Chicago, then," said Lou. He went in the bedroom and called up for more seltzer and put in his call to Mary. He had left word with the operator not to disturb him for the last two hours and now she told him that Ebie had called twice. He had figured out Ebie as good enough sport not to regard last night as anything but a momentary lapse, but he might be mistaken. Sometimes these girls that talked like such good sports were more trouble than the other kind. Even while he had the receiver to his ear the operator said, "Will you take Miss Vane's call now?" and there was nothing to do but say yes. He went to the living room door and nodded to Jay.

"Long distance," he said and closed the door between the two rooms.

"Listen," said Ebie's voice, "do me a favor, will you?"

All right, now it was coming. Buy me some Tidewater stock, please, and I'll send you a check later. Lou braced himself.

"Rosenbaum's there with you, isn't he?" she asked. "Don't be so damned cagey, this isn't going to hurt you. The point is that he's going to suggest my little permanent guest to you for some promotion work and for God's sake say yes to it, will you?"

Lou was slow getting it.

"Who? What do you mean promotion work?"

Ebie was impatient.

"This Kameray dame I have on my neck. She knows too damn much—especially after last night."

"Oh."

"She doesn't know it was you. She only knows it wasn't Jay. Anyway it's getting me. You know. Not knowing when she's going to pop out with something when he comes in."

That was easy. Lou was relieved.

"What do you want me to do?"

"Get her out of town, keep her in the West, I don't care. Rosenbaum's sort of afraid to push her into something for fear you'll catch on to his position, so you help him out."

"That's a cinch," said Lou. He was glad of the tip. Some way to please Rosenbaum, who after all, represented the Major. "How do you feel today?"

Ebie groaned.

"Awful. Butterflies in my stomach, you know. I had to turn in two drawings to the agency this morning. That's where I saw Rosenbaum. I shook so I could hardly hold a pencil. We drank a whole bottle of Hennessey after we got back here, you know."

Lou hadn't remembered that.

"You kept telephoning everybody," Ebie said. "God knows who. Then you passed out."

The operator cut in and told him his call to Chicago was ready so he told Ebie he'd call her back and waited.

"Hello, Mary," he said briskly, "I thought I'd better let you know I'm tied up here. Some things have turned up and it will take me a few more days to get them cleaned up."

"Yes?" Mary said coldly.

It reminded Lou they were not on warm terms, so he tried to think of something personal to tell her, the sort of thing he seldom told her but which she loved to hear.

"Oh, by the by, I had a nice talk with your uncle on the train," he said. "He was on the same car."

There was a silence and he rattled the receiver.

"Mary, are you there?"

33

"This is the third time you've called me and told me all that in the last twelve hours," she said quietly.

This stunned Lou.

"You called me twice last night," she said. "Once at four o'clock and again at four thirty. It seems to have left no impression on you."

Lou mopped his brow. That was something he had never done before. Must have had his conscience working overtime.

"I forgot to tell you about seeing the Judge," he said.

"The conversation has been exactly the same all three times," said Mary.

Lou pulled himself together. If she was trying to get his goat he'd show her.

"Supposing I call you when I get back in town, then," he said coolly. "No use my wasting long-distance dough. So long."

At that he'd forgotten to ask after the kid. That would burn her up. It was funny, too, because he was fond of the kid. The only thing was that Mary had sort of taken it over from the minute it was born and made it her special personal property, none of his, until he had gotten out of the habit of even taking it on his knee. He occasionally surprised himself wishing he had a child of his own, and then he'd remember why he really had one, only it was Mary's and he didn't dare touch it. Some women took their children that way. It didn't matter, really, and it filled her life all the time he was on the road.

He was about to call Ebie back and get more dope on Rosenbaum when Jay opened the door.

"Flo and her mother went to Atlantic City," said Jay.

Who the hell cared?

"Nice for you," said Lou.

"I didn't have a chance to thank you for pulling me out of the jam there at the station," said Jay. "I sure appreciated it. Flo didn't bat an eye."

"Flo know's what's good for her," said Lou. "I'll bet if she didn't know what was up yesterday she did today when you handed her that hundred dollar fitted bag."

"She didn't say so," said Jay and then astonishment lit up his ruddy tan face. "How'd you know I gave her a fitted bag?"

Lou laughed.

"A shot in the dark," he said. "I ought to know how you work by this time. A woman would have to be mighty dumb not to notice your tracks."

Jay sat down on the bed, and lit a cigarette.

"Bring your drink in, Rosenbaum," Lou called. "We're holing in, in here."

"Listen, Lou, you didn't pull a fast one on me with Ebie, did you?" Jay muttered in an undertone.

Lou was hunting for a fallen cigarette and did not answer at first.

"She said you took her out, and I was wondering," Jay said slowly.

"What the hell are you getting at?" Lou exclaimed, and then Rosenbaum came in.

"I was just wondering if a good smart girl couldn't help us interest the right people in the Castles," Lou said. "Not just the pushing average looker, you know, somebody a little different, higher class, maybe, different."

Rosenbaum went over to the window and looked out.

"I could get you a very competent young woman who answers your description," he said. "Part German, part

35

Russian. Exiled here. She brought my cousin's little girl over from Germany last year and we feel grateful and of course very responsible for her. As I think of it she would give the right continental class to the thing. Discreet, smart —a very unusual personality."

"Sounds perfect," said Lou easily. "Let's hire her. What's her name?"

"Mrs. Kameray," said Rosenbaum, still not looking around. "I'll have my office get in touch with her and send her here."

It struck Lou as funny that Jay Oliver sat there, knowing who the woman was but not speaking up for fear Rosenbaum would then know about him and Ebie, and Rosenbaum, who knew perfectly well through Mrs. Kameray all about Jay Oliver and Ebie, did not dare mention where Mrs. Kameray was staying for the same cock-eyed reason.

Jay lay back on the bed smoking, shading his eyes with his hand.

"What's eating you?" Lou upbraided him. "Here I give you a nice bit of business and you act as if you'd just lost it."

"I feel lousy, that's all," said Jay. "Can't a guy feel lousy?"

Rosenbaum picked his hat and stick from the dresser-top.

"You people will want to celebrate at some hot spot, I suppose," he said with a sigh. "I'm a family man. I stay home tonight with my family and my little Hilda, and listen to the Jello hour."

Lou saw him to the elevator. When he came back he winked at Jay.

"Family man, oh, yeah," he said. "You should have

seen him doing the rhumba up at La Conga last night."

"Oh, was that where you and Ebie went?" Jay asked.

"It's a good orchestra," Lou said lightly.

"I should take Ebie dancing more, I suppose," said Jay. His tone was so mournful that Lou was annoyed.

"Go ahead, but don't act as if it was such a chore," he said. "After all I see you dancing with every other chippy in town."

"So Ebie's a chippy," said Jay.

"I never said any such thing," said Lou, and that was the way it went on till finally Lou called up Ebie to show how much he respected her and he asked her and Mrs. Kameray to come out and have a cocktail with Jay Oliver and himself.

"Wherever you want to go," he added.

"Trina would like to go to the Rainbow Room," Ebie said with a patient air. "She says she's never seen twilight come over the Rainbow Room."

"For Christ's sake, isn't that too bad?" said Jay, when this message was relayed to him. "Tell her to hustle herself up there then right now before it's too late."

Jay took a shower and borrowed one of Lou's ties and they were pals again.

"We can shake 'em at eight or so and go have a good time," said Lou. "We don't want to get into anything."

IV

THE Kameray woman wasn't bad. She wasn't bad at all,
Lou told Jay in the men's room.

"That phoney accent throws me," said Jay.

"I think it's cute," Lou said.

"Sure, that's why she hangs on to it," Jay said. "She's
a liability if you ask me."

Jay was still worried because he hadn't been able to get
back on Ebie's good side. Just as she was beginning to
mellow and was hinting at lunching with him tomorrow,
Jay recollected that Flo would probably be back by then
and he didn't dare commit himself. So that made it worse.
It was the longest Ebie had ever been mad with him. All
through the cocktails at the Rainbow Room and the dinner
at the Trouville she had been high-spirited and charming,
always a bad sign in a woman who has every reason to
be sulky. She had been brightly interested in everything
Jay said, exclaimed "How amusing!" after his anecdotes,
and all in all showed such a pointedly polite, agreeable
side of her nature that Jay feared the worst. As a feeler he
made some remark about wives popping up in unexpected
places, but Ebie merely laughed gayly and said, "My dear
man, if you'd known as many married men as I have you'd
know they all have to jump when the little woman appears." And she added parenthetically to Mrs. Kameray,
"After all, you can't blame the wives—it's not their fault
they're always getting left at home."

"I'll bet Rosenbaum would do a burn if he knew we

had the Kameray woman out tonight," Jay said to Lou in the johnny. "He was saving her to spring on you tomorrow, wasn't he? Poor leetle Meester Rosenbaum."

"Her accent isn't phony," said Lou. "She's foreign, isn't she?"

Jay made a face.

"Nuts, she spoke English perfectly when she got here," he said. "Then she caught on to this accent business and how it gets the guys. So she's been doing this-how-you-say-in-English, and-eet-ees-zo-how-you-say stuff ever since."

"She's got a right to an accent if she is foreign, hasn't she?" Lou said. "Anyway, she's a darn smart little dame, if you ask me."

Jay brushed his hands over his coat.

"What she says with that cute accent would sound dumb if she said it straight," he said. "Don't be a goddam fool. The dame's a phony of the first water."

"Phony or not she'll be okay working on Castles-in-the-Woods," said Lou. "Snap out of this, will you? I throw a nice bit of business your way, and here you are, griping."

Jay did not smile.

"I got worries, Lou. Flo popping up all over the place. If it was anybody but a wife it would be blackmail, because she never comes right out and accuses me, she just sort of hints until I give her a check to shut her up. And now Ebie's sore. I know you don't like Ebie but———"

"All I got against Ebie is that she's too good for you," Lou interrupted. "What do you want to mess around with somebody like Ebie for?"

"I don't know," said Jay, dolefully. "I'm not messing. It's just that I like to go back to Ebie, that's all."

"That's the trouble with you, Jay," Lou told him frankly.

"You're always getting into fly-paper. Take me. I drop in the Spinning Top, pick up Tessie or Fifi, slip them a fifty-dollar bill and that's the end of it. I can meet them on the street with my wife, they never bat an eye."

"Ah, they got no feelings," Jay argued. "What's the fun of sleeping with some little tart with no feelings?"

"Once you got feelings you're in trouble," Lou warned him. "Those girls are all right. No talk. Nothing. But what do you do? You get some dame that's restless, mad at her husband, maybe, too high-class for a fifty-dollar bill so you got to give 'em a diamond pin. Then the trouble begins. Oh, Jay, this is Mrs. Friedman——"

"That's all washed up," Jay said.

"Never mind, it's always somebody like her. Oh, Jay, she says, I'm here at the fur storage and I'm so embarrassed, I'm short a hundred dollars cash for the alterations on my mink. Do be a lamb and loan me a couple hundred —send it over, will you? . . ."

"Ah, shut up," said Jay.

"Or else she has to get her car out of hock, or she wants to pay her dues at the Golf Club," Lou went on relentlessly. "Too high-class for fifty bucks a night. It's just five hundred a shot, that's all. And then she talks, and her friends are your wife's friends and then you're in. Don't you ever learn anything, Jay, for God's sake?"

Jay looked sorrowfully in the mirror at his brown face, now a little haggard from a combination of hangovers and woes.

"Can I help it if I like high-class women?" he asked. "I like a looker, sure, but I like a little class to them, a little intelligence. To me it's no fun unless the woman has a little intelligence."

"They got more than you can use, believe me," said Lou. "It's that intelligence that costs you money, boy."

When they got back to their table Ebie and Mrs. Kameray had their heads together whispering about something furiously, but drew apart when the men sat down.

"How you women dish!" said Jay. "Clothes and men, that's all you women think of."

"I suppose the subject of clothes and sex never came up in the forty minutes you two have been in the little boys' room," said Ebie snippily.

Lou took charge of that one.

"Men don't have the time to discuss sex when they're alone, I assure you," he said.

"Well, then, I don't know where they picked it up," Ebie said. She turned to Mrs. Kameray. "Wonderful, isn't it? They never talk sex and they never listen to sex talk. They just learn it by Braille."

Ebie getting nasty was a good sign, so Jay cheered up. No man was more miserable in the doghouse, than Jay, Lou reflected, and no man in the world did more to get himself into the doghouse. Figure that one out. They danced a little more happily together this time, but Mrs. Kameray was too tired so Lou sat with her, wondering what to talk about that would keep her seductive accent going. He couldn't imagine why that got him so, but it did, just like Ebie's apartment had got him. Some quality there he had never encountered.

"We were talking about our fren' Meester Rosenbaum," Mrs. Kameray explained. "The feeling about Jews is so strong I say he should make his name Gentile, like Rosetree or Rosebush."

Lou laughed loudly.

"Is it fonny?" Mrs. Kameray inquired innocently. "Meester Rosebush, he laughed too, but I say I am going to make the start until everyone will think he is a good Meester Rosebush and not a bad Meester Rosenbaum."

Lou laughed until the tears came to his eyes. He looked around for Jay and Ebie to come back so he could repeat the story but could not spot them on the floor. They must have gone out to the bar for a private quickie. It was just like Jay Oliver,—here he could easily seize this momentary break in his relations with Ebie to cut it off for good, but no he had to get his head back under the axe again, in a good position so that Flo or Ebie could take turns whacking.

He looked at Mrs. Kameray and wondered curiously why Ebie disliked her so much. Here was a lady, definitely a lady, you could tell that, nobody to be a nuisance around the place, yet Ebie was catty about her. She was different from American women he had known, about twenty-eight, he thought, or less, but tricked out to look like a dainty little woman instead of the youthful college girl type that the twenty-eight-year-old American girls tried to imitate. She had brown sleek fine hair parted in the middle with a little bun at the back, a fine bust, tiny waist, rounded thighs and slender legs, like old-fashioned women, he thought, and small in stature like old-fashioned women. Her little flowered hat dripped a silvery veil over her smooth white forehead and even over the nose—a strong New England nose like his mother's with the same full high cheeks and rich full lips, pouting a little but all the more provocative. He liked her slender sloping shoulders, the long slim forearms, he liked her slim ankles with their slow breath-taking ascent into plumpness, and more seductive than that was

42

her poise, her calm acceptance of her own charms, the cool glaze over her dark brown eyes. He had been a long time trying to figure out what gave the piquantly artificial air to her person, and decided it must be the foreign flavor of her clothes, smart with lacy jabots, and the painted ivory ear-rings must help, for to his surprise she wore no make-up at all.

"Don't you wear lipstick?" he was impelled to ask.

She smiled deprecatingly.

"Everyone looks at me so when I wear leepsteek," she said. "I don't like it when everyone looks at me so. And my eyes are so beeg I cannot put on the stuff they put on."

"Ebie certainly lays it on," said Lou.

Mrs. Kameray lowered her eyes.

"Ebie is so nice," she said. "Ebie is a very nice person."

Lou couldn't help thinking how decent this girl was, nothing catty about her, when Ebie had put *her* on the pan all right behind her back. You didn't often run into women with any loyalty to each other. He saw Ebie and Jay standing out by the bar talking earnestly. They were getting along now, he could tell by their faces.

"Ebie's all right," he said, "when she isn't drinking."

Mrs. Kameray did not reply.

"I wonder what Rosebush would say if he knew you were out with Jay and me tonight," Lou kidded her. "He's arranged for me to meet you tomorrow, you know."

Mrs. Kameray's eyes danced.

"We wouldn't want to disappoint Mr. Rosebush, then, if he's made himself so much trouble about the introduction. Let's pretend tomorrow we don't know each other," she suggested.

Lou laughed again and agreed. He could see Jay and

Ebie craning their necks to look at him and thought they were probably surprised to see him laughing so much. He was usually pretty deadpan, but then he didn't get a girl with such a dandy sense of humor often.

"What's your business like, Mr. Lou?" asked Mrs. Kameray, earnestly, hands locked beneath her chin. "I so want to know."

"Take a hotel," said Lou. "Or take a tavern or a resort. It's got to have equipment, hasn't it—furniture, orchestra, cigarette girls, maybe palm trees? And it's got to have good roads leading to it, good neighborhood around it. All right, I'm the man they consult."

"You do all that?" she was wide-eyed.

"I have small office staffs, sure, but I got investigators all over the world, people making maps, people shopping for equipment, people wangling local politics to clean up bad sections around a hotel,—they report to me. I keep a finger on everything, I'm the works."

"Like an emperor," sighed Mrs. Kameray wonderingly. "Oh, how you must be a genius! Yes, like a czar!"

Jay and Ebie had disappeared for a long time before Lou realized it and even then, he went on explaining his business to Mrs. Kameray for hours, sipping brandies to her Rhine wine and seltzer, glowing in the unexpected pleasure of talking business to a woman, and though he did not even touch her hand he felt more disloyal to Mary than he had ever felt in his six years' married life.

V

ON SUNDAYS Ebie lay in bed and thought what a mess
she'd made of her life. She had been in the habit of
thinking this every Sunday for years and it struck her that
she hadn't run through these Sabbath meditations for
weeks. Why was that? By Sunday she still had done enough
things to be sorry for, she hadn't stopped making a mess
of things, that much was certain. It must be she had turned
off the routine during Trina Kameray's long stay. That
was it. All during Mrs. Kameray's stay she had waked up,
at first irritated and finally furious at the mere sound of
somebody breathing in the next room. The shower running
made her think jealously—"my new red-and-silver shower
curtains, damn her hide!" The smell of coffee reminded
her that it would be made in Trina's way with a twist of
lemon peel which Ebie loathed. The phone ringing made
her snatch the receiver and snap "Wrong number" before
the person had a chance to ask the infinitely grating question, "Is this Mrs. Kameray's apartment?" All these little
things had made Ebie irritable and continuously filled with
Christian intolerance. No one could have been more unob-
trusive than Mrs. Kameray around the house, and after
all it wasn't as if it was a tiny apartment, there really was
room and to spare for two people. Nor was Ebie a selfish
person, she told herself, she was perfectly candid with herself, if she'd been a selfish person she would have been the
first to admit it. It was just that what was hers was hers.

45

All right, she'd brushed the woman off. There wasn't a shred of her around, she had been shipped off on a three months' tour of the country for Castles-in-the-Woods, representing the Louis Donovan Service. Therefore now Ebie hadn't any hates and Sunday rages. She had doldrums. The same set of doldrums she'd had for ten years,—ever since she had started being twenty-four, in fact, an age she had loyally stuck to socially for these ten winters. Professionally she admitted twenty-eight, and a maidenly fear of thirty. No reason why not, she looked better than she ever did, that is, dressed up. A commercial artist got a lot of graft, especially when she did clothes, as Ebie did. So even if her income hadn't been enough to dress her handsomely her graft would have. And presents. One thing and another.

The chimes from St. Thomas' told her it must be around eleven so she rolled over and checked this with her little musical alarm clock which had been tinkling "Lazy Mary" for the last half hour. It was the chimes' fault she had such bad Sundays, Ebie decided. They nipped into her sleep, dimly reproaching her for being late to Sunday school at the M. P. Church on Elm Avenue, Greenpoint, Iowa. She would struggle to wake up because although she didn't care about Sunday school she did want to wear her new pink dotted Swiss with the toast-colored straw hat so that the little boy who played in the yard next to the church would see her. Finally she would manage to wake up. And here she'd be in New York and not Greenpoint, and then she'd think of what a perfect mess she'd made of everything since those dotted Swiss Sundays, and that had been, roughly speaking, ever since she'd been ten. No sir, she thought mournfully, she hadn't had a pink dotted Swiss since her tenth birthday, unless you counted that dotted

Swiss kimono with the china blue silk lining. Nothing Sunday school about that, of course. Still, it was dotted Swiss.

She threw off the cover—it had been a warm night but there had been a little cool breeze with a pleasant hint of autumn and burning leaves. The kids in Greenpoint used to burn leaves on September evenings, she recalled. On Sundays, too. She wondered why anybody wanted to burn leaves but anyway it was fun and smelled wonderful. She must tell that perfume company to put out a Burnt Leaf fragrance. They'd say women didn't want to smell like a small-town bonfire, but she would say look at Russian Leather. People had said women didn't want to smell like Russian Leather but it turned out they did. Well, there was a constructive thought. Burnt Leaf Parfum. Only you couldn't say "parfum" any more unless it was made in France, because of that new law. All right, call it Burnt Leaf Smell and see where you got. She got out of bed and walked into the adjoining room, barefooted in her new high-necked nightgown, the one with the train, the one she had been presented with after drawing it for the manufacturer. She wanted to see what the work-room looked like, being a work-room again and not a guest-room. It looked wonderful, the couch a couch again instead of a bed, the table a desk instead of a dressing-table.

"My God, I really am getting selfish," she admitted, and then she decided this joy in the house to yourself was not selfishness but just pleasure in self-preservation, a New York characteristic. In a town full of people the New Yorker's only haven was home, she thought, pleased at being so clever and philosophical with just her own thoughts, and then she wondered if that was what she really thought. That was another angle to her Sunday soliloquies, this thinking things then wondering if that was what she really thought or what she had made up her mind to think, and if so, what was she really thinking behind her thoughts.

Ebie had two small rooms, the bed-room and the work-room, opening on the balcony over the living-room, but the work-room was so dark she usually worked in the sunny living-room below and used the upstairs room just for storing and filing. She had had this apartment for five years and was still amazed and delighted with its magnificence. A woman cover-designer had first had the place, it was a co-operative apartment, and it was still filled with the little touches that had finally bankrupted her,—the concealed lighting, the built-in cozy corners and trick bookshelves on the balcony, the specially made door-knobs, wall fixtures, ventilating gadgets, all things the poor owner could not take with her or resell. Moving in here had represented a big change in Ebie's life, a definite decision to play the commercial game, drop the old artistic crowd downtown and the Village nonsense. She'd spent enough time sitting at the feet of somber soon-to-be-great painters having them lecture her about taking her talent seriously, urging her to make good the promise of her Art League days, and decrying the advertising art she was making a living at and incidentally which they couldn't do. She was a sap for some of those boys, no doubt about that. She used to cook midnight supper for them while they kept her up all night talking art and she was flattered that they allowed her around. Then she met Jay Oliver with one of the advertising men she knew at an Illustrators' Ball and it was a moment in her life all right. The change from art talk to hard-boiled Middlewestern business talk seemed marvellously refreshing. Her ten years with Art seemed a long expedition into a foreign, fuzzy, phony world,—it was fine stepping out of it into straight commercial world, hearing Jay's straight talk. Money. Money. All right, there it was, the thing everybody wanted, artists, too, only it was wonderful to have people come right out and say so. It was like the simple dotted Swiss days, all one, two, three.

Ebie reflected now that she had begun thinking life was a mess ever since she'd made up her mind not to be kidded any more about life or to kid herself about it, for that matter. So here she was, not knowing when she was kidding herself and when not, whether she liked this handsome independent plush life her income brought her or whether she had had more fun, while she had it, out of the old rowdy-serious Bohemian life. The thing she had decided was that a girl alone had to have an above-reproach background in which to be Bohemian. You could slide down banisters yelling "Whoopee" in a palace and you might and could be a gay visiting duchess, but a little gay solo dance in a Greenwich Village basement made a girl out either a nut or a tramp. A good address was a girl's best mother in New York. A man saw a place like this and thoughts of marriage came out on him as obviously as freckles.

Not that Ebie wanted marriage. She'd had chances enough but where would she get off, marrying somebody and then scramming out every time Jay Oliver called up? Still she'd like a little affection, she thought with a modest dab at her eyes with her kerchief, maybe you didn't want a husband or a mother or a father or a child or a dog but you did have to have something. You did really have a right to have something belonging to you, something you could kick around and say, now that, that is definitely mine and nobody else's, and nobody has the right to kick it around but me, and that's security. What did she have secure in her life? I mean tender, true security, not financial security. That set her thinking some more.

Ebie put on the taffeta housecoat and slippers that Hannah had laid out for her and turned on the radio. She felt like a little companionship. If you could only skip Sundays! Her bed-room was rather bare in comparison to the heavy-carpeted luxury of the living-room and it was not so much that she had run out of money by the time she had furnished the downstairs as that she did not like to wake up in a clutter of ruffles. She couldn't quite explain this but if you waked up to bare walls, uncurtained windows, Venetian shades of course but no drapes, you could map out the day's work with no interfering images. The little white radio on the night-table bleated out a sonorous sermon and again Ebie shivered and turned it off. She might as well go down and get breakfast. Hannah never came on Sundays so she got her own.

In the kitchenette off the living-room, shelves were prettily stacked with black-and-white checkered canisters, a glass cabinet of all manner of goblets, tumblers, ballons, liqueur glasses, all betraying the old Southern hospitality standards, and the shelf of fancy canned goods, pickled walnuts, brandied peaches, smoked salmon, pickled mussels, shredded cocoanut, black and red caviar, teas—oolong, jasmine, mate, revealed a nice imagination in food.

"And to think," Ebie reflected, "I'm the girl that used to eat sugar and vinegar on my lettuce."

As a matter of fact Ebie, when she cared to, could whip up a nice little dinner, a gift that had made her quite popular as a Sunday night hostess for her father back in

Greenpoint, and later on as an art student living on Washington Square. She wondered now, as she plugged in the percolator, whether Lou Donovan ever let on to Jay what had happened the other night. Men were always such gentlemen with each other that any dope could tell what they were hiding. She wasn't mad at Jay, as he thought, for the stupid mess about his wife,—though she had let him think she was still mad. She was really mad at herself. There was the telegram on the table cancelling one job, all because she'd delayed it by rushing out to Pittsburgh to meet Jay. She could blame Jay for that if she wanted to be unfair but of course it was all her own fault for being such a fool about him. Here she deliberately sets out to be a success instead of an artist and then lets a married man make a mess of both things! All right, that was bad enough, but then she ought to keep the love part secure, since she messed up her life for it, but no, she had to make even a mess of that by letting the man's best friend stay all night.

"How did I get to be such a louse?" she wondered out loud. "If it had to be somebody why did it have to be his best friend?"

So she decided to blame it on the brandy, but then there were more self-reproaches there. That meant she was making a mess of her life by drinking too much. Drink ruined a girl's looks in short order, Rosenbaum had told her that much. On the other hand, as she had pointed out to him, she could show him girls who had never had a drink in their lives and yet were no balls of fire so far as looks were concerned. She turned the downstairs radio on to WQXR and got the Fifth Symphony. She always got the Fifth Symphony. She could almost write it herself now,—boom boom boom, begin the beginning over and over till every instrument has got in a few well-chosen remarks, then begin again, and again, ah now we're getting into it. But no, just where the middle should be the end begins with each little instrument saying a few last words, then altogether, amen, amen, good-bye,—ah but wait a minute, just a last minute suggestion, then good-bye, but wait, one more final nightcap of finales, boom da da boom, then another (now I really mean it this time, we really must go after this last one). That was the Fifth Symphony and that was what art and culture finally rattled down to—too much spinach, take it all and say you like it, or else throw your weight with people like Lou Donovan and Jay Oliver who made fun of culture because they didn't have any. She had kidded the pair of them the other night at dinner, the night she brushed off Mrs. Kameray.

"What'll you have, baby, a steak?" Jay had asked.

"A steak for God's sake," she had mocked. "These two bums clean up a fortune today and they can't think of anything better than a steak to buy for us."

"Anything you say, baby," Jay said. "You can have quails on toast just by lifting a finger."

"That deal today is nothing," Lou said. "By the time we're through, old dear, we'll be buying you angels on toast."

The waiter stood at attention and Jay looked up.

"Four angels on toast, waiter," he said, "nothing too good for us."

Angels on toast, my eye. Ebie sat eating toast and sausages with sliced pineapple, listening to WQXR and looking over the Art Section of the *Sunday Tribune*. Whenever she got disgusted with her affair with Jay she cried a little over the art columns. That helped along her Sunday doldrums as much as anything. Here was Royal Cortissoz or Jewell approving "Dunes," "Kansas Dirt Farmer," "Apples and Bible," "The Old Captain," "Upstate White Church"—(as if she hadn't practiced them all herself ages ago)—by her former art school colleagues. She too might be in that blessed company—"heavily influenced by Kenneth Hayes Miller," or "under the domination of the Midwest School," or "reminiscent of Cézanne but lacking of course both his gusto and his inspiration." Yes she could be among those contemporary immortals instead of here in this elegant apartment, last night's orchids and tomorrow's breakfast all on ice, her life a mess,—yes there could be no doubt of that, though her gift for prostituting her art had always made those old companions strangely jealous. She dried a tear again, and turned to the society page, for no reason, except that there could be nothing certainly in those small periodic sentences to make her think of either the futility of love or of art. Or so she thought until she was idly glancing down "News of Resorts" and after "White Sulphur Springs" came to the first item under "Atlantic City":

"Mr. and Mrs. Jay Oliver and her mother Mrs. Mac-Alister are at the Hotel Traymore."

Ebie put the paper down and lit a cigarette. After the way he had tried to make it up with her. After the way she had almost forgiven him and really intended to at the right moment. Then he goes down to Atlantic City with his wife and mother-in-law of all people. No reason why not. A wife was a wife. She shouldn't flare up at Jay. The fault was her own for giving up her simple old life as a real artist—(work away at it even if it takes years! That's what she should have done)—and started distorting all

53

the decent·things in life with commercial art, married men, Rainbow Rooms. Hopping all over the country at a word from the man. Kicking her work over. Kicking over her ideals. Her little old dotted Swiss ideals, she thought sadly. Served her right that he should pass her up now for his wife and a little family stroll down the old Boardwalk. Served her right for picking up with a fellow like Jay. Visiting fireman. That's what fellows like Jay and Lou were called. Fellows the old crowd would have laughed at. Fellows you took to Luchow's for dinner then to Jimmy Kelly's for the midnight floorshow and they shouted "Greenwich Village—whoopee!" And your crowd sneered at them and didn't appreciate that they might be smart in their own line to make all that money, and the visiting firemen looked at your friends' and your own art works and said, "How long did it take you to copy a picture that big?"

You fell for them for a while of course, the firemen, because maybe you got a little too much art talk, a little too much literary conversation, a little too much brain work instead of dancing and fun. But a person was a fool to let them get you. Here Ebie pulled up the shades and saw that the day was fine, it was wearing its finest Sunday clouds, white, calm, substantial, and a stern blue sky, and the sun was all polished up and glittering, throwing eye-stabbing reflections on windows across the court, shining away fiercely, working hard to make a good impression so that it needn't come back after lunch. No, nothing to prevent her picking up her old life, she could always go back to it, just as Jay and Lou could always go back to their wives. Jay and Lou with their big respect for marriage. Doing anything they pleased on the side but keeping up the great marriage front. The Show Must Go On. That was the phony part of the visiting firemen. And just as Ebie had gotten very suddenly fed up one day with artists' life in Greenwich Village she now got fed up with her present. She dialed the garage for her car and then raced upstairs to dress. She rummaged through a drawer till she came upon a dotted Swiss dance set with blue ribbon bows. If you couldn't wear it outside you could at least wear it next you. Then she turned on the radio full blast to a recorded program and sang with it, "I Can Dream, Can't I?" softly along with Bing Crosby while she hurried into a suit. She suddenly felt like kicking over every trace of the present.

"I'd almost go back to Greenpoint," she thought, "only it wouldn't work out because I'm not ten years old any more."

Outside the apartment the doorman opened the door of her little blue Plymouth for her.

"Glad to see you can get away such a fine day," he said heartily. "Sure fine weather for getting out in the country."

She must certainly have had the look of going some place all right.

The little blue Plymouth with the red wheels rolled down Park and over the Grand Central ramp and down Fourth. On Sundays Fourth Avenue below Murray Hill was a deserted street except for the little comings and goings of the Vanderbilt Hotel. There was a nice hotel, Ebie thought, it had Wedgwood medallions all over the doors and a dark mezzanine where you could lunch with one man and see over the balcony rail the man you were going to dine with that night being a big shot with the boys—(cigars, brandy, do-you-know-the-one-about-the-derby-hat-and-the-plumber)—at a table down in the dining-room below. A nice hotel, the Vanderbilt. Caruso had a floor there once, but there were other things about the place, too, Ebie recalled with a reminiscent smile. She had forgotten to salute the old Murray Hill Hotel a few blocks back, but there were memories of that, too. Brass beds, for instance. Bay windows. In the dining-room, publishers, agents, travelling salesmen, and Hartz Mountain canaries, a pleasantly out-of-town flavor to it that made you able to guess the type of man he was if he suggested this restaurant.

A little blue car is very becoming to a young woman as every young woman knows, so the casual pedestrian today turned to look after Ebie as she drove on down and over to Irving Place where the Sunday hush fell on old well-kept brownstones, handsome old apartment houses;—people really lived here, there was even a father out wheeling a baby, a rare spectacle in Ebie's life so she leaned out to see whether the pram really contained a baby or a publicity stunt. Now the lights changed and stopped her directly in front of the house she had once roomed in with her girl friend from the League named Honey. Ebie was surprised to see the house still there, an old brownstone, one of Stanford White's designs (she remembered the land-lady pointing out the house around the corner on Gramercy Park where Mr. White had lived before his murder),—oh, yes, and it was there that young musician had shot down the author, David Graham Phillips. It was a romantic murder belt, this section, sometimes famed as the home of Washington Irving though he had never been murdered so far as she knew.

56

From a fine old mansion this house Ebie once knew had deteriorated into "Furnished Rooms" with an Armenian restaurant in its basement. Odd spacious black walnutty rooms, Ebie recalled, with dark mahogany stairs up and down from one wing to the other, elaborate balustrades, little balconies in the great foyer as if for a small orchestra, so that the bleak rooming-house atmosphere blended with the dim fragrance of long-ago balls. You could almost shake out echoes of "Kiss Me Again" from the dark velvet hangings. Oh, yes, it was an old waltz house, Ebie thought, definitely that. She wondered if Honey still lived there and looked at the door intently, half expecting the old girl friend to walk out as big as life, but there was no sign of her. Just as well since they had parted on very chilly terms for no reason at all except that they either disliked each other's men friends or else liked them too much. At any rate they had a habit of spending the last hour before retiring, the Stocking-washing and Cold Cream Hour, in snarling at each other over each other's dates. Honey was a virgin (at least you couldn't prove she wasn't), and was as proud as punch of it. You would have thought it was something that had been in the family for generations so that no matter what the circumstances she could never quite bring herself to hock it. Honey took courses in oil at the League and modelled for a commercial photographer for money, and Ebie took black-and-white courses and did fashions and illustrating for money. They had a living-room with quite nice furniture, at least like Honey's virtue you couldn't prove it wasn't, since it was always encased in bright chintz slip covers. There was a fireplace with fires forbidden, a little bedroom and bath and kitchenette, all for eighteen a week. Since all they ever cooked in was breakfast or a canned hash supper their expenses were very little, unless they were being rushed by League boy friends at their own expense since the boys there were usually poor. Ebie and Honey used to try to break even by taking out a Visiting Fireman one night and a League boy the next. They even had their moments when they had no dates at all but just went on a girls-together-spree. They'd wait around till almost eight pretending they wanted to finish a detective story, or that they weren't hungry really, then face the fact that there was no dinner date coming up tonight, so they would go round the corner to a tavern where O. Henry used to go, and they'd sit in the dark smoked-wood booth drinking old-fashioneds and telling each other things they certainly wished later they had never told, and bragging about their families, sometimes making them very hot stuff socially back home and the next time making them romantically on the wrong side of the tracks. The families must have been on wheels back in the Midwest, whizzing back and forth across the tracks at a mere word from the New York daughters. The thing about this restaurant, too, was that there was nothing tea-roomy about it, so they felt very sophisticated being the only women in it often. Honey loved literary men so other times they went to a literary hangout on Eighth Street where you could see your favorite author in the sidewalk café. Honey usually carried a magazine with her "work" in it to impress the strangers who usually barged up trying to promote a date. They drank Planters Punches here, a specialty of the place, one that usually brought all the men's eyes to their table, and eventually the "Pardon me, I hope I'm not a nuisance, but would you mind telling me what the name of that wonderful drink is? . . . Planters Punch? . . . Thank you. Look, you won't think I'm fresh I hope, if I suggest buying a round of them. Seriously, I'm just curious about them."

What a drink! The waiter bore the glass with snow a foot thick all around the glass and a mountain above it topped by a miniature fir tree of mint, and extra long straws through which you drilled for rum, and it seemed to come up from the damp bowels of the very earth, you could almost get Floyd Collins on a clear day as somebody had once remarked. After things got going Honey would whip out the magazines and show her Work. She was the girl on page 98 in the nightgown holding her hands to her head and remarking in capital letters right beneath the picture, "Oh, why didn't I take a Selzamint and Wake up Happy?"

"There," Honey would cry, "would you believe that's me? My other profile is much better—the right side of my face, I mean, but they liked this side for a change."

Then she'd eagerly leaf through the next magazine. There she was on the back of the cover page in three colors in three different poses. ONE: Ball gown. Dancing with white-tie man who averts his face. Balloon coming out of her mouth saying, *Let's go home, dear, no one will dance with me, yet I look every bit as nice as Emily.* Balloon from white-tie man says, *Yes, dear, but why not see our family doctor?* Two: Doctor Troutman's office. Honey in street clothes. Balloon coming out of Honey's mouth saying, *But, Doctor, is there nothing I can do about Body Aroma?* Doctor balloons back, *Fortunately, Mrs. Flashman, there is a secret formula known to physicians for many years but only recently made available to the public. It is ——*" THREE: The Ball. Different ball dress for Honey and this time surrounded by half a dozen men all holding out their hands as she is wafted triumphantly into the dance by her proud husband. *Well, dear,* he balloons at her, *I notice you had every dance tonight. What has changed you? Bodyjoy,* she radiantly balloons right back. *Ever since using Bodyjoy my pores have been breathing properly and I am once again the girl you used to know.*

The strangers were always impressed and usually told Honey that her acting in these three little vignettes from real life was so good she ought to be in pictures, and she always had the snapper ready, "But I AM in pictures, only not the kind you mean. I'm an artist."

Honey was such a feeb Ebie couldn't understand how she'd stuck it out with her those two years. It got so just the sight of Honey on a Sunday sitting around painting her toenails and brushing her red hair one hundred strokes was enough to drive her crazy. When the hairdresser burnt off a big hank of this prized hair in a permanent wave, Ebie did feel sorry for her and tried to comfort the poor girl as she lay sobbing on the bed, the handmirror face down beside her.

"Never mind, Honey," Ebie had said, "you never were the conventional type of model anyway, you're not dependent on a glamor-girl haircut. You've got a different style, see, not the regular model type of face."

At this Honey sat up and looked eagerly into her mirror again.

"I know," she agreed with satisfaction. "I'm more the elfin type. My face is a perfect heart-shape, isn't it?"

Even if it was kidney-shaped Ebie didn't want to hear about it and she moved out almost at once before she started screaming. She took a place then on Washington Square North East with a back door on the Mews. An enormous, high-ceilinged room it was, panelled walls, great windows through whose perennially dirt-stained panes the sun threw a stingy little light. There was an oil-heater to combat the strange blasts and drafts that wolfed around the baronial room on winter nights, whistled through locked doors, walls, closed windows, barred fireplaces. But a great cathedral chair, a vast sofa all bought at auction around the corner and ready to crumble at a glance, and her easel, drawing board, and reproductions of Daumier, Steinlen, Breughel, Grosz, and a few of her own sketches, pinned on the wall, gave the place quite an atmosphere. In fact the studio was so romantically Bohemian, so much the artist's dream, that Ebie did less and less serious art here and more and more discussion of it. The more commercial work she did the more of her old studies did she pin up with pride, and the more money she made the more she enjoyed the company of the arty boys and girls. "My God, but I was bright then," she reflected now with astonishment, "I certainly threw away a good brain when I started up with Jay and Lou's crowd." But of course it was her own fault, she knew that.

Further down the street the blue Plymouth drew up before an entrance labelled simply "BAR and GRILL." It was the tavern entrance to a somewhat mediæval looking hotel, whose time-and-soot-blackened façade was frittered with fire-escapes racing the dingy windows up to the ugly gargoyles on the roof. For Ebie this hotel too held certain associations and for a minute she looked out of the car thoughtfully at it, wondering whether to rouse these sleeping memories. Even on a bright noon like this the BAR and GRILL was a sunless cavern, its dark oak wainscoting rising high to meet grimy black walls, its ship-windows covered with heavy pumpkin-colored chintz, so that entering the room you seemed at first in a cellar fog till a feeble ray of gray light from a window above the door permitted you to grope your way down the long somber bar. Once in you were in for no mere moment, and Ebie, aware of this legend as she was, gave a slight start on seeing that same ruddy but glum man in the derby at the foot of the bar who had been there five years ago day and night, his coat always over his arm as if in the act of flight, a flight that never took place.

It was after twelve, the hour when the bar opened on Sundays, and the elderly lady residents of the hotel were without too much obvious haste taking their places in the grill-room, nodding and smiling to the waitresses, carrying their knitting and a slender volume of some English bard, anything to prop against their first Manhattan. If you ever had asked yourself "What ever became of that famous old suffragette who chained herself to the San Francisco courthouse? What ever became of that lawyer who saved Killer Mackay? What ever became of the girl who survived Niagara Falls? What became of the author whose one book sold so many million copies he never wrote again? What became of the first wives of these now famous men?" the answer would be—"Look at the BAR and GRILL." Here they dwell, as remote from life as if they were in Bali. Coming out at noon to the Grill they retreat at dusk into the even dingier caverns of the upstairs, grope their way through narrow silent hallways to their small dark respectable rooms. Seldom speaking to each other they are comforted by each other's presence and if in the night the lady who had once sung with Caruso should feel once and for good that wild pain in her left auricle she could always rap on the wall and thus summon the ex-eminent architect who had been freed of the charge of strangling a whole family twenty years ago near Albany.

A stained-glass window behind the bar gave a saintly glow to these resident lunchers as they sipped their drinks and dipped into literature. It was sip and dip, sip and dip, until cocktail time was proclaimed by the arrival of the little cocktail sausage wagon, and by that time the barriers that prevailed at noon would be brushed aside, privacies violated, discreet bits of personal information exchanged, letters from absent nephews or far-off celebrated friends read out loud while Music by Muzak played Songs From Cole Porter Hits. Another curious thing about these small, venerable, respectable hotels, there seemed no appeal here to the average customer. BAR and GRILL for instance, appealed to seemingly genteel widows and spinsters of small incomes because there was an air of musty piety about the management, a lady could be a dipsomaniac here under the most genteel conditions,—very quiet, very hushed, this place; then there were these tired flashes in the pan, the one-shot celebrities, and on the other hand there was a gayer younger group whose loyalty to the BAR and GRILL was based on the cheapness of its martinis. Over their simple dollar lunches (four martinis and a sandwich) this livelier set snickered at the old residents, whispered nifties to each other when the small very, very fat little old resident waddled in and was assisted with great dignity to a bar stool by two courtly gentlemen near-by who appeared unable to get a real hold on the gelatinous little creature and must scoop her up by handfuls.

The sight of the smart little blue car drawn up outside joined all groups in a common excitement, heightened by the unusual spectacle of such an uptownish and well-turned-out specimen as Ebie Vane coming in to this ancient cavern. Not that many of the residents did not have friends as splendid as this in other quarters of the city, but these friends were understandably loath to contact them in this dark hole. Who was she meeting—what brought her here instead of to the Lafayette, the Fifth Avenue, the Brevoort or one of the other more expensive and certainly more suitable rendezvous?

Ebie, after a brief glance around, took a stool at the bar and ordered a Dubonnet with a dash of brandy by way of eye-opener.

"What happened to Willie?" she asked the bartender, a beaming rosy young man, a chain grocery store clerk, she thought.

"Willie? Willie's been gone these five years," he said in a pleasant Scotch brogue.

The glum man in the derby with his cane hooked over the bar-rail, the fat lady, and the two gray-haired men drinking Scotch silently at the other end of the bar all were eyeing Ebie in the bar-mirror. She saw their eyes reflected between the mirrored stacks of bottles, their quietly questioning faces. She certainly must look out of place, there, the only normal-looking visitor in the whole joint. She looked around more carefully and then saw in the dim little stall in the corner where the livelier set was lunching the person she was seeking. She paid for her drink and walked over.

"Hello, mama," she said.

"Why hello, Ebie," said her mother pleasantly. "Sit down—these are friends of mine—I didn't catch their names. I was just telling them how perfectly ridiculous this article on Edgar Arlington Robinson was, so don't interrupt."

Ebie nodded to the others and sat down on the end of the bench beside her mother. The others, who had been sitting with resigned, unhappy faces, exchanging hopeless looks with each other, up to this point, now brightened. No good deed of hers was ever more appreciated than this simple appearance at the table, for her natty plaid suit and simple good looks gave point to her mother's endless anecdote as well as excuse to her mother's mere existence, something the group she was now entertaining had doubted could be done. To tell the truth the lively set had just about decided to give up Ye Bar, in spite of its twenty-cent drinks, because of Mrs. Vane. The three of them, two men and a girl, had been hilariously comparing notes on last night's party, burying their heads in their hands as they were reminded of the perfectly awful things they had said and done, and to so-and-so of all people; they had reassured each other that it didn't really matter since the so-and-sos had been known to misbehave themselves on occasion.

"But at Mrs. Whitney's!" the girl kept exclaiming. "At Mrs. Whitney's of all places! Oh, Foster, you shouldn't have! After all, you can't go around tweaking every Van Dyke you see."

"How did I know it was General Vanderbilt?" complained the young man, and then he sighed. "But what hospitality! Two footmen to each guest, pouring up your glass as fast as you could down it till finally they kicked us out. Why aren't there more homes like that?"

"You can't say anything, my dear," the other young man chided the girl, "after you pushed that dealer into the chocolate cake."

They buried their faces again, roared with laughter, reproached themselves, roared, and then Mrs. Vane appeared, as indeed, she appeared to almost every guest in the Bar and Grill at some inopportune moment, and for this reason was known as The Haunt. A tall gaunt woman of sixty, she looked like a witch, black eyes, dyed oily black hair, and strange drapes pinned together somehow on her person with little oddments of jingling jewelry and bracelets which served to set off her amazingly long fingernails. As a wit-butt Mrs. Vane had served her purpose more than well in Ye Bar and Grill, but it was her flair for society that was ruining her and in fact almost ruining the hotel. Mrs. Vane loathed the lonely women of the hotel and yet a literary woman of violent opinions has to have someone to talk to, and frequently Albert, the bartender, was too busy to listen. At those times she would raise her lorgnette and examine the room for suitable companionship. Today she spotted the intelligent young group in the end stall and at once descended upon them.

"I love laughter," she said by way of introduction. "May I join you? I am so outraged by this article on Robinson, Robinson, the poet, you know—let me read you what this absolute fool has to say about him—hmm . . . let's see— here . . . listen to this."

She was in, the young lively set was crushed, and there she sat, ordering her dry sherry, very very dry please, Albert, one after the other because she was not a drinking woman and could only take a dash of sherry or in cold weather a medicinal dose of brandy. Of both these liquors she drank very little but all the time. Her companions were imprisoned, their laughter stopped, gloomily they foresaw hours passing with this sort of thing and no decent escape. Ebie's entrance at least permitted them to watch curiously

the smart stranger at the bar, without having to fasten
their eyes on Mrs. Vane's witch-face. Then to their amazement the handsome stranger walked up to their very table
and was Mrs. Vane's own kin and they respected Mrs.
Vane, then, and listened eagerly to her, lest she take their
pretty guest away. In a pause during which Mrs. Vane
lifted her glass to drink, one of the young men said, "Are
you and your mother in town for long?" hoping to draw
Ebie in and freeze mother out but it proved to be the
opposite, for Mrs. Vane hastily set down her drink and
switched at once from reminiscences of Robinson to her
own life story.

"Goodness me, young man, I've lived in New York ever
since I found I couldn't get a decent psychoanalyst in Iowa.
I've been here since 1924, off and on. A few years in
Europe, of course. I met Freud. Speaking of Freud, Ebie,
what do you hear from your father?"

"I got a Christmas card," said Ebie. "Nothing since then.
It was just signed Father and Daisy."

"Probably married again," mused Mrs. Vane but the
subject did not seem to interest her for she immediately
launched into her life up to a treasured evening she had
spent with Gogarty, the great Irish writer, who, she stated,
definitely was the wittiest man she had ever had the pleasure
of meeting. The young people looked curiously at Ebie,
trying to fathom her connection with the weird old bore,
and Ebie looked at her watch. Mrs. Vane described in
detail the violent prejudices she had mentioned about
George Moore, James Joyce, Bernard Shaw, and other
great figures to the sparkling Mr. Gogarty on her great
evening with him.

"What did he say?" politely inquired the girl.

Mrs. Vane's yellow face lit up.

"Gogarty? He didn't say a thing," she exclaimed triumphantly. "Not a damned thing all evening! Where was the card from, Ebie?"

"Greenpoint," said Ebie. "He still lives in Greenpoint. He still has the store, you know. Look, mama, how would you like to take a house in Connecticut with me?"

The inquiry served to silence Mrs. Vane's monologue as nothing else could. She lifted her lorgnette and frowned intently through it at Ebie.

"Connecticut? A house?" She was suddenly aware of the amenities for she turned to the three now embarrassed young people and said graciously, "I don't believe I introduced myself. My name is Mrs. Vane. You must excuse my daughter for bringing up personal matters at a public luncheon. What kind of a house, Ebie, do you mean a boarding house?"

"No, not a boarding house, nor a bawdy house, either," Ebie exclaimed, exasperated. "A house."

Mrs. Vane now rested her chin on her hand and studied Ebie seriously.

"I suppose you mean a salt-box. That's the kind of houses they have in Connecticut. Salt-boxes. No, Ebie. I don't see why I should have to live in a salt-box. Not at my age."

The girl saw an opportunity now to escape and nodded significantly to her companions.

"Mrs. Vane and her daughter want to talk family matters, boys," she said. "They don't want us intruding."

"No, no," protested Mrs. Vane reaching across the table toward her escaping companion, "it's my daughter who is the intruder. I had no idea she was coming in. Why didn't you telephone me, Ebie? After all, one doesn't just drop in on a person."

"I've left messages," Ebie answered, "but you never called back."

"Probably had nothing to say," said Mrs. Vane. "I see no reason for using the telephone just because there's one handy. If I had had something to say, naturally I would have called. Don't go."

She urged this last in a most hospitable voice as if it was she who had arrived early to snatch this prize corner and had graciously permitted these strangers to join her. The Lively Set, however, climbed over her draped knees with alacrity, the men with a last wistful glance at Ebie. As they hurried out into the little oblong of light that revealed the mouth of the cave Ebie heard the girl say clearly, in answer to some murmured comment from the man, "Yes, but don't you think a little too, too Harper's Bazaar?" All you needed to be Harper's Bazaarish down here was a tweed suit and a loud muffler, she thought.

"Who were they, mama?" Ebie asked.

"I don't know their names," said Mrs. Vane, with controlled ill-nature regretting her loss of public, "After all, Ebie, I have lived around here for some time. It's natural that a great many people should know me without my knowing them. Now what is this about a salt-box?"

"I was just thinking today," Ebie explained patiently, "that here we are, the only two Vanes in New York and we ought to see something of each other. I thought we might have a house in some little village the way we used to out in Greenpoint, and go there when we're sick of New York."

It sounded so perfectly foolish after she said it that Ebie

was not surprised to see her mother twist her mouth into a wry grimace and examine her sidewise, with head cocked, like some curious old barn-fowl.

"I'm sick of New York, right now," Ebie added.

"I'm not," said Mrs. Vane. "I'm not a bit sick of it. Why should I want to live in a house again? I was analyzed out of a house once, I don't want to get back in one. Do you realize what a house means, Ebie?"

"I've got some money, that's all right."

"It isn't money," said Mrs. Vane with a certain amount of passion, "it's the grocery list, the bread-man, the coal-man, the garbage-man, the children."

"I haven't any children," Ebie said desperately.

"There are always children," said Mrs. Vane. "I've never seen a house that children didn't get into sometime or other. A salt-box. That's characteristic of you, Ebie. Typically, typically Vane."

As Ebie had never made any suggestion in her life that even approached the fantastic normality of this one, she let her mother's remark pass.

"We could have a station wagon and on a Sunday like this we could even go to one of those little churches, the kind you used to make me go to when I was little," Ebie said.

Her mother was still looking at her as if expecting a more actively violent evidence of insanity.

"The only reason I sent you to church was to have a little quiet in the house," she said. "That's the only reason people send their children to church. Besides, my property's here in New York. I take a great deal of interest in my property."

Mrs. Vane had used "the property" years ago as an excuse to stay in New York and Ebie recognized the argument now. She had in fact traded her house out in Iowa for first payment on a made-over tenement in New York, and this deal had obliged her to make her first trip to New York, a trip which turned out to be one-way. The "property" was in back of a bakery in the Italian quarter and was tenanted by impoverished artists and writers who seldom paid rent and who left word constantly at the BAR and GRILL for Mrs. Vane to please fix the hole in the roof, the rats in the wall, the boiling water in the toilet-bowl, the two old panhandlers who slept on a newspaper every night in the vestibule, the explosions in the furnace, the roaches, the bugs, the boys playing baseball in the court, and other minor matters. These little messages, written on the hotel's pink memorandum slips as the calls came in to the operator, were brought one by one by the lone hotel bellboy, an elderly negro of sixty, to Mrs. Vane every day at twelve when she reported for her first sherry in the bar.

"Goodness me, Albert," she would say, examining these pink slips with the complacency of a star looking over fan mail, "Two B says the girls up in Four A are streetwalkers and wants them either thrown out or a carpet put on the stairs so the tramping up and down all night is hushed."

"Better throw them out," Albert advised at this point.

Mrs. Vane was astonished.

"Indeed not, I shall throw out Two B instead. They're the ones that are always complaining."

"You can't throw 'em out if they paid their rent," Albert said.

"That's the nice part," Mrs. Vane responded. "They

haven't. I can always throw anybody out I want to because nobody ever pays their rent. Except Four A."

Even Four A complained one day. They wanted Mrs. Vane to come over right away and see about the roof. They did not so much object to the hole in it as to the bricks falling through it. God knows whom they might hit. Mrs. Vane decided to regard this summons and, arrayed in her most splendid vestiges of rabbit and imitation leopard with a green scarf wound round her head to set off her long hooped ear-rings, she went over to her Property and rang Four A's bell. But every time the door opened a crack and a girl peeped out she cried out, "Go way, go way." Mrs. Vane, mystified, finally went downstairs into the little court-yard between the bakery and her house and made noises till the girl looked out the window and again made frantic gesticulations of dismissal. Mrs. Vane shrugged and went home, found a call waiting to come over to see Four A's room at once.

"I was just there, my dear girl," she said. "You wouldn't permit me to enter."

"Oh," said the girl weakly, "we thought you were a gypsy."

It was this very property that was now holding Mrs. Vane in the city and keeping Ebie from living a fresh wholesome family life in a simple village far from Jay Olivers and commercial art. It was not the first time her mother had disappointed her, but Ebie was still able to be surprised.

"My life is here, my dear child," said Mrs. Vane. She tapped her magazine pointedly. "I was just reading this article when you interrupted with this salt-box notion. I like to keep up. I read everything, no matter how mad it makes me. You ought to read more. You're always chasing about. You ought to read and find out what life is all about."

There didn't seem to be much more to say. Every few years Ebie remembered her mother and tried to revive the acquaintance but it was always the same. There was nothing to say to each other, and definitely no need of each other any more than there had been years ago when Mrs. Vane was the leading clubwoman of Greenpoint.

"Now, why," asked her mother, suddenly interested in Ebie's fingernails, "would anybody have fingernails like that?"

"Because I like them, that's why," snapped Ebie.

"I'm glad it's a matter of choice, then," said Mrs. Vane. "For a moment I thought it was doctor's orders. I must go upstairs and see if that little snip that does my hair has come. Good-bye, my dear."

"Are you having your hair dyed again?" asked Ebie.

Mrs. Vane looked pained.

"Not dyed, Ebie, restored. There's a great difference."

She rose and wafted away, her magazine under her arm, and Ebie gave up. She thought she might as well have a drink to revive her spirits and stood at the bar after her mother had floated into the hall.

"We met on the General out of Chicago," a voice said at her elbow. "I believe we have a mutual friend in Mr. Donovan, Mr. Louis Donovan."

Ebie started and drew back. Beside her at the bar was a middle-aged gentleman in the newest-looking suit imaginable, soft gray hat pulled jauntily down over a weather-beaten face now illuminated by an ingratiating toothy smile. Ebie didn't remember ever having seen him before.

73

"My name is Truesdale," he said, and lifted his hat briefly. "Here's my card."

Bewildered, Ebie looked at the card thrust into her hand.

"T. V. Truesdale," it said, and down in the lower left-hand corner, "Personally representing Louis Donovan, Pres. of the Louis Donovan Service."

"Well, for God's sake," said Ebie. It was quite true as her mother had pointed out, you never knew who knew you until it was too late.

VI

Mr. Truesdale had been nipping in and out of the Hotel
Ellery for many years without attracting either the respect
or the interest of the management. He had a seventy-five-
cent room on the first floor, that is the floor above the
Bar and Grill, and since this was the only seventy-five-cent
room in the whole place and was originally intended for
the colored elevator boy, its possession by Truesdale did
not automatically endow him with great prestige. He knew
this, of course, and did not draw the manager's contemptuous eye by entering the palm-riddled lobby, but instead
scuttled in and out by the delivery entrance in back, over
ashcans and stray cats, and whisked through the court up
the back stairs to the little dark hole over the kitchen.
Steerage, that was what it was, and he was used to it, you
could hear the hotel machinery throbbing all night, dishes
rhythmically clattering, cooks fighting, ashcans rolling
about, milk bottles clanking, delivery trucks backfiring,
trunks galumphing up and down stairs, and hearing this
you felt you were really going some place, if only into another tomorrow.

The fact that Mr. Truesdale was not a drunkard or
woman-chaser or a noisy guest with pets or violins, that
sort of thing, did not particularly enhance his position.
Sometimes those abstinences from the ordinary vices merely
indicated the man was a pauper or possibly a law-avoider
for obscure and sinister reasons. Honest, yes. But even this

was not too much respected ever since the time he had doled out his two-nights' bill with a dollar in dimes, thirty-eight pennies and twelve cents in postage stamps. The dollar and a half was paid, all right, but supposing one of the fancier guests had seen the exchange offered! It would make the Ellery seem like a flophouse, and decent guests would run like mad.

The manager of the Ellery had a selection of greetings for his customers. For the old gentlemen permanents he had a gravely respectful, "Good day, sir. How's the arthritis today, sir?" Usually he leaped ahead of them to hold open a door and on icy winter days looked out the door after them, calling out "Are you all right, sir?" and none of the old gentlemen permanents thanked him for this apprehension that they would drop dead any minute. With the old lady permanents he was fatherly, humorous, kidding them about their flirtatiousness, complimenting them on their spryness, patting them a good deal, scolding them lightly for not wearing their mufflers, and pleasing them mightily by his assumption they were all feeble-minded. He was especially concerned over his old ladies, though they were a niggardly lot and wanted everything for their money, but he had sense enough to know that women were the ones with the money, old women, anyway, and nobody minds miserliness in guests that have it tucked away in a sock. It's when they don't have another cent that stinginess is a vice. The manager—his name was Mr. Lowry, —had another greeting for the neighborhood husbands who put up at the Ellery when their wives were away or their apartments being done over; these were business men, family men, with daughters in college, and Mr. Lowry treated them as equals; shaking his head over business,

the fate of the Dodgers, European conditions, the damn
Reds, and gravely making it clear that he too had a home,
a family, a Buick, and a cocker spaniel like any other law-
abiding citizen, he was not to be mistaken for a fly-by-night
whippersnapper just because he was in the hotel business;
with these equals Mr. Lowry often had a beer or two in
the bar, and if they were really solid men he occasionally
got drunk with them on a summer night; you could safely
bet on his companions' good bank standing if you ever
saw Mr. Lowry weaving about in glorious abandon; with
such good men Mr. Lowry even permitted himself to get
drunk in his own bar, but he never drank with a drunkard,
that is an ordinary drunkard, and he made it a rule never
to drink for pleasure. For Mr. Truesdale, who was relentlessly remembered as having paid his bill in three-cent
postage stamps once, Mr. Lowry had a democratic nod,
or more exactly a half-nod, unaccompanied by a smile or
direct gaze, a preoccupied busyman's nod, but at least it
was something, better than his brusque half-nod to debtors.
Mr. Truesdale, however, stalwartly refused to accept any
nod, marching past the manager when they did meet, with
a stony face, though afterwards in the hall or in the
privacy of his room his lips moved soundlessly in a brief
imprecation. "Bastards! I'll get the bastards!" Mr. Truesdale, by throwing Mr. Lowry in the plural, indicated that
he was not so much a solitary enemy as a mere private in
an army of enemies.

The Hotel lobby was even darker and drearier than the
Bar and Grill, not a whit brightened by its palms or cir-
culating library stand that was rarely open for business
and when it was only had twenty or less books. A stand
of picture postcards, five cents each, showing the Hotel

Ellery did not require any attendant inasmuch as the Ellery residents obviously were never tempted to advertise to the folks back home their present fortunes. Through an avenue of palms the guest strode or crawled to the desk for mail or bills, and here Mr. Lowry usually stood checking on the work of his employees, or handling the guest himself. For ordinary routine he placed himself behind the mailboxes and frowned out at his telephone operator or the room clerk as if it was his frown that did the work, not the assistants at all. Occasionally Mr. Lowry laughed, a booming fine laugh that made everyone feel better. He had his fond chuckle for the old residents, his good sport laugh for equals, but these were nothing to his laughter when he heard a genuine bit of wit, a good story or a snappy comeback. People were often telling him anecdotes or some merry fellow would toss out a good crack and Mr. Lowry laughed and laughed, that is if the guest had paid or was paying his bill. If the fellow was in arrears Mr. Lowry shrugged at the jest and muttered "Hmm. A wisecracker" sarcastically after him. But what could be wittier or more refreshing than the remarks made by a man paying his bill? Mr. Lowry had a dandy sense of humor and did not consider it his fault that nothing witty was ever said by a party that owed you money, or passed out a rubber check.

In Mr. Truesdale's scuffed Gladstone bag under his bed there was—and this would have astounded Mr. Lowry—a large index card with brief bits of information about Mr. Lowry and indeed in the same package of cards were snippets of news about other figures in the hotel, about Mrs. Vane, for instance. Mrs. Vane was listed, with a few personal remarks about her tastes, under "Automobile Prospects." Mr. Truesdale had been able, on occasion, to turn an honest dollar by selling a list of "Interested" Prospects to an auto company salesman. Mr. Lowry, it would have embarrassed him to know, was a potential toupée customer, being a self-conscious bald man instead of a debonair one. Under "Suggested Approach" Mr. Truesdale had jotted "Toupée would add dignity necessary to hotel manager besides making youthful appearance attracting younger clients, also relieve L.'s tendency to head colds." It can be seen that Mr. Truesdale, even when seeming to be unemployed, was in reality never idle, profiting by any overheard conversations as well as by his own sharp little eyes. Mr. Truesdale never forgot a face nor anything about its owner that he'd ever known. This was not really so remarkable since his bread and butter so often depended on this memory, aided by his dossier of tidbits. It was not that Mr. Truesdale was a lover of humanity or an observer of the contemporary scene, either. If he ever got two cents he could rub together, he often mused, he would rejoice in never speaking to anybody, he would shrug his shoulders when anyone asked for recognition and say, "I meet so many people!" He'd have the great pleasure of minding his own business and telling everybody else to go mind theirs. However, he was fifty now, and the chances of ever having two pennies to rub together were less and less. Twenty years ago he might have been optimistic over his little finger-hold on Lou Donovan. Now he accepted it as a bit of luck for today but tomorrow it might vanish. While it lasted he was playing it for all it was worth, never mind about that. There was always a chance of a bit of permanent luck. Within the last three days he'd made more money than he had in the last two months. He'd had a couple of tens and three fives in his worn wallet—in fact he'd gotten a new genuine pigskin wallet at a chain drug-store for ninety-seven cents, ten cents more with his initials. Lou had prescribed a decent suit of clothes, advanced forty bucks on it. Forty bucks for a suit of clothes! Truesdale hated to spend money on clothes, but it was an absolute fact that the trouser seat of his present suit was worn to such gossamer thinness that he had to rise with the utmost caution. So he went down to Division Street and selected a natty extraordinarily aquamarine-colored suit for fourteen-fifty.

"I wouldn't pay a penny more than twelve for this quality suit any other time," he told the salesman sternly, "of coss, as you see my bucket's out in my old suit so I can't bargain with you."

He bought a Paisley-patterned shirt, ninety-four cents with tab collar and came across a rare bargain in bow ties, three for fifty-nine, blue polka dot, green polka dot, and a more severe black polka dot, all absolute rayon. Shopping further at a "PRICES SMASHED! BUILDING COMING DOWN! FORCED OUT OF BUSINESS!" place down by Brooklyn Bridge he was able to pick up half a dozen colored handkerchiefs with "Lawrence" embroidered in the corner for nineteen cents. He could have gotten three with his own initials for the same money, but economy prevailed over egotism. Very few people looked at the name on your handkerchief, and if a manufacturer's mistake about the popularity of the name "Lawrence" could be profited upon, then by all means proceed to profit.

No doubt about it, the new outfit did give him quite a kick. He went to the stationers on Fourteenth Street and bought a new brief case, eighty-nine cents, a beauty, zipper style; he also bought a handsome fountain pen and pencil combination, one buck, a brand new set of index cards, and four bottles of ink named "Aztec Brown," "Patrician Purple," "South Sea Blue" and "Spanish Tile." These were business improvements, for he had decided to use each color on a person's dossier to denote certain things, the blue, say for automobile prospects, the purple for piano or radio possibilities and so on. He placed the ink bottles in a neat little quartette on his dresser-top and laid the two ties with his old one in the top drawer, and felt the first genuine thrill of possession he'd had in years.

"Of coss, it's only a beginning," he reminded himself.

On the Sunday he met Ebie Vane he paid his week's bill with a twenty and was rewarded by Mr. Lowry telling him a joke. He rewarded Mr. Lowry by saying calmly, as he picked up his change, "Yes, as I recall it that anecdote was quite a favorite with the old Maharajah—quite a favorite, as a matter of fact. He's told it for years."

He left while the manager muttered "So. A wiscracker, eh!" quite disgruntled at the rejection of his good-will offer. The good-will was not offered solely because of the new show of affluence on Truesdale's part, it was due also to the sudden series of phone calls, telegrams, incidental indications of a guest's rise in the world. Mr. Lowry was even willing to suspect that the three-cent stamps episode was the gesture of an eccentric rather than a pauper. But if he was prepared with friendly overtures, Mr. Truesdale on the other hand was not, stalking into the Bar and Grill with head high quite as if Mr. Lowry was merely a servant of the hotel, as was indeed the case, not the owner as he liked to imagine himself.

In the Bar and Grill this Sunday Mr. Truesdale found

the conversation between Albert and the glum man in the derby going on about houses in the country, a conversation which Mrs. Vane's raised voice on salt-boxes had given the cue. The glum man wished to God he could get rid of his farm near Danbury, Connecticut, speaking of farms, and this one only raised chickens and taxes. If he could get rid of the place he'd take the dough and buy a forty-foot tub, a sea-goer, and by golly, he'd never get off it. He'd fish from Newfoundland to Bimini and the Keys, he'd go after every damn fish there was. He'd never do a stroke of work, he'd call in his insurance policies, he'd lie on every beach from here to hell-and-gone, and for food he'd eat fish, it wasn't bad, and he'd wash it down with beer, or, if he had it, some plain old Dago red. Albert, the bartender, however, never could see a thing in fishing. So far as he was concerned fish was only something that came in cans and could stay there. He had a lot at Northern Beach, Long Island, bought with newspaper subscriptions and a hundred bucks down, and if he saved some more he'd turn that over with his old Chevy and buy a double house in Bensonhurst, rent out the top floor, keep the bottom, make it pay for itself. Mr. Truesdale made a note of these two desires for his dossiers on each of the men, exchanged cards with the glum man, who was a Tompkins of some paper manufacturing company. Even while his ears were picking up this information his eyes observed Ebie Vane, the lady he spotted on the train with Lou Donovan, and the other fellow. She looked a darn sight better than she had the morning he saw her get off the train; he had marked her then as a high-class tart. Maybe he was wrong. She looked fresh as paint today. What she was to Donovan he could not figure out, whether a train pick-up, a regular secretary, an accidental encounter, or an old friend. Being in the Ellery Bar made the pick-up theory seem the strongest, since Donovan was certainly not the kind of man to park a genuine lady friend in such a dump. After a few minutes' observation, however, Truesdale marked the car, the mother, and the comments of the other customers indicating that Ebie was a stranger here. The old dame was her mother, that was made clear. Mr. Truesdale, always loyal to his many employers, observed everything with the greatest care in case there might be something here Mr. Donovan might care to know. No matter what her connection was with Donovan, friend or employee, there might some day be some complication that a word or two of straight data might clear up. No harm, certainly, in speaking up to her. His new turn of luck gave him confidence, for he was not one ordinarily to accost strange young ladies; on the other hand Ebie's gloom made her more receptive than was usual for her. She looked at his card and then looked over the man curiously. Lou's promotion activities she knew had strange wires out all over so this man was probably all right. Not that she cared much about the references of men she met in public places. The world after all was not a private club, thank God. You could talk or not as you liked with any stranger unless they started making passes or being a pest.

"I didn't know Mr. Donovan had a representative in this hotel," she said.

"I'm in and out here," said Mr. Truesdale. "The cuisine, of coss, is not of the best."

"What is the cuisine?" Ebie idly asked. "I don't eat here, thank heaven."

Mr. Truesdale pondered this only a minute.

"Irish," he stated finally. "Personally, I find East Indian cooking the finest in the world."

He signalled Albert for a beer.

"You're having Dubonnet, I see. May I suggest another with this time a dash of Campari bitters, a favorite of my old friend, the Duke of Malleywell, at one time a resident of Calcutta?"

"I'll chance it," said Ebie, with a shrug.

It struck her that the man might be a detective. He might be a detective for Jay's wife, using Lou as an opening wedge. That was it, of course. The wife flying to New York with her mother, trying to get the goods on Jay, planting this fellow on the train even, so as to have further evidence. Probably right now he was checking up on Lou's alibi that she was an interior decorator doing his office, no connection of Jay's at all. She tried to remember what else Lou had said that day in the crisis. That she'd met him at the train. Well, this man knew differently so she'd have to fix that up a little if he should ask any questions.

"I dassay most of you New Yorkers think you know curry," said Mr. Truesdale. "But what do you get for curry here? A cream sauce with a sprinkle of the powder! No Bombay duck. No shredded cocoanut. A touch of Major Grey, perhaps, perhaps not. Depending. Have you known Mr. Donovan long?"

Ebie braced herself for the witness stand. She was, she decided, a very old friend of Lou's. She had gotten on the train in Pittsburgh, since he must have checked that. She was a commercial artist, since he must have checked that also, but was hoping to branch out in decorating, hence the opportunity to do Mr. Donovan's New York office. She had met Mr. Oliver for the first time on the train with her very dear friend, Mr. Donovan. She was now calling on her mother at the Ellery to discuss settling in the country.

"But why is it me that has to be on the spot?" Ebie's resentful second thought came. "Why don't I get the goods on Jay's wife, instead? But oh, no, it's me that's the criminal. It's me that has to save the home for Jay. Lou Donovan and me. The old marines."

Mr. Truesdale, using a little running sideline of comments on Siamese versus Ceylon dishes, as a siphon, managed to painlessly draw off Ebie's prepared information. The declaration of her friendship for Lou verified his feeling that she was the girl-friend, her mother explained her connection with the Ellery. The matter that interested him most, however, was the desire for a farm. It was a long shot that the lady who wanted to buy a farm would want to buy the very thing the glum man wanted to get rid of and indeed Mr. Truesdale had never known of a case where such a pat deal ever came through. But it was worth a gamble. A word here, a private tip to Tompkins, and there might be ten or twenty bucks in it for the informant. Mr. Truesdale had no lofty notions of his value, a few dollars picked up here and there, no responsibility about further complications, no duties, no ties. Pick up any time and move on to the West or East, unless he had something that looked pretty steady like his Lou Donovan contact.

"A commercial artist makes a lot of money," said Mr. Truesdale, eyeing Ebie thoughtfully. "Maybe more than a decorator."

"It's too high-pressure," Ebie said. "You can't ever catch up. And I never save. No matter what I make."

"Best thing for a type like you, then, is to put it in possessions," advised her new companion, authoritatively.

"Cars. Diamonds. Of coss, you ought to safeguard your future, roof over the head, and all that. It's a tremenjus comfort to a New Yorker to know he's got a little place out somewhere he can retire to if bad times come."

"It sure is," said Ebie. She looked at him suspiciously. Was this a quiet warning for her to get out of town? Maybe Jay's wife was out with a gun. Sometimes wives did get hold of a gun and the first thing they wanted to do was shoot down all the other women, never the guy that needed shooting. Maybe this little dick was tipping her off. Of course she had given him that lead about wanting to settle down somewhere in the country with her mother. He certainly picked it up fast, though. There was some reason for that. Calling her bluff, maybe.

"Of coss, it's a matter of finding the right place," said Mr. Truesdale judiciously. "You might want a showplace —or you might want a self-supporting sort of place. Of coss, if you aren't dependent on your own salary, if you have other resources to count on——"

"I haven't," Ebie nipped that one in the bud. Jay's wife wanted to see if Jay was passing out any of the family silver, evidently.

"I happen to know Mr. Donovan's business is very good so the decorating of his office is bound to be well paid," said Mr. Truesdale with a large gesture, as if the emolument was to come from his own pocket.

"If I should take the job," Ebie said cautiously, "I know Mr. Donovan would be generous. Particularly to such an old friend as I am."

She thought she'd better clear up everything now so she added, "Perhaps all Chicago people are generous, I don't know. Lou is the only person I know really well out there."

Mr. Truesdale blinked and then recovered himself. Ebie thought it was from surprise that she only knew Lou, but then reflected that he might assume she was out to get Lou. It struck her as funny. One on Jay and the little woman. She would not let Truesdale pay for her drink, which she gulped with considerable distaste for the overdose of bitters. She was relieved when the old bellboy came in with a message that if Mrs. Vane's daughter was still there her mother would like her to step upstairs and see her for a moment.

"If I should hear of a place in the country, I'll get in touch with you," Mr. Truesdale offered, affably. "Sometimes I hear things. Not my business, of coss. But sometimes I hear of things. I dassay I can always contact you through Mr. Donovan's office. That is, if you're seriously in the market."

"Oh, I am," Ebie assured him. "Indeed, I am."

"A genuine pleasure to meet you again," Mr. Truesdale said, bowing. "It would be a privilege to be of any assistance."

Ebie gave him a friendly nod and departed into the interior lobby. Mr. Truesdale paid for his beer and glanced around alertly to see what had become of his other friend with the boating desires. Mr. Thompson was at that moment seated in a booth having the dollar steak luncheon. He did not encourage Mr. Truesdale since it is one thing to mix at a bar and another thing at one's board.

"Just a word about that property of yours, friend," said Mr. Truesdale. "Is it in good condition?"

"Forty run-down acres, house leaks, garden gone to pot, chickens dying off," said Mr. Thompson readily, without slowing up the terrific eating pace he had set for himself, eating being merely a necessary stoking of the body to strengthen it for further drinking. "My wife sold all the decent furniture in it before we separated and the rest my daughter took when she got married so it's half-bare. Damned uncomfortable. I stay here mostly but there' the place. Yelling for repairs. Got a nigger out there, shiftless cuss, but he half-tends to it and makes a little, gardening."

"How much would you sell it for?" asked Mr. Truesdale.

Thompson looked more friendly. He thought a minute.

"Four thousand five," he said. "It would cost me that much to fix it up. I'd rather get rid of it."

Mr. Truesdale looked around.

"How much would it be worth to you to know of a good prospect?" he asked in a low voice.

"Not a damn cent," said his friend readily. "Unless they bought it."

"Supposing they bought it?" asked Mr. Truesdale.

"Sit down," said Thompson. "Have a beer."

VII

Mrs. Vane had a seventeen-dollar-a-week room and bath at the Ellery. It was a fair-sized room on the fourth floor front with two big windows and a respectable bath. Through these great windows the sun, at certain glorious moments around noon on certain days in December and late in the afternoon during the summer solstice, flooded the apartment across the street with its radiance and the grateful house at once flung the radiance back by reflection into Mrs. Vane's fortunate chamber. It was a time worth looking forward to, and the lady was always disappointed if a little errand kept her out during this magic interval.

"Oh, dearie!" she'd exclaim poignantly. "I've missed the sun today!"

The furniture was imitation maple, with a day-bed to give a sitting-room effect. This desirable effect, however, was at once offset by the piles of hat-boxes, bulging battered suitcases, and one open wardrobe trunk which took up most of the room and the huge Victorian walnut dresser with pier glass mirror, and marble top, an item Mrs. Vane had salvaged from a country auction somewhere and which she said was worth a perfect fortune if the right person came along. It had cost a small fortune already to have it crated and delivered and hauled to her room at the Ellery, that much Ebie knew.

"Is that you, Ebie?" called her mother. "Come in."

The old lady was in the bathroom, draped in Turkish towels, seated before the washbowl while the "little snip" from the next-door beauty shop worked the dye into the ancient scalp, with dabs of cotton. The snip nodded to Ebie and winked.

"This ain't a dye, you know," she said naughtily, "it's just a tint, if you please."

Ebie pulled up a chair to the bathroom door and lit a cigarette.

"Why don't you have it brown, mom?" she suggested, "it's more softening. I mean, if you must dye it."

"What do I want to look softened for?" irritably asked her mother.

"See?" said the snip.

The snip was a wiry little Irish girl with a big pretty doll's head, blue-eyed and curly-haired, attached to her small, tough little body.

"The old lady's got a bee, today," she whispered to Ebie. "Look out."

"I feel low, mom," said Ebie, "got any brandy around?"

"Now, Ebie!" upbraided her mother. "How did you know I had any? Besides I'm saving it."

"I sent you some not long ago," Ebie said defensively. "Where is it?"

Her mother heaved a sigh.

"I can't keep a thing," she said. "Look in the closet behind the shoe cabinet."

Ebie found the bottle and some glasses.

"Want some?" she offered the girl.

"A half one," said the snip. "I learned that in Ireland. I went back last year, and my dad thought it was awful I didn't drink. 'Come on, Maureen,' he'd say, 'a drop'd do you good, just a half one.' He'd put away a dozen half ones. I'd say, 'Why don't you take a full one, pop, you want it, and he'd say, 'No Maureen, I only take a half one, I'm no drunkard, my girl.' "

"So long as you're passing it out, I'd better have a touch," said Mrs. Vane. "After all it's my brandy."

"Soon as the old boy'd get a snoot full he'd start telling me the stories," said the snip, smacking her lips with pleasure over her glass. "All about the little people, not like your fairies, but little people with beards, dressed up with red shoes, all cocked up. There's a little man dressed up like that in Queenstown in the church, a real little one, he plays the chimes."

"Yes, and you never brought me back the colleen cape," Mrs. Vane remembered reproachfully.

"Your ma's always asking for a colleen cape like she seen once in the pictures. No good telling her the colleens don't dress that way. Like dad wanting me to bring him over an Uncle Sam suit, like the Americans wear."

"Never mind, get busy on my hair," Mrs. Vane ordered peremptorily. "I want to speak to my daughter."

"Fire away," said the snip.

"What's on your mind, mom?" Ebie asked.

"It's that antique," said her mother. "Look at that, Ebie. That's a beautiful thing, isn't it? You ought to know, getting around, what a thing like that is worth. It's genuine antique."

"It's old, but that doesn't keep it from being a pain," said Ebie. "What do you want with a thing like that? It looks like a ferryboat, all bulging out on the sides that way. All it needs is a whistle."

"That's the God's truth," agreed the snip.

"How do you know about antiques, my dear girl?" coldly asked Mrs. Vane, as the snip wrapped a towel around her head.

"My boy friend," said the snip.

"That upholsterer?" Mrs. Vane inquired, then added sternly. "I should think he would have asked you to marry him by this time, Maureen."

"Now, mama!" Ebie scolded. "Girls don't have to be getting married every minute. Times are different."

"I'm not an octogenarian, my dear," Mrs. Vane snapped.

"Sure, my boy friend and I figured we'd just live together," the snip giggled, with a wink at Ebie.

Mrs. Vane struggled to turn around and wither the girl with a look but it was too much with the firm hands now holding her head in a vise.

"A nice Catholic girl like you!" she exclaimed, outraged.

"What's the harm?" innocently asked the snip.

"I wouldn't do it, that's all," Mrs. Vane said, trapped. "I wouldn't do it. He'll leave you, sure as fate. And what if you have a baby?"

"I won't," said the snip.

"Leave her alone," said Ebie to her mother. "I'm the person to worry about. I'm your daughter."

"I hate young people," said Mrs. Vane sincerely. "You two seem to think any older person is someone to be mocked, and ridiculed. Neither one of you has a dime's worth of intellect. Ebie, about that tea-room you were planning . . ."

"Not a tea-room, mom," Ebie protested, now beginning to feel tired of the whole idea of the country what with everyone pressing her about it.

"Whatever it is, I begin to think it's the best idea you

ever had," Mrs. Vane went on, surprisingly. "I'm only surprised it didn't occur to you before."

"You kicked it out when I suggested it downstairs," Ebie said.

Her mother dismissed ,this.

"I've thought it over. I think it could be a gold mine."

"A gold mine?" Ebie was startled at this angle.

"Certainly. Take that beautiful old dresser there. I have a flair for that sort of thing. I'd like nothing better than whipping about the country picking up a piece here and there. I'd make a mint."

"Like you do on your apartment house," jeered Ebie.

"Never mind about that," said Mrs. Vane. "I can do two things at once. Or I might even sell the place and put it into antiques. You run the tea-room, say by some old mill stream, and I handle the antiques."

Ebie got up.

"That's a perfect whiz of an idea," she said, "and I can see right off where you make a million, but skip the tea-room part. The place I want to get is to use for a home, see, a home."

"A home," Mrs. Vane repeated, puzzled.

"Well, skip that part, too, then," Ebie said with resignation. "I just made the suggestion because I'm fed up with New York. I'm tired of the works. I want to lie around the porch all day like decent folks and dig in the garden and read serials in the *Cosmopolitan.*"

"Ebie, you're not yourself," said her mother, shaking her head. "But I'm serious. We'll find a place and I'll take the piece out as a starter and snap up a few bargains here and there and make a profit."

"Isn't she a one?" the snip marvelled, working away at

the old head as if her manual operations over the brain centers were helping this wave of inspiration.

"It's the first genuine inspiration I've had in years," stated Mrs. Vane proudly. "I'm really excited for once."

"I guess the Ellery'll be glad to get that thing out of the hotel," said the snip with a nod toward the dresser. "You don't need a house, Miss Vane. Just park that thing on a lot somewhere and move in."

"When will you find out more?" eagerly Mrs. Vane inquired, ignoring the girl. "I'm really intensely serious about this venture."

Ebie felt weak and as if fate was pushing her into something she had no right to fight. Once, in her early days with Jay Oliver, she felt like slashing up her wrists and ending the whole mess. Since then worse things had happened than mere lovers' quarrels, and she only felt now like running away, not poking her head in an oven or anything like that, just walking out of her present life quietly with no fuss, no good-byes, no quarrels. First her mother hadn't liked the country idea, all right, then, that was out. Then that funny little man at the bar, undoubtedly somebody hired by Mrs. Jay Oliver to watch her, challenged her about the country idea again, as if it was either that, or else. She didn't much care. But now her mother was hopping on the idea. The antique gag would occupy the old lady, maybe, but she'd get over it when it was time to really work on it.

"Don't let this old girl bully you into buying her a house," advised the snip jocularly. "I know how your folks are. Believe me, I stopped mine. They write me from the old country and they say, 'Maureen, we miss you, send us your picture and p.s. you might put a bit with it as times is hard here.' So I send 'em pictures of breadlines here in New York and I say, 'There's me, third from the end, with the tin cup up high.' That stops 'em."

"I don't blame you, Maureen," Mrs. Vane said. "You'll need every cent you make for your baby. But Ebie here——"

Ebie and the snip laughed.

"Okay, mom, I'll look around," said Ebie. "We'll see about the antique business when we get the place. I don't care what you sell so long as I'm not in it."

"You'll miss New York, believe me," said the snip.

"The hell with New York," said Ebie and went away, even more depressed than when she had come.

VIII

WHAT a week, what a week, Lou thought, yodelling "ya-ya-ya-ya-dee-die-dee-ya" in the shower bath, what a perfect honey of a week he'd had. What a town, New York, he thought, lathering his head with the piny-scented suds, what a beautiful, big-hearted honey of a town. No place in the world like New York. Everything had gone tick-tock, not a hitch. Call it the town, call it maybe a little bit Lou Donovan knowing how to handle it, too. That was the kind of guy he was, big town stuff. Little things floored him, but give him a big problem, give him a big town, the biggest, and he could swing it with his hands tied. People, for instance, the same. Little people, small fry, they only got in his hair, but give him the presidents, the managers, the thoroughbred women—(take Mary, for instance, his own wife)—and he knew just where to scratch.

He stepped out of the shower and doused himself with cologne. He had decided to plane out at one but first there were some matters of office equipment to settle (the receptionist really did turn out to have white hair, premature, sure, but it did give a high-class touch to the place) and arrangements had to be made to send Truesdale down to Maryland to look things over for him, quite sub rosa. The man could be valuable to him. Then there was the luncheon Florabella Cosmetics, Inc., was throwing for its officials and the press at the Ritz, at twelve. He promised to take a peek in and say hello to the boys before he took the car to the airport. Florabella was in the class with Elizabeth Arden and Rubenstein, and Lou was happy at being able to recommend such high-priced products to his clients. Most of them couldn't afford the prices wholesale but for Castles-in-the-Woods nothing was too good. Florabella Arbutus Soap and Florabella Arbutus Bathsalts in every bathroom, Florabella Make-up and Arbutus Tissue in every powder room, a fountain of Florabella cologne in the Tea Garden of the hotel. He'd already signed the order and it was a pip. A joy indeed on such a fine September day to have an unlimited treasury to dip into, not your own.

He whistled as he selected a gray tie with a small yellow dot, eight-fifty, a gray suit with the merest flicker of a darker stripe, one forty he paid for that suit, gray silk socks, —he looked all right, maybe a little tell-tale crinkling around the eyes, still he looked better than the run of men you'd meet. Nothing flashy, just quiet good taste. Mary had taught him that, she hated loud clothes, it was all he could do to sneak in an occasional pin-stripe.

"I don't know why it is," she said once, shaking her head humorously, "Lou always *looks* as if he had on a plaid suit even if it's the plainest dark blue."

He knew what she meant,—that he could give anything a certain air as soon as he put it on his back. Even in the old days when he paid twenty-two fifty for a suit he could wear it as if it was something.

In the florist's downstairs he selected a neat freesia for his buttonhole, ordered a batch of chrysanthemums, twenty dollars' worth, sent to the Major's wife with his card—ah, those were the touches that counted!—whom he hadn't met but who had just arrived on the *Normandie* according to his informers. He went to the telephone operator's desk to put in a call to Jay Oliver, find out if he was back yet from Atlantic City but he wasn't, so he called his Chicago office and told Miss Frye out there what to do and what to say.

"I'll be back tonight, but better tell Mrs. Donovan I'm not expected till tomorrow," he said, thinking ahead that he might want to date up Mrs. Kameray when he got in town, since she was already in Chicago. There it was, he thought, the difference between him and Jay Oliver,—he paved his way in advance for any little adventure, so he always had an out.

"The first Mrs. Donovan came in again," said Miss Frye over the phone. "She's still on your tail."

Francie again. You'd think you could brush somebody off after fifteen years, and true enough she hadn't crossed his path for ten years till this last month when she and her consumptive husband had hit Chicago. He had nothing against Fran, she was all right, only she made him feel so damned uncomfortable, always reminding him that once they did this and that, and there was always the danger of her spilling the beans to Mary. Why couldn't the past stay in the past quietly?

"What did she want?" he asked.

"Said she was broke," said Miss Frye. "You know. Wants to take the husband to Arizona. Hocked the car here for hotel rent."

"Arizona, hell, I'll bet he wants to get to Santa Anita," Lou growled. "That guy never learns. Dropped all his bonus money at Hialeah in two days, all right, so now he's set for Tia Juana and the West Coast tracks. No wonder he's broke."

"Well, she said she wanted to get him to Arizona for

98

his health," Miss Frye said non-committally, "I don't know what's on the level with her. She's coming back in later."

"How much she want?"

"Enough to get the car out and a couple weeks' board. Sixty—seventy bucks."

"Seventy bucks is a lot of dough," said Lou. "Give her twenty and tell her I said scram. I'm no Rockefeller."

He was feeling too good this morning to be bothered by Francie still hanging around. He remembered there was a hotel men's convention at the Stevens this week and some business friends might be around.

"Line up whoever calls up for a little party tonight," he said. "I'll be in late this afternoon. Open house. You might check up on the Scotch."

"Mr. Oliver was in," she said. So Jay was home already. "He helped himself to the bar a while ago and left on a high note."

"If he calls again tell him to drop in around sixish," he said.

"He will," said Miss Frye. "He says he's got to check stories with you as soon as he gets in. What goes on there in New York anyway?"

"Never you mind," Lou laughed. Smart kid, Miss Frye.

He paid the telephone operator, a cute trick with bangs. On her mark every minute, too. A kidder, but no funny business. At least that was Jay Oliver's report. Jay never could see a telephone operator without trying to promote.

"Don't you look grand with the posy!" she said. "You certainly do look happy. Is it the flower?"

"Sure, it's the flower," he said. "What else would I have to be happy about?"

"If that's all it takes!" she sighed. "Maybe I ought to

wear a flower myself if that's all it takes to be happy."

Smiling, Lou went back to the flower shop and ordered ten dollars' worth of red roses and a spray of gardenias sent to the hotel telephone operator.

"Not the blonde one," he specified, "the one with the bangs and the Southern accent."

"That's the one that likes sweetheart roses," said the boy wrapping a corsage in waxed paper standing near.

"All right, send her sweetheart roses, too," said Lou. "Let the girl be satisfied, by all means."

He wrote "Now, will you be happy?" on a card, signed it with his room number and "Donovan" and slipped it in the envelope. On second thought he slid a twenty into the envelope, too. That kind of thing gave him a big kick. He could never understand stinginess. These fellows that figured out ten per cent for tips, never tip unless you have to, and all that. All right, he had to figure close that way twenty, even fifteen years ago, but Christ, he was only making fifty or sixty bucks a week then. He was playing the horses then, too, and they certainly were doing him dirt all right. That was another thing. Some men never learned. Some men, like the punk Francie was living with right now, went on following the races year in, year out, losing and never knew when to stop. After three or four years of bad breaks he pulled out. Give him a wheel, the bird-cage, roulette, or even poker, at least there was some fun in the game itself. He usually managed to walk out with a little more dough than he went in with. But the horses— well, horses just didn't like him. The hell with them.

He walked up Park, holding his stomach in, feeling so fine that he was surprised to see so many glum faces about, glum-faced doormen in uniform walking tenants' obstinate little dogs on leash, grim nursemaids holding yelling little boys in sailor suits and little girls with a mere ruffle for a dress above little knock-knees, holding them by the hands but plainly wishing it was by the necks. What was the matter with people all so glum today?

He felt fine all morning, approved his receptionist, approved the rug, sofa and chairs that had come for the inner office. Not much was really needed,—just a front, an address. He probably wouldn't see it more than two or three days a month, if that. Unless the Castles-in-the-Wood thing took more time than he expected. He thought he'd drop in the Florabella Show Room over on Madison and pick up old Florabella himself, otherwise Bill Massey, and go on to the lunch from there. The Florabella Show Room was a sweetheart all right, you had to hand it to these guys, they knew how to dress up a cake of soap till it looked like the Hope diamond, all encased in jewelled tinsel paper in a satin box, and the rest of the stuff the same, all displayed in a satin-walled scented showroom with beautiful girls in different flower-colored satin play-suits making you order more than you ever intended. Lou sat down on a dainty pink sofa while Florabella products, exquisitely mounted on little gold stairs, revolved slowly under a glass bell in the middle of the room. Bill Massey came in from the rear offices, which were a far cry from the elegance of the front, but nobody cared. The pretty girl who had summoned him for Lou smiled at them both and departed gracefully. Massey, a big Irishman built like a prizefighter, thick neck, big nose, red curly hair, looked after the girl frowning.

"Was she giving you the eye?" he asked.

"Why the hell not?" Lou wanted to know. "I'm a customer, ain't I? Doesn't the customer get any breaks around here?"

Massey sighed.

"I hire these girls for their sex appeal but I'll be goddamned if I'm going to let them use it," he said. "I got a problem on my hands, believe me. They make the business, but they aren't supposed to make the customer. After all some customers got women in the family. It wouldn't be the first time if a wife walked in right now and started bawling hell out of me for selling her husband a bill of goods. That was Nettie, I'll tell her to lay off, you got a wife."

"Ah, leave her be, she didn't give me the eye," Lou said.

"It was a double take if I ever saw a double take," Massey said firmly. He sighed and rumpled his red hair. "I give 'em a pep talk every morning. Just gave 'em one now. 'Get in there and fight,' I said to 'em. 'It's for Florabella, your old alma mater. But for God's sake, kids,' I said to 'em, 'slow up the hips once in a while.' I said, 'Can't you take your mind off it for say just an hour a day?' "

He went back to get his hat and Lou started talking to the girl who had now come back and was going through her little routine of passing around a silver tray of samples, prettily boxed, stepping about prettily with the rhythm of the professional model, carefully toasted legs very appetizing against her aquamarine satin play-suit with its advantageous little flare-ups at front and back.

"Too bad you've only got two legs," said Lou.

"Thank you," she said courteously with a little bow.

"Don't thank me, thank God," said Lou. "Would you mind loaning me the pair of 'em to pin up in my office?"

She giggled, and wriggled her foot in its silver sandal.

"Yes, sir," said Lou, "if you were a centipede, by golly, I'd marry you."

"Don't be silly, I *am* married," she giggled.

Lou shrugged.

"Okay, you turn me down. How old are you?"

"Nineteen," she said.

"Hell, what would I be doing with an old hag of nineteen?" he wanted to know. "You'd only be good for a couple more years. I'd be out time and money. Make out I didn't say anything."

"All right, Mr. Donovan," she tittered. "I didn't know you were looking for a wife."

"I'm always looking for a wife," he insisted. "I'm fresh out of wives today. Too bad you're not my type."

Massey came back, hat on the back of his head.

"We're early for the banquet," he said, looking at his watch. "Let's drop in the Men's Bar and I'll match you for drinks. I could use a whiskey sour after the helling I did around town last night. Remind me to bump myself off next time I go up to Harlem, will you? Make a note of that, Nettie."

"All right, Mr. Massey," she obediently said.

Lou tucked a ten on her tray and lightly flicked her chin with his forefinger.

"You're in," he said. "Next time I'm in town I'll shoot it out with your husband. How big is he?"

"Six feet," she said, "he was a fullback at Dartmouth."

"Six feet? Then I'd better make friends with him," Lou said. "The way I pictured him was about four feet two. You can tell him it's all right. Come on, Florabella."

"You slay 'em, don't you?" jeered Massey. "A killer-diller. If you had as many of them around as I have day and night you'd be so sick of glamour girls you'd hunt down the plainest fattest woman in the world just for a thrill. Or turn nance. Why, I heard a story just the other day that I—me—mind you, was supposed to be a queen."

"Well?" Lou asked. Massey banged him on the shoulder. "That'll be enough," he said.

"I don't have to flatter you, boy," Lou said. "I threw you an order, now I can sit back and insult you all I damn please."

In the Men's Bar at the Ritz they ran into Rosenbaum reading the *Journal* and waiting for some client of his. He offered to buy a round but Florabella insisted on matching for it.

"Christ, the match game is the only exercise I ever get," he pleaded.

Rosenbaum shrugged. He didn't know the match game so Florabella patiently explained it, you guessed how many matches the other guy had in his hand and if you were right it was a horse and when you got three horses you won the round.

"Listen," said Rosenbaum, "do you mind if I just buy the drinks and save us all that trouble?"

Lou and Florabella wouldn't let him, however, so he regretfully won and it was Florabella's check. When Florabella went out to see if the guests were coming to the luncheon yet, Rosenbaum drew Lou aside.

"I want to thank you for giving our family friend, Mrs. Kameray, that job," he said in an undertone. "She was very happy about it, and I think will be darn good at promoting. I was especially flattered that you took my recommendation without even bothering to interview her. That's confidence, all right."

"If you say somebody's all right, they're all right," said Lou heartily. "That's how much I think of your opinion, Rosenbaum."

The little rascal! She'd never even peeped to Rosenbaum about being out all hours with him that night.

"I think you would have been very satisfied with her if you had met her," Rosenbaum continued. "She has poise and charm—all the stuff."

"Hell, fella, I can't meet everybody that's recommended," Lou said heartily. "She may be Helen of Troy but when a guy's only got four or five days in New York he doesn't have time to meet all the people he'd like. You say she's okay—all right, then, she's okay."

Florabella came back and said they had to go in to their luncheon party. Nobody was there yet but as host he had to be there. And if Lou could only stay a few minutes he'd better come in now.

"Wish you could join us, Rosenberg," said Florabella.

"Rosenbaum," corrected Rosenbaum.

Florabella waved his hand carelessly.

"Rosenberg, Rosenstein, Rosenbaum—it's all the same, pal, so long as the old heart's in the right place."

"Call him Rosebush the way I do," Lou chuckled, but he ended his guffaw by clearing his throat for a sudden startled expression had come to Rosenbaum's face. Lou was uneasily aware of Rosenbaum's eyes following him thoughtfully as he went out with Florabella. He could have kicked himself for the break. It was just the kind of fool break a fellow like Jay Oliver might make, a dead give-away if the other man was even half-smart. From the reflective look in his eye Lou was rather afraid Rosenbaum was more than half-smart.

"Now why did I have to pull that Rosebush gag?" he lamented. A fine crack to set a guy thinking, all right. As bad as being too quick knowing a wrong telephone number. Lou was so annoyed with himself for spilling Mrs. Kameray's little Rosebush joke that he did himself no credit with Florabella's early guests. He stood around for a few minutes with the bunch, laughing perfunctorily as Florabella wowed them with anecdote after anecdote, shady limerick after shady limerick. Usually Lou jotted down any new gags in his notebook for future edification of clients, but today he only half-heard. Later, on the plane, he tried to remember some of them but couldn't think of a single one.

IX

IN THE dead of night wives talked to their husbands, in the dark they talked and talked while the clock on the bureau ticked sleep away, and the last street cars clanged off on distant streets to remoter suburbs, where in new houses bursting with mortgages and the latest conveniences wives talked in the dark, and talked and talked. All over the country the wives' voices droned on and on about the bridge prizes, the luncheon, the hollandaise sauce, the walnut surprise, the little defeats, the little jealousies, the children, the grocer, the neighbor, and husbands might put pillows over their heads or stuff their ears with cotton, pretend to snore, sigh loudly with fatigue, no matter, the voices went on and on, riveting the darkness, hammering into the night hush, as ceaselessly and as involuntarily as cricket noises.

Jay Oliver sometimes comforted himself with the thought of all those other husbands, and he forced himself to admit in all fairness that perhaps he would not be so dead tired when he spent a night at home if he hadn't been up to plenty mischief elsewhere lately, so that listening was a just penance for past defections. Flo's nasal voice went on in the dark from her bed on the other side of the night-table while she worked Helena Rubenstein's tissue cream into her relaxed pores and laughter lines; Jay could almost tell now by the changes in her tone whether she was working on chin or nose or throat. Tonight through his dozing

there ran something about a Tossed Salad. Eleanor, it
seemed, whoever Eleanor was, and God knows he'd heard
enough about her so he should know by this time, Eleanor
had insisted on a Tossed Salad. Everyone else had wanted
Waldorf at the club luncheon but Eleanor had absolutely
insisted on a Tossed Salad. Sleepily Jay pictured this
Eleanor Whosis stamping her feet in the middle of the
dining-room, throwing the Waldorf apple-and-nut con-
coction smack on the floor and screaming, "A tossed salad,
or else! I insist on a tossed salad!" He pursued this melo-
dramatic scene in dreamy fancy, half-asleep so that the
images changed from normal size to dream proportions
and just as Eleanor herself had become a Statue of Liberty
in a dining-room as big as the Grand Central Station, in
fact a dining-room that was exactly that with trains shooting around under the table on two levels, just then he heard
another familiar cue, a phrase that on innumerable other
occasions had threaded Flo's bedtime monologues.

"If I could just set foot in that house, just once," she
was saying. So then he knew she was on her perpetual
grievance about the Lou Donovans, and the cool way
Mary Donovan kept her at a polite distance, and of course
there's never anything a husband can do about this, even
though he harbors the same secret grudge himself.

"Oh, I've passed the place plenty of times, I know the
outside," Flo went on mournfully. "It's all right, it's a
nice house, if you like Normandy Cottage style. Personally,
I think Southern Colonial like ours is a lot prettier and
more American looking. And even if this neighborhood
is falling off a little at least it's nearer town and that's what
I like. I mean I've seen the place outside, but I just want
to know for curiosity's sake how she's fixed it inside. She's

supposed to be so darned cultured and have such wonderful good taste and being a Harrod, my goodness, you'd think it was royalty the way Lou goes on about 'My wife, of course, is a Harrod.' I guess my folks are just as good as anybody's. My grandfather owned the biggest store in Taylorville, I could have gone to Vassar if I hadn't been fool enough to fall for you. I could have gone to Europe. What I mean is that it seems funny that all of your business friends have had us at their homes for dinner or cards except the Donovans, and here he is supposed to be such a pal of yours. I'd just like to set foot in that house, see what's so wonderful about it that they won't let anybody in. Not that she snubs me, she was just as nice as pie today at Eleanor's, and she asked me all about the petit point I made for Eleanor's dining-room chairs. I must say it is unusual, whether Eleanor appreciates it or not, so we talked about that, I mean Mary Donovan and I, and then I told her all about our trip, and do you know she didn't know a thing about Lou having an interior decorator to do his New York office? I said, 'My yes, she met him at the train in New York,' you know, that hard-looking girl with the pink veil over her hat, that Miss Vance or Vane or something."

Jay's eyes and ears opened so sharply at this last name that he felt as if they must have made a terrific noise. He was suddenly wide awake, and gripping the covers.

"Vance?" he said hoarsely.

"Well, Vance or Vane, anyway, believe me, Lou is in bad about that, I could tell by her expression," Flo went on complacently. "As soon as I mentioned her and how Lou said she was decorating the New York office for Lou, Mary Donovan pricked up her ears, so I knew something was up, and then she said, 'Oh, yes, that must be the one Uncle mentioned meeting with Lou. I'm sure I hope she does as nice a job on the New York office as Marshall Field did on his Chicago office.' Just like that, you know, very smooth, very easy, only you can't kid me. I could tell right away that I'd spilled something that was on her mind already. I could tell something was up right there at the station. So could Mama. Mama said the same thing, when she saw how funny Lou acted. She said, 'That girl's no decorator, she's Lou's girl friend.' "

"Oh, I don't think so," Jay's voice sounded so faint that Flo said, "What?" and he said, "I just said you might be right but I hardly think so."

This irritated Flo so much she sat right up in bed and raised her voice.

"You don't think so, oh, no, of course you don't think so, you men always stick together, you stick together instead of sticking to your wives, you know damn well Lou has a girl friend in New York, you're just afraid to tell me. Well, you don't need to, Mama and I are smart enough, we caught on. An interior decorator doesn't have to meet the customer's train, does she, if you ask me I'll bet she was on the train all along, probably came all the way from Chicago with him. Lou gets away with murder just because Mary is too refined to keep her eyes open. But you wouldn't admit it. You men are so darned afraid to tell anything about each other. Believe me, you don't even need to. Mary Donovan's no fool, though, she's on to him."

Jay lay very still, afraid to trust his voice, wondering irritably what was the matter with him that he couldn't stand up for Lou and defend him the way Lou had for him, and he felt mad at Lou for showing such superior guts in a crisis.

"You won't admit she's his girl friend," Flo said resentfully, "because you do the same thing, probably, and you're afraid I'll find out. Well, listen, old thing, you don't hide anything from me, at all, at all. I have a pretty good hunch about things like that. Now what's the matter? Where are you going? What are you getting out of bed for?"

"I'm going to get a drink," Jay said patiently, sliding his feet into bedroom slippers. "I'm thirsty, that's all."

"It's that ham we had," said Flo. "We had ham at Eleanor's for lunch, too. Baked with pineapple, like a casserole, and mashed sweet potatoes with marshmallow whip along the edges. And then the tossed salad and banana-almond ice cream with strawberry sauce and fudge cake. I was so nervous when one of the girls dropped some sauce and it nearly stained the petit point seat but fortunately it went on her dress instead. Eleanor says when she has men for dinner she protects the petit point on the dining-room chairs by putting an oilized napkin over the seats the men use so they can't drop stuff on the petit point between their legs; of course with the women their skirts protect the petit point. Mary Donovan said they were the most attractive chairs she's seen, and I offered to show her how to work them, so maybe she'll ask me over there sometime. I feel kinda sorry for her, so big as you please and so darned sure of herself, and all the time Lou keeping that Vance girl in New York and pretending it's business. Believe me, if I was in her shoes I'd have it out with him, I'd march myself right along to New York next time he went and I'd follow him wherever he went till I got the goods on him. I'm going to tell her so, too, if she asks me."

"I wouldn't," Jay wanted to say but no sound came

from his lips so he gave it up and pattered out the bedroom door, relieved to stumble over a hooked rug in the doorway so that he could relieve his feelings by cursing and upbraiding the stupidity of the maid, and even the mistress for overwaxing floors and having rugs skating all over the place. The counterattack successfully silenced Flo.

"I'm too tired to argue with you, Jay," she complained. "I've been flying all over the country for the last four days and then the lunch today and I'm honestly dead. It's just mean of you to start something when I'm trying to get a little rest. Go on, get a drink, if you can't sleep, but let me get a little rest, for a change."

He heard her turn over and he drew a breath of relief. In the sunroom he found the drink he was looking for and it was not water either. He sat in the wicker chaise longue, smoking and sipping a brandy for an hour or two, gloomily reflecting on how miserably he was repaying Lou for saving his life. All right, he was a bastard, but what could a man do once his wife sets out to make a bastard of him? God damn fool, that's all he was, he muttered to himself a dozen times, fool of the world, ought to have a rousing good kick in the pants, serve him right. Lou, though, was the regular fellow, a real friend, a pal, the man who saved him when he was on the spot. Well, the least he could do was to tip him off about what Flo and Judge Harrod had told Mary. In a way, though, he didn't see any real reason why Lou Donovan shouldn't get in a little hot water now and then. Other men did. Other men got caught every time they tweaked a stenographer's chin or snatched a kiss behind a kitchen door. A fellow—even a smart one like Lou Donovan—couldn't expect to have everything work out like velvet every minute. It wasn't normal to go through life with never a slip-up in the arrangements. Lou was a fool to expect his luck to always hold. Still, he'd tip him off to watch his step as soon as he got back in town. He owed him that much.

X

At six o'clock who should show up but old Francie. She would! Lou, back in Chicago, was in the "office bar" shaving himself and getting a kick, as he always did, out of the elegant little hideout he had created out of a dirty old fileroom. One of these days he'd put a bartender on the payroll, boy would that be something! More like a yacht than a business office! He had a small handmirror rigged up against a highball glass on a card-table; his coat and vest and gray shirt hung over the chromium chair-back. He was in his stocking feet, because he'd handed his shoes over to Mike the building bootblack so he wouldn't lose any time.

"Well, she's in again," said Miss Frye, closing the door to the office behind her. "What do I say now?"

What could anybody say?

"Now, how did she know I just got in town?" asked Lou. "I get off the plane at five forty and in fifteen minutes she's right on my tail."

"I told you," said Miss Frye. "I warned you."

"Did you give her the check I told you?"

"She wouldn't take it," said Miss Frye. "She said she had to see you personally. I couldn't say anything."

"What she want to hang around Chicago for?" groaned Lou.

"You men," said Miss Frye. "You want to step out of your past as if it was an old pair of pants."

"I wish it was that easy," Lou sighed. In a way it was

a relief to have Miss Frye know about all his private affairs, even to that old marriage. She knew how to ward off trouble, then, and she was dependable. No sex there, nothing but hardboiled efficiency. If he ever got into trouble, he could count on Miss Frye all right. It was worth sixty a week to him to know that.

"Anybody with her? What was the situation, anyway?"

"Well," said Frye, "she's still got the Ford; that means she's not so hard up. I saw her parking it across the street."

"How's she looking—the old girl, I mean?"

Miss Frye's sharp little pixie face went up, sniffing the air, hunting the right word.

"Tacky?" prompted Lou. "Weepy?"

"No," said Miss Frye. "On the make."

On the make. Worse yet. Miss Frye seemed to think so too for she shook her head sympathetically.

"I'll give her ten minutes," said Lou. "She can see I'm rushed, and then when the fellas come in it'll be easy to brush her off. That convention crowd will scare her off."

"Are you sticking around here all evening?" Miss Frye asked.

Lou shrugged. One thing Miss Frye didn't know and wouldn't if he could help it, was that he had fixed up a date with Mrs. Kameray for that evening. Let the fellows use the bar, let them have a good time there, do as they pleased with nobody in town to spy on them. He'd give them the keys, let Jay Oliver be host, and he'd slip off to the Stevens and pick up Mrs. Kameray, get acquainted.

"Maybe, maybe not," he said. "Anyway, if my house calls up I'm not back yet. Give me some cash, too, before you go. Get it in fifties."

As soon as Francie came in, Lou saw what Miss Frye meant. She had taken off ten or fifteen pounds since the last meeting ten years ago, and had a bunch of cornsilk curls sticking out of a black satin lid that looked like an opera hat with an extravagant veil floating around it. Her flaring plaid skirt was way up to here (her legs stayed good and did she know it, for she took one of the bar stools right away where she could swing them to good advantage) and if the swirl of her skirt showed more knee than was necessary they were good enough knees to justify it. A chiffon scarf was tucked around the neck of her black velvet jacket with polka dots to match her poppy-red lips and fingertips. She must have put in some stiff work on her face because it did not look old, not even thirty, only it had that desperate set look that a woman's face always gets when she's decided to show the world she's not afraid of it. It was a brave thing to see, but pretty grim as an invitation to the male. Or maybe he just felt that way, knowing Francie so well. It was a blind spot. Maybe she'd never look or be anything but five hand-to-mouth years, 1920-to-1925, Newark, N. J., to Coral Gables, to Coney. God, he almost forgot that Coney Island rooming house! Maybe to him Francie would never be anything but Lady Bad Luck. Even if she hadn't had a thing to do with his bad luck he still thought of her that way because as soon as he broke with her his luck sprang high. Not her fault. Couldn't really blame old Fran. Still she was always Friday the thirteenth to him, and you couldn't laugh her off.

"Excuse the undress, Francie," he said, deciding to take it very natural. "Just got off the New York plane and rushing right into conference with some big restaurant men."

"Never mind the undress," said Francie, laughing. "An old married couple like us!"

Socko. Just like that. Always bringing up that they used to be married, that so far as that went they still were. Lou couldn't help shooting a look around the room as if Mary or the Harrods might be somewhere behind a curtain, listening, horrified. You'd think he and Francie had never even had the divorce to hear her talk. Just as if he didn't have Mary and the kid now and Francie herself had the punk, but Francie had always managed to take a line somehow that would embarrass him. He really had nothing against Francie—they'd had a couple of good years and three bad ones, but why in the name of heaven did she have to pop up right now in his life? Why did she have to take in Chicago after all these years? Why did she have to walk across his path like some black cat just as he was having the biggest break of his life? Sure, he felt sorry for her, his luck coming and hers going as soon as they broke up, but he'd been decent enough there for a while, sending her a check once in a while when she wrote, not as much as she wanted, maybe, but hell's bells, what was the matter with the punk supporting her?

It would have made him more comfortable if she raised the roof or bawled him out now, but instead she just sat staring at him, smiling and managing to remind him of old intimate things. It was indecent and he could feel his neck getting red. Undressing him with her memory, that's what it amounted to. He wished she would get down to brass tacks and say what she'd come to say—that she was broke again and she hated terribly to ask but this was just a loan, she'd get it back to him the tenth of some month or other. He braced himself for defense against this, he braced himself to remind her that he'd handed out a check twice in the last month to her, after all he'd better make it clear he was no sucker. He knew damn well it was the punk putting her up to put the bee on him.

"This is a new angle," she said, looking around the cozy little lounge. "Bar right next the office. What's the idea? Can't you wait to get to the one downstairs?"

Lou looked at his lathered face in the mirror.

"This is a convention town," he said. "Visitors like a little hideaway where they can drink and talk deals over privately. Have some fun without some big customer watching them. It's all good business for me. I had it fixed up last year."

Francie walked around and looked over the tables.

"Roulette, even," she said. "And look at those bottles!"

She pointed to the glistening array behind the Chinese-red bar.

"Reminds me of the time we had getting enough dough to buy brandy for that Senator who was going to let you in on a deal. He never came through, anyway, that was the joke. I knew he wouldn't all the time."

"Yes," said Lou quietly. "You always knew they'd never come through, didn't you, Francie?"

That stopped her. Without turning his head he felt her grow very still.

"I know what you mean, Lou," she said in a low voice. "If I'd had sense enough to believe in those wild schemes of yours we'd be together right now and I wouldn't be broke while you're riding high. We'd both be in the money. And we'd be—together. Like we ought to be."

Lou finished his shaving, folded up the mirror and put it in his bag on the chair. He didn't look at her because he knew well enough she had her handkerchief to her eyes.

"Still shave twice a day?" she said a little shakily.

"I got up early," he said coldly. The only way to stop this sentiment-fest was to get tough right away and he did.

"O.K., let's hear it," he said. "What's the punk let you in for this time? I told you I got big expenses on my hands, the kid's got mastoid trouble, Mary's had to cut short her cruise, the income tax people are after me. Money's mighty scarce."

He saw her stiffen and turn her head away. She was trying to pretend this was just a social call for old-times' sake, and if money came into it the idea was just casual, on the spur of the moment.

"Too bad about the kid," she said, and there was that again. All the time they had been together, he recalled now, she had wanted children—one, anyway,—and they used to fight about it. If he could put two hundred down on a car he could afford to pay for a baby, that was always her argument. His line was that he couldn't stand kids, they'd break up the marriage. And the crazy life they lived, rooming houses, a jump ahead of the sheriff or the landlady,—no, he said, no kids for him. So now he was crazy about the little girl Mary had presented him with. What was wrong with that? Was it his fault he had human nature?

"Like a drink?" he said. "Oh, no, that's so, you never could take it, could you?"

He was glad he could remember something that wasn't too personal.

"One drink and you hit the ceiling, remember?"

"I'm different, now," she said. "Sure I'll have a highball."

He went behind the bar and mixed her one. Where the hell was Jay Oliver or somebody, somebody to break this thing up?

"Look, do you mind not saying anything about being my ex?" he asked, trying to act offhand about it as if it hadn't been on his mind ever since she blew in to town. "I mean there's no point in bringing it up now. You're Mrs. Thomson now and there's a new Mrs. Donovan. You know. Might look funny."

She nodded slowly. Her eyes travelled around the room, studying the silver Venetian shades, and the nudes outlined in silver on the scarlet walls. Through the gleaming silvery curtains you could see the lake, blue and cold and smooth as metal.

"Pretty swell place," she said. "It's a wonder you don't stay here every night instead of going home."

"Lots of times I do," he said. "The out-of-town fellas are keen about it, naturally. Gives 'em a sort of private spot to drop in between trains, put in some phone calls, catch a few drinks, do business or line up a hot date. Like an old-time speakeasy, that's the charm of it. I had a crowd of advertising men here couple weeks ago and they were shooting craps up here till Sunday afternoon. Never left the place. Boy, was it a shambles! Shooting for five hundred a throw. I won three grand but I was the host so I had to let 'em take it off me."

She was sipping her drink and he could tell the way she went at it that she still didn't know how to handle it. Small-town, that was Francie, even to the devilish way she smoked a cigarette, little finger crooked, head cocked, like a stock-company vamp. The Girl from Rector's—that was Francie with a drink and a cigarette and her legs crossed. It had once rather tickled him, he recalled now with amazement. Maybe it was because he could in those early days measure how much he was learning in the world by what Francie was; she stayed exactly where he started, and once this had pleased his ego, now it embarrassed him to think he was ever that much of a hick.

"I'm planning to do a little branching out on my own," she said. "It's this way, Lou. I know you don't think much of Frank——"

"Right!" Frank was the punk she married.

"But honestly, Lou, he isn't well! He's got that bad lung and there isn't much work a guy with a bad lung can do. A little cold and he's laid up all winter. The climate's bad."

Now it was coming.

"Why didn't he go out West with his bonus money instead of dropping it all at Hialeah?" barked Lou. This was the same old fight. "I got no sympathy."

"Listen, Lou, the race track is all he knows. He can lie in bed and study it, and that's all he can do. Gee, that boy knows all there is to know about horses and tracks. You did once, but, honest, you'd have to take your hat off to him, if you could hear him. He knows every stable, he knows which horse likes mud and which likes sand; he has everything figured out. Everybody in the neighborhood comes around wherever we are to hear what he has to say."

"Maybe they didn't hear how he come out at Hialeah," said Lou sarcastically. "Seven hundred bucks in two days."

"Lou, you know you can't do much with seven hundred," said Francie plaintively. "You got to have something to play with. If he'd had a thousand now——"

Lou laughed harshly.

"Seven hundred bucks is a lot of money, baby," he said.

"Can I have another drink?" Francie asked suddenly.

Lou looked at his wrist watch.

"These fellas ought to be here any minute, but O.K. Same?"

"Maybe I'd like it better straight," said Francie. "Or look, maybe you got some absinthe. I got crazy about absinthe in New Orleans. And then in Havana I always drank ojen."

"Been around a lot, haven't you?" said Lou. "You'd better stick to Scotch."

He poured two fingers in a glass. Every minute seemed torture. He didn't want to see her, no reason why he should have to, it downed him, somehow, brought back every bit of the old desperation under which they had lived. If she just would stand up, act as if she was going. Anything. And it made him suddenly see the perfect awfulness of Mary or the Harrods suddenly finding out about a previous marriage. Nothing criminal in it. But why in God's name hadn't he ever mentioned it? How would he ever be able to explain that?

"So your marriage turned out all right, then," Francie said slowly. "I read about it in the papers, of course. She was a somebody, I guess. What'd it say—adopted by her uncle, old Judge Whosis? Anyway I got the idea that you'd married into some class."

Lou started talking hastily, trying to keep her off this tack. He talked about the new house in Winnetka, how the decorator soaked him, how the electrical fixtures alone cost ten thousand, it was criminal, but in this business you had to make a show, entertain the boys, put up a front. You had to look like big money to make it, a funny thing that was, and besides he dealt direct with the big shots, the presidents, the general managers, why only yesterday he lunched in New York with Major— well, not to mention names, but later on the world would be hearing about Castles-in-the-Woods, one of the biggest— Lou stopped as suddenly as he had begun, for in his anxiety to get away from personal matters into business he was making his business so prosperous that he was letting himself in for a bigger touch than ever. Francie, however, did not press it then.

"I should think those convention boys would go some place where they could get girls instead of just drinking here with no fun."

"I get girls for them all right, never mind about that," said Lou shortly. "Never let it be said! I date up a half dozen live numbers from the Spinning Top down the street or a couple of dancers from Giulio's Grotto. They drop in between floor shows over there and keep things moving. Most of them leave with a hundred-dollar bill stuck in their pocket. These guys are the real thing, you know, and do the babes know it!"

Talk to her as if she was a man, that was it! Forget the personal thing entirely. Don't let it get you!

Francie kicked her slippers off.

"I don't know why liquor always makes me do that," she said laughing. "All of a sudden I got to take my shoes off."

Miss Frye opened the door and Lou jumped.

"I'll betcha it looks funny coming in and finding us both with our shoes off," Francie giggled.

Miss Frye smiled uncertainly. Lou tried to signal her to try getting rid of Francie but Francie kept her eyes on him so he dared not try anything.

"Mike brought your shoes back, Mr. Donovan," said Miss Frye, and the dwarfed old bootblack crept in behind her and set the shoes down on the chair.

"Is there anything else before I go?" she asked.

"Can't let you go yet, Miss Frye, sorry," Lou said hastily. Good heavens! Leave him alone with Francie? God knows what she'd do. Cry. Scream. Anything was possible. "See if Mr. Oliver's left his office. Or try him at the store. Or the Drake. That's right. He might be at the Drake with old Whittleby. Tell him I'm waiting. And phone the café to send over canapés, olives, chips—get plenty of everything. There may only be half a dozen of us and there may be twenty."

"Some conference," said Francie.

Lou shrugged.

"Just a routine, that's all. All right, now, what's on your mind?"

And Francie plunged.

"I was figuring if you could let me have sixty-two dollars we could get the car out of hock and drive to Arizona next week," said Francie, all in a breath. "Don't say no, Lou. I know you've been good to me and I realize how you feel about Frank, but this time it'll work out. I'll leave him in Arizona with his aunt and maybe he'll get his health back. Then I'll go on to Los Angeles to pick up a job—I don't mean pictures, I realize I'm too old for that, but maybe in some church or something. They must use organists somewhere; you hear 'em all the time on the radio. After all, when you knew me first I was getting seventy-five a week there in the picture show—more than you made taking tickets."

If there was one stage of his life he wanted to forget

124

it was his ticket-taking days in that lousy movie house in Jersey. Next she'd ring in the stuff about his being pin boy at the bowling alley when he was a kid, all the stuff he wanted to forget—not because he was ashamed of it, hell, anybody might have to work their way up the ladder, but the days it brought back were so wretched, days of being kicked around, days when he was dumb, too, afraid to speak out, even, just remembering them gave him an inferiority. Oh, sure, she'd have to bring all that up. She couldn't let a fellow be happy in his present. That was Francie for you.

"I was a darn good organist," said Francie. "You said yourself I could get more out of 'I Love You Truly' than anybody you ever heard."

Now the old organ stuff was going to come out, about how long she studied to be a movie organist and had that swell job just a year when sound came in and threw everybody out. It was too bad, sure it was too bad, he'd said so then over and over, day in, day out, but women and elephants never forget anything.

"I hear that in some of the high-class restaurants they've started using organists," she said. "So far as that goes I got my figure back now and might get a hostess job some place. Maybe in a night club."

Lou didn't say anything. If she thought she could compete with the glamour girls he wouldn't remind her how old she was. Two years older than he was.

"How do you make it sixty-two bucks exactly?" he asked. "Why does it have to be sixty-two?"

He was being nasty, all right, he knew it, but there was something about her coming in and hanging around this way that made him feel that way. Coming in, spoiling his wonderful week, his top moment, reminding him that once he was a small-town dumb-bell, taking the rap from every-body, afraid to call his fritter his own.

Francie fidgeted with the chiffon scarf.

"I figure a dollar fifty a day for food for the two of us, forty to get the car out of hock and we're set for about two weeks, long enough to get West. Something'll turn up in Santa Fe, maybe."

"You just might drive on to Santa Anita or Caliente, too, mightn't you?" Lou inquired softly. "Race tracks handy there, for the punk. And supposing you didn't have the car in hock at all, supposing you had it parked around the corner right this minute, you could put that forty bucks on a horse, couldn't you?"

She was trapped and she knew it.

"Okay, I lied about that," she said, looking down at the floor. "A person's got to lie about things once in a while. God knows you ought to admit that. Anyway, you're so down on Frank I can't talk straight to you. Honest, Lou, I can't be mean to a guy that's only got a year or two to live. If talking track makes him feel like a big he-man when I know damn well he isn't one—well, gee, I can't explain, but if you heard him crying sometime because he can't take care of me right——"

"You can't expect me to keep some guy just because you happen to be crazy about him," said Lou, and was sorry he said it right away.

Francie looked straight at him, very solemn.

"You know I was never crazy about anybody but you," she said. "You knew it when you walked out. You'll always know it. Frank was sick in the house and I was low—well, that was all there was to it. You got to have somebody.

Look, Lou, take it this way. If it hadn't been for my marrying him, you'd have had to put up alimony. I ain't ever bothered you much, you got to admit that, I never let out a peep since you been married, not till now. I ain't bothered you."

Those "ain'ts" made him squirm as much as her sorrowful eyes. You'd think women would get over a thing after a while, but no, by God, they hang on to every damn thing in their lives, hoard every little ancient romance as if it was a Liberty Bond. He tried not to see how her eyes followed his hands as he buttoned up his shirt, and he reddened, knowing what she was thinking, that this was like old times, old times she was always remembering, and he was always trying to pretend never had happened. It was funny how a man was so ashamed of having cared for somebody once and funny how a woman never got tired talking about it.

"Sixty-two dollars is a lot of money, Francie," he said briskly. "Maybe not if you don't have to slave for it, the way I do. You can just go back and tell the White Man that Red Feather says if he had to pay the government what I do he wouldn't be shelling out sixty-two bucks to every mug that wants to put the bee on him."

Yes, and that was another thing that made him detest this whole scene, himself, and Francie and everything about it. The little reminder that he had ever had anything to do with a dame that could go for a down-at-heels mug like that dope she finally married. That was the kind of thing that got a man down.

Francie stopped swinging her legs and wriggled the toes in her stockings. Her silence rattled him. Then she spoke in a very low voice.

"You talk about your house," she said. "I've been past

there lots of times. I've seen the baby. I've seen her, too. Mary."

Lou's blood ran cold. Had she talked to Mary? And the thought of the eyes watching him, watching him and Mary when they didn't know they were being observed. The sad jealous eyes of old Francie.

"Oh, I never went in," Francie said bitterly, as if sensing his uneasiness. "I never said anything to her. I just wanted to see, that was all."

Lou suddenly felt he could endure no more.

"Miss Frye!" he bellowed. "Miss Frye, where the hell are those things from the café?"

Miss Frye hastily opened the door and the boy from the restaurant was right behind her with a great tray of hors d'œuvres and a basket of tidbits to spread out in little silver dishes along the bar. Lou mopped his brow.

"Your house just called," said Miss Frye.

"Call back and say I'm expected on tomorrow's plane," said Lou. "And call the Colony. Maybe Mr. Oliver dropped in there."

"Okay," said Miss Frye and again Lou could not give her a signal because of Fran's watchful eyes.

The door to the office closed.

"So you're brushing Mary off, now," said Francie. "Through with her, eh, through with her, too."

Lou gave his necktie a furious jerk.

"Certainly I'm not through with Mary, too," he snapped. "What put that in that little pin head?"

"Staying here nights with all those girls," said Francie. "What kind of woman is she, allowing you to do that?"

"Allowing me!" Lou shouted. "How would she know about it?"

"Lying to her," said Francie. "That's one thing you never did with me. You thought too much of me for that, I'll say that for you."

Lou gripped the table with both hands.

"I'm not lying to her," he expostulated. "I'm merely saving myself explanations, that's all. Explanations take time and I'm a very busy man."

"You never did that when *we* were together," said Francie. She said "together" as if it meant everything. "Honest, Lou, you were happy with me, then, you got to admit that much, you really were happy. I used to call you 'pussy,' remember?"

"Every man that's called 'pussy' isn't the happiest man in the world," muttered Lou. "Can't you drop this, Francie, for God's sake?"

"We were never even separated," went on Francie dreamily, looking out the window over the lake, "except the time you went to Toronto about that advertising job and the time you and your brother went to Texas for that oil deal."

"I've never been in Toronto in my life," said Lou grimly. "And this is the first time I ever heard of my having a brother."

He realized what he had done the next minute, but it was too late.

"Oh!" gasped Francie, clutching her heart. She looked straight ahead for a second then carefully stooped over and picked up her shoes. She wiggled her feet into them silently. She looked pinched and stricken.

"Good Lord, everybody has to alibi once in a while just to save a lot of talk, that's all it means," Lou bumbled along.

Francie straightened her skirt out now and fussed with her scarf. She gave a little laugh that was like cracked ice in a glass.

"I don't know what could have been eating me," she said. "I knew you did a lot of things I didn't like, but I was perfectly certain you never two-timed me. That was the nice thing. I just *knew*. I used to say to myself, never mind how things turned out in the end, at least when they were right, they *were* right. A person has to have something to kinda go on, you know, especially. . . . The brother in Texas. . . . How dumb I must have been. It's a laugh. It was right when we were really crazy about each other, too. I—I—I mean. . . . Funny how you hang on to some things no matter what happens, then it turns out those are just the things you should have skipped."

So now she'd have to cry a little.

Lou scowled and folded his arms. Where were these fellows that should have come in now to save him?

"Snap out of it, Francie," he growled.

"Oh, it isn't that I care so much about that forty dollars," she sniffled into her handkerchief. "Maybe he would lose it right away like he did at Hialeah, but in a way it's your fault. I keep remembering that if I had believed all your talk about buying up hotel concessions, then selling them, and all those other wild notions of yours, you and I would never have split. Now I make it up, see, by believing what Frank tells me. I think maybe if I walked out on him it would be just the time for him to strike big dough just the way it was with you. I don't want to make the same mistake twice."

"You would compare a business genius with a turf tramp," said Lou sarcastically.

He kept himself from screaming at her to get the hell out and stop making his insides squirm this way. He felt like half a cent. He might as well never have made good since the movie house days. Francie could do that to him in just ten minutes.

"Here," he said, inspired, and rummaged through his pockets. "This is all the cash I can spare right now. The checkbook's in the safe for the night. This will help."

He put three tens on the table. Francie looked at it a minute without touching it, then suddenly brushed it on the floor and stamped on it.

"Say!" he blazed at her.

He was so surprised and indignant that he could say no more.

Just as unexpectedly Francie the next moment bent over and picked up the three bills, straightened them out carefully and put them in her pocketbook. He saw a nickel and an aspirin and two one-cent stamps in the coin department.

"Even if it was only a penny," Francie said wearily, "I'd have to end up scrambling for it."

She powdered her nose and fluffed the new blonde curls over her ear. At least she was going. At least that. Thirty bucks was enough to get her out of town. He could have given her more, he would have only she made him so boiling mad the way she got his ego down. It was a gift with some women. But he shouldn't get mad, not show it, anyway.

"So long, Francie," he said. "I'm sorry about things, but you can't blame me, considering everything. It's a tough world, some of us got the touch and some haven't, that's the way I see it."

"Got it all figured out, haven't you?" said Francie. "Mr. Dale Carnegie."

He saw she was looking at him in a sorrowful, still way, and he might have guessed something was coming, but somehow he didn't expect her to do this, fling her arms around his neck and kiss him wildly. It was the worst. thing that had happened so far, and of course that was the exact moment Miss Frye chose to open the door and let some men barge in.

"Hot dog!" yelled Jay Oliver.

Lou pushed Francie away from him and tried to grin, wiping lipstick off his face.

"Will you look at old Lou," jubilantly cried Jay. "Damned if he isn't in conference!"

There were the two promotion men from Denver and the Canadian whiskey baron. They beamed and waited for introductions which Lou mumbled through, conscious of Jay's gleeful enjoyment of his embarrassment. Francie quietly picked her bag up.

"I'll be with you fellows in a sec," Lou said, trying to act casual. "I got to see this lady to the elevator."

"Thought you were having some babes in," said the Canadian.

"Oh, the babes will be along any minute," Lou reassured him. "Come on, Francie."

"Why do we lose this little lady?" Jay demanded genially. "What's the matter with keeping her here for a little drinkie or two? Or is she your private property, Lou you old rascal?"

"No," said Lou, "only she's got to——"

His eyes fell before Francie's sardonic smile.

"Look, you can stick around, can't you, Halfpint?" Jay

caught Francie's arm jovially. "What's the matter with playing around for a while? We're all good guys. You tell her, Lou."

"Sure they are," said Lou with a sickening sense of defeat. Outside he heard the shrill giggles and scampering of the girls from the Grotto just getting out of the elevator and it sounded to him like the marines coming. He breathed a sigh.

"Ah, here they come. Here come the babes, now, no need holding you any longer, Francie, if you've got to go. The lads will have company."

"Ah, come on, anyway, and stay," urged Jay, thoroughly happy now that he sensed Lou's uneasiness. "Can't you stay?"

"Sure, I'm staying," said Francie. She yanked off the opera-hat lid and threw it playfully at the big Canadian. "I'd like to play with a good guy for once in my life. Set 'em up, Lou, let's get going!"

Friday the thirteenth, Lou thought numbly, trying to smile, black cat cross your path, new moon over wrong shoulder. Lady Luck. Lady Bad Luck. Okay, shrug your shoulders, take it on the chin.

"Don't I get any caviar?" complained Francie reaching for the tray. Lou passed her the caviar canapés.

"Angels on toast if you ask for them, sweetheart," he said easily. That was the way. Chin up. Always leave 'em laughing.

XI

IN THE middle of the morning after a party Lou always got a craving for creamed marinierte herring and breakfasted on it at the Old Heidelberg, with a glass of beer. He felt depressed and it wasn't just the hangover, either. A little ammoniated bromoseltzer had fixed that an hour ago over at the Stevens Hotel where he had spent the night. Little things, little things again. He'd muffed the date with Mrs. Kameray last night, simply because, believe it or not, he was afraid to leave the office party last night for fear Francie would tell something she shouldn't. She'd been all right about not mentioning their old marriage, but what was so good about that discretion, after all? Her doting glances and embraces, the little clubby cracks about past intimacies, made the thing look even worse. They all ended up at Giulio's, but it was too late then to meet the little Kameray. When he called her up to explain she was sore as the dickens. That was all right, when he had time he'd smooth her down. She wasn't the type, as he figured her out, to stay mad. But it was simply plans going wrong that irritated him. And old Francie. She'd gone off finally with Jay Oliver and that was safe enough, he thought he could count on Jay even if she told him the whole business. Jay wouldn't tell, but the mere fact that he even knew was disagreeable enough. Well, he'd just have to keep reminding Jay of how he fixed up the Ebie business for him. On days like this the least little thing could set him up or throw him. The waiter fussing around, giving him the "Mr. Donovan" this and "Mr. Donovan" that, was soothingly satisfactory, but then there was the little encounter with old Grahame, the head of a hotel chain and friend of Judge Harrod. Lou had waved genially to him as he passed him.

Grahame, who was about to squeeze his two hundred and seventy-five pounds behind the wheel of a Packard coupé, actually got out of the car and waddled back to the restaurant door to shake hands with Lou. It was the warmest greeting he had ever given Lou and Lou's flagging spirits soared.

"Great seeing you, Mr. Grahame!" Lou said happily.

"Great seeing you, too," said Grahame in his panting breathless squeaky little voice, "and doing fine, now, I can tell by your looks."

"Thanks, Mr. Grahame," said Lou. "Nice of you to say so."

"Always glad to see one of our old bellboys make good in the world," said Grahame, still pumping his hand. "Good luck, Cassidy, and if you're ever around the hotel look in and say hello to the old crowd."

He had waddled back to his car, happy in his democratic little interview, before Lou could think of anything to say. Of course he really had only seen Grahame a couple times at the Harrods' and the old boy was over sixty and probably stone blind. Still that "Cassidy" was a burn. He was glad to see one of Grahame's managers, a fellow named Pritchard, having a late breakfast at the next table, so he could take out his wounded feelings. Pritchard was all right, he thought a lot of Lou and they'd had some deals together.

Today Pritchard, too, was gloomy.

"How do I know what makes the old boy say things like that?" he said, when Lou complained. "Imagine you or me being able to get away with a crack like that! 'One of our bellboys'—can you imagine it! The only thing is that he isn't smart enough to have meant it as an insult."

"He's not so dumb," said Lou. "You don't pile up four million by being dumb."

"The hell you don't," said Pritchard. "Old Grahame's typical old-time success. When he was twenty-five his old man handed him the business. He married dough, and so now he gives a sales talk once a week on how kind hearts and coronets are all you need to get to the top. It's a pain."

"He could have been an ambassador," said Lou, still smarting. "He's travelled all over."

"Not all over. Only where there's a Ritz," said Pritchard sourly. "Why, that old bastard hasn't been off his fritter in twenty years. When he goes to Paris he drives straight to the Ritz and then he has his meals sent to his room till it's time to go to London. Same there. 'Where's the Ritz?,' he says when he comes out of his stateroom, and then they shoot him there and he says, 'Where's my suite?' and then he's done London. Why, he won't go any place there isn't a Ritz. 'Where's the Ritz?,' he says when he gets off the boat or the plane, 'take me straight to the Ritz.' If there isn't any he climbs back on the plane. Oh, sure. The brains of the business and all that. From the bottom up and bottoms up and all that."

"What's wrong with the Ritz?" said Lou. "It's a good hotel. Or wouldn't a bellboy know?"

It seemed funny now, or sort of funny.

"What's on your mind now?" Pritchard asked when Lou was silent.

"I was just thinking I might move to New York," Lou said reflectively. "I don't know. As soon as I get back home here something comes up, some little thing, that throws me. I'm not the small-town type. I'm at home in New York or travelling around."

"Chicago's a small town, then, all of a sudden," Pritchard mocked.

"I mean I care about things here, as soon as I get off a train, that don't matter any place else," Lou explained.

"Nuts, it's just your conscience," Pritchard said. He sighed. "Nobody has their conscience around much away from home. It's like a garage. It ought to be handy to your house. Believe me, I know."

Lou didn't encourage the confession he was pretty sure was coming up for the simple reason that it was his experience that men were always sore at you after they opened up their hearts. As if you'd asked them. He didn't want to find out. He never asked. But try and stop them telling you.

"Last night, for instance," said Pritchard, true to form. "What a mess that turned out to be."

"Yeah?"

"I took my wife and daughter, you know Barbara Lucy, you met her at the races, well," Pritchard took a gulp of beer, scowling, "here it was Barbara Lucy's sixteenth birthday so we took her down to the Chez Paris. I was dancing with the kid or trying to, I'm no dancer, and who should I bump into on the floor but Jay Oliver with a floozy."

Francie, thought Lou. So that's where they went.

"I was kind of high, you know how you have to brace

yourself for the old family outing," continued Pritchard, wiping his moustache, "I'd have one with the little woman —the kid only has sherry—then I'd have a couple of quick ones at the bar. So Jay and I make a few cracks, just good-natured you know, on the floor, and end up switching partners, Jay with Barbara Lucy and me squeezing up the floozy."

So Jay didn't even have sense enough to take Francie to a little out-of-the-way spot. No, it had to be Chez Paris. Why he might even have had Mary there—that is, if Mary would ever have been willing to go out to night-clubs or for that matter, if he himself had been anywhere near her last night.

"Well, of course the wife was sore at Jay, because she knows Flo, and she thought it was laying it on for him to bring a floozy out in public like that. I was too high to care, and the kid got a kick out of changing partners on the floor that way, so I was squeezing up the floozy— I can't dance worth a damn, all I do is sort of march around and love 'em up a little if they're the type, and all of a sudden my wife prances up to the dance floor and calls Barbara Lucy off first, then she tries to catch me by the arm as I'm floating past with the floozy. Well, you know me. I was feeling no pain by that time, so the upshot was that the wife took Barbara Lucy home and left me with Jay and the floozy, and when I got out to Evanston I was locked out. So I spent the night at the Stevens. What the hell I do next I don't know."

Lou lit a cigarette, admiring the way his fingers hardly shook at all. Two up for old Francie, then.

"Wonder where old Oliver stands now at his house," was all he said.

Pritchard shook his head sorrowfully.

"He hasn't got a chance. Not if Eleanor has anything to do with it. I said, soon as we spot the floozy, I said, look, now Eleanor, I know you know Flo and I know how women stick together so far as telling each other any bad news goes, but skip it this once. Let's have a gentleman's agreement, that you don't tell Flo. So she said okay, I'm mad, she says, but at least I'm no troublemaker. So we had a gentleman's agreement she shouldn't say anything."

"Think she said anything?" Lou asked.

This was all old Francie's fault. Typhoid Mary if there ever was one.

"Listen, the thing was all over town by ten o'clock this morning," said Pritchard gloomily. "That's what comes of my wife not being a gentleman."

"I'll hear more about it from Jay, then," Lou said. You bet he would. He'd have to fix it up with Flo again. And Flo would bully Jay until he'd say he was only taking one of the girls home from a party at Lou Donovan's office, and then Flo would say, why I understood Mrs. Donovan to say he wasn't home yet. Or no. There was one salvation. Mary, his dear, dear wife, snooted Flo, thank God. Mary snooted all his business friends, Mary was too high-class to be a little helper to her husband and what could be sweeter than that? She never saw Flo except at some card club they all belonged to, thanks be to good breeding. He suddenly felt safe again and it was all because of Mary. He was glad now that things had' turned out so he hadn't had the date with Mrs. Kameray last night. At least that was one thing he needn't feel guilty about. He thought now he'd better fix up the whole business before he went out to the house that night.

"I got a man from New York coming in at twelve," he said. "If you see your boss tell him his bellboy wants a new uniform, will you?"

"Ah, don't mind what that old fathead says," said Pritchard. "I swear to God I've worked for him fifteen years and he still calls me Mitchell. Listen, I was out taking some visitors through my brother's paper mill one day, by accident, when who should I see sweeping through the place but a Chamber of Commerce delegation led by old man Grahame. He didn't even know me. I spoke. He gives me the old handshake and then he says, 'Well, Mitchell,' he says, 'the working man has a better time today than when I was a young man.' I burbled something or other and then he says, 'Are you satisfied with your work here, Mitchell? Have you got a good foreman?' Hells bells, you're bellboy crack is nothing new. Forget it. You're in."

Lou laughed. The hell with Grahame. Next time he ran into him he'd let him have a little bit of the old stuff right back.

"If you see old Oliver tell him we're not friends any more," Pritchard called after him.

Back at the office the sun was pouring in the great windows as if nothing had happened. The false book-cases that formed the door to the bar looked innocent as could be, never for an instant hinting that a mere push of the button could make them swing open into a world of unlettered temptation. Miss Frye was busily typing at her huge oak desk, reading goggles perched on the tip of her sharp nose. Lou tossed his hat in the closet and got on the phone. He got the Building Superintendent.

"What's the matter with this water cooler? Get more ice in it, will you? Right away. Donovan's office."

"How do you know?" Miss Frye queried, looking up from her typewriter. "You haven't even tried it yet."

"Never mind, I go by hunches," Lou said.

Miss Frye looked him over thoughtfully.

"So that's the way it is," she said. "Maybe you should have gone to a Turkish bath."

Lou made an impatient gesture.

"Don't argue with me, Miss Frye," he begged. "I got things on my mind. What's new?"

He went to his own desk, a large kidney-shaped handsome affair in the corner, set between two long windows hung with heavy blue. This blue frame against the oak-panelled walls was a fine spot for a blonde, Miss Frye had often remarked, and had prophesied that one of these days that was just what would happen. Lou picked up the telegrams. One from Rosenbaum advising him to check up at once on Mrs. Kameray, one from the New York office girl advising that the office furniture was now in. Telegrams from his personal scout, old T. V. Truesdale, Personal Representative of Louis Donovan Service.

"PERSONALLY INVESTIGATED MARYLAND VENTURE STOP WHOLE COUNTRYSIDE ANTAGONISTIC STOP FEEL TOO COMMERCIAL VIOLATING SOUTHERN IDEALISM JEOPARDIZING EXCLUSIVENESS OF LOCAL CLUBS AND RESIDENCES STOP ALREADY LOCAL MERCHANTS PREPARING RESISTANCE BY RAISING ALL COMMODITY PRICES STOP PARTICULARLY HOSTILE TO ROSENBAUM STOP WOULD SUGGEST HE LEARN TO RIDE OR DRINK BEFORE FURTHER SOUTHERN PROMOTION WORK COUNTRYSIDE FEARS CASTLES WILL CHEAPEN LOCAL

REAL ESTATE STOP WOULD SUGGEST GOOD WILL SWING THROUGH THIS REGION. SIGNED T. V. TRUESDALE."

"Sweet," said Lou and tore open the next one.

"HOW ABOUT DREAM ANALYZER AS FEATURE OF CASTLES COCKTAIL ROOM? JUST MET UNUSUALLY GIFTED ARMENIAN PRINCESS HALF EGYPTIAN ADAPTABLE TO SOUTHERN SOCIAL LIFE ALSO READS CARDS HANDS AND STARS AND DOES CLASSICAL DANCING AS POSSIBLE DINNER FEATURE IN GRAND HOTEL BALLROOM. JUST A SUGGESTION. SIGNED T. V. TRUESDALE."

"Isn't that just ducky?" Lou exclaimed. The old boy was jumping right into it. And still another one.

"RELIABLY INFORMED MAJOR AND WIFE TIFFED OVER SECRET ADMIRER SENDING TERRIFIC FLORAL GIFTS WIFE MOVING TO AMBASSADOR GO SLOW IN CASE OF DOMESTIC RIFT. SIGNED T. V. TRUESDALE."

"Would you mind telling me who that screwball is that you took on in New York?" inquired Miss Frye, observing Lou as he read the Truesdale works.

"He may turn out handy," Lou answered judiciously. "Right now he's just found out about Western Union."

"They've been coming in every ten minutes," said Miss Frye. "They don't make sense to me. Not unless you've got a syndicate gossip column that I don't know about."

"I got no secrets from you, honey," said Lou, "except a few little things I keep to myself."

There were three phone calls from Mary. That was funny since she'd been told he wouldn't be in town till this afternoon. Somebody must have told her something. Something had slipped up.

"Did my wife say anything about what she wanted?" he asked.

She hadn't. But she must be worried about something to have made three calls in one morning. Mrs. Donovan wasn't one to call up the office much. Lou frowned. A horrid suspicion crossed his mind.

"Look, Miss Frye, do you think Francie might have called up my wife? I'd like your guess on that."

Miss Frye gave a whistle, screwed up her little face in an intense effort at concentration, then shook her head.

"I doubt it," she decided. "She was feeling too good last I saw her."

"Where'd you see her? You left here before seven and she wasn't off the ground till around nine."

Miss Frye tossed her head.

"Listen, I go places like anybody else. Boy friend and I dropped in Chez Paris after the movies and there was the old girl with Mr. Oliver."

"What was she doing?" asked Lou.

"They were trying out a new kind of rhumba, looked like," said Miss Frye. "Mr. Oliver stood still and clapped his hands up over his head and she was doing the bumps."

Why in heaven's name hadn't he given her a couple hundred and told her to leave town? Lou groaned. He called the house. Better not experiment with any fancy lies if Mary was worried. He wouldn't tell the exact truth, of course, but he would shoot around it.

Whenever he heard Mary's cool agreeable voice on the telephone he had an exultant pride in having won her. There it was, sheer class and no mistake about it. It was in the way she walked into a room, in the clothes she wore, in her simple reserve, a man didn't need to say a thing, just "This is my wife" and his stock went straight up.

"Hello dear," he said briskly before she could say anything. "Got in so late last night didn't want to disturb you, so I parked at the Stevens. How's the kid?"

"That's what I wanted to ask you about, Lou," Mary said. "The doctor says she's perfectly well but a little rest would help her. So Aunt Felicia wants to take her with her to Arizona next week."

There it was, as usual. His wife and his daughter belonged to the Harrod family. Aunt Felicia and the Judge were in charge of them. He, Lou, was just a sort of chauffeur, so far as they knew his name was Cassidy. If he hadn't shelled out so much on his home and family it would be different. Then they could rightfully step in and say, "That bastard husband of yours doesn't treat you right, he's not taking care of you, but we'll see that you and the kid get three meals a day." Sure, then it would be all right. He'd still be mad, but at least they'd have a right. But no, they have to nose into a perfectly well-to-do happy family that he's looking after up to the hilt. But there was never any use talking to Mary this way. She never understood or, when she did, understood wrong, thinking he didn't appreciate family feeling because he himself never had any. She sympathized with him but said he must learn that other people did have strong family feelings reaching out even to fourth cousins and even to old servants of fourth cousins. He must recognize his narrow-mindedness there as a forgivable fault but nevertheless a fault.

"What does the doctor say?" he asked after a pause.

"The doctor thinks it would be splendid. He thinks it will build her up."

"Too bad he couldn't have suggested it to me, then, when I paid the bill," snapped Lou, but never mind that, he mustn't get mad. "How long will you be gone?"

"Not more than three or four weeks," said Mary. "Of course Baby is perfectly happy with Aunt Felicia if you think I'd better stay here. I'll send the nurse along, of course, and she won't miss me at all, really."

"Oh, no," Lou said. "You'd be worried without her. I wouldn't want you to stay home and be worried."

"You're sure you'll be all right?" Mary asked.

"Oh, sure. I may not go out to the house. I may stay at a hotel in town."

There was a pause and then Mary said, "Oh."

"When do you want to go? I'll get tickets and make arrangements."

"No no, dear, it won't be necessary. Uncle will attend to everything."

The usual brushoff. Old Cassidy, the bellboy, mustn't try to muscle in on the Harrods' exclusive family affairs.

"You're quite sure you'll manage all right alone?" Mary asked.

"Oh, sure. You do when I'm away, don't you?"

"Of course, dear."

There seemed to be something else she wanted to say but whatever it was she hesitated. Lou was afraid to ask, for it might be something he didn't want to hear. She might explain what troublesome news had made her so unusually cold to him when he left town. It was better for both of them not to have these things out in the open.

He admired her far too much to give her direct lies and it was not becoming in a person like Mary to descend to the nagging, niggling questions that wives like Flo were always putting to their husbands.

"That all?" he asked.

"Yes. . . . You had a nice time in New York?"

"Nice time? Listen, do you think I go to New York for a nice time? My dear girl, I'm on my toes every minute there. I've been working like a dog. New things in the fire. I'm dead tired."

"We'll have a quiet evening tonight, then. It's Aunt Felicia's Chamber Music night but I'll stay home with you instead."

Ordinarily Lou would have taken the opportunity to line up a date on the side since his wife was going to be busy. But now he thought it would be a good thing for the Harrods to know that when he was home Mary preferred his company to theirs. Let them know who was running the Donovans.

"Want some people in for cards?" he asked.

"No," said Mary. "I'd rather we talked. I'd like to talk to you alone. Some things that are on my mind. You know."

So there was something. So now it was coming. He stared out the window after she hung up, beating the desk with his fingers.

"Miss Frye," he called out finally, "I want you to get out all the Castles-in-the-Woods material, pictures, everything, and order all the Florabella samples you can get, and give me copies of the orders we've given out in the last month."

Miss Frye looked up surprised.

"I want to take them out to the house tonight to show Mary," he explained.

"I didn't know you talked business with your wife," she exclaimed.

"Tonight I will," said Lou.

XII

LATELY Mary had thought more and more about going to a psychoanalyst. Something was going queer in her mind, but the trouble was she was not having hallucinations, she was having facts. What could the doctors do about that? Well, doctor, she would say if she went to one of Them—(she always thought of the psychoanalysts as Them) I was perfectly normal for the first twenty-nine years of my life, I lived on a normal diet of hallucinations; an unusually intelligent and cultured upbringing enabled me to conduct my life decently blindfolded, but lately my mind seems to be shaking. Doctor, I think I'm going sane. Then the doctor, of course, would say, Nonsense, Mrs. Donovan, you can't tell me that an intelligent woman like you is beginning to doubt your insanity. Why, Mrs. Donovan, he would say, smiling indulgently, I assure you on my word of honor as a medical man you are as insane as anybody in this room. Forget it. You're tired, perhaps, you've been worried about your child's illness, that mastoid operation, natural, perfectly natural, you've overdone your music, gotten yourself in an emotional stage about it, that's all. These Truths, which you describe as disturbing your night dreams and your day thoughts, will soon pass. Why not go to New York on a shopping binge?—forget yourself, don't think about your husband for a few days, don't wonder about these problems; I'll guarantee you'll be your happy smiling insane self in no time.

The difficult thing about Truths was that, unlike Hallucinations, they could not be shared with anyone else. Truth
came in little individual portions and that was all there
was to it. For instance she had always been able to talk
to people about her husband's shrewd business genius,
his great reserve of wisdom, his generous heart, but there
was absolutely no one with whom she could discuss the
sudden blow of doubt, of genuine distrust, that had come
to her. Doctor, she would say, though of course she would
never in the world dare go to a psychoanalyst, Lou would
be horrified, but just supposing she did, Doctor, she would
say, can you suggest some harmless powder to restore
Hallucinations? Is there some dietary cure for loss of
complacency, is there some hypodermic needle to inject
self-deception?

For the life of her, Mary could not understand exactly
what moment had brought this unwelcome blaze of per-
ceptiveness to her life. It may have been a glance inter-
cepted, a word overheard, but whatever the starting point
was it had happened and now everything she heard or
saw in her day's routine had significance. There was his
calmness, of course, in leaving her for a week or two
weeks, any time business called. She was calm, too, about
those absences, but she had thought till recently that they
were calm in the same way, with their unhappiness locked
up inside. Well, his was calmness inside, too, it seemed.
There was his lack of responsiveness, the cool kisses, the
casual love-making. She was not responsive exactly, perhaps, she too gave cool kisses, but then that was all an
impetuous man demanded. It was when he was no longer
impetuous that the anemia in their relationship became
apparent. Certainly both could not be passive. But what

else could she be? It would be more than she could do to
confess that she could never sleep when he was away and
that she often got up in the night, quite lost without him,
and played phonograph records till daylight. And she
could never say love-words the way other wives did or
hold hands, but it seemed to her Lou would not have
liked that anyway. It had always seemed perfectly suitable
to her and she had assumed—to him—the man to be the
lover and to voice their love, the lady to be acquiescent
and shyly passive. But what did you do when there was
nothing to acquiesce to, no stormy advances to be passive
about? Well, she would never know, for she would never
dare ask. Maybe someone could teach her how to kick
down her own reserve. Maybe, instead of the psychoanalyst, she should go to a School for Etiquette. Professor,
she would say, I should like to know how to forget good
breeding. Is there a short summer course in forgetting
the gentlewoman's code? Is there a little home study extension course in how to operate like a human being
instead of a lady? But then she did not *want* to shout her
feelings to the housetops. That was the trouble.

Perhaps it was a surgeon she should consult. Surgeon,
she would say, how long would I have to be in the hospital
for a minor mental operation? How serious is it to cut
out that little section behind the brow that separates what
a Nice Girl Sees and Hears from What Really Happens?
The night that the woman called up for Lou, for instance,
and left word for Mr. Donovan to call her.

"Is this his mother?" the lady had inquired in a foreign
accent.

"This is his wife," Mary had answered. "Is there anything I can do?"

There was a brief pause and then a "No, thank you" that sounded almost embarrassed. That was how she guessed he was already in town, though he had said he would not be in till next day. But she could not for the life of her bring herself to mention this, no, you could not deliberately accuse someone of deceiving you. She had wanted him to insist on her staying home and letting the baby go West alone with Aunt Felicia, but she could not propose it herself. And he had merely said, "How long will you be gone?" Then one of the women at a bridge party had declared Jay Oliver had a mistress in New York, and in a flash she was certain this was true of Lou too. But she knew she would never mention it, she could never ask him, she could never spy, whatever suspicions she might have would have to freeze up inside her along with the evidence.

Now that everything about him had new meaning Mary was astonished to realize that her aunt and uncle had never for a moment liked or trusted Lou. She knew they had reservations about him, but she had thought it was merely their disappointment that he was not their sort. She did not dream it was active dislike. He had been new to Chicago and no part of Aunt Felicia's Eastern background, either. He had seemed to Mary just the rugged hearty salt-of-the-earth American that her uncle had always publicly praised and privately patronized. She had discounted their coolness to Lou as just the natural jealousy of the man who took their darling niece away from them. And Lou's loud pooh-poohing of the Judge and Aunt Felicia she took with loyal understanding, as his perfectly unnecessary feeling of social inferiority. She assured him over and over that he was more brilliant, more admirable in every way than anyone in the Harrod circle, he mustn't have a chip on his shoulder about them, he must only understand that they were spoiled, fortunate people who could never match his self-promoted achievements. Now, suddenly, she saw how genuinely they despised him, when Aunt Felicia said, "Your uncle doesn't encourage divorce, my dear, but he often says that if you suffer too much from your mistake he would do anything in his power to get you free."

Mary was too surprised to be angry. It happened the very day after Lou had told her about the friendly meeting with the Judge on the train. She mildly spoke of this now to her aunt.

"Oh, then he told you about that," said Aunt Felicia with a peculiar smile. "The Judge didn't think he would want it mentioned."

Aunt Felicia meant something, and the obvious implication was that Lou was in company he should not have been. Mary dared not ask. Her aunt would have said no more, anyway. Instead they listened to the Simon Barer records that had just come from England, until time for Aunt Felicia to go to her fitting.

When Lou called up later in the afternoon to ask if she wouldn't like a little company for dinner, she did not remind him that they were to have a talk alone that night. It was another mark of change in him that he disregarded their old taboo against unprepared entertainment, at home. Unexpected social demands on him he nearly always took care of by staying downtown and excusing Mary from the picture. She had always taken this as consideration for her shyness and dislike of crowds. Now, he was considering only his uneasiness at being alone with her.

"If you like company, by all means let's have it," she said.

"It's the Olivers," he said. "You know. He's Whittleby Cotton. I do a lot of business with them. You've met her. Sure it's all right?"

"Perfectly," she said.

It was the night of Aunt Felicia's Chamber Music group, which she loved but always gave up when Lou was home. She knew she would be thinking of this and the peace of music all the evening when she would be straining to be gay or merely friendly with Lou's friends. Already her head began to pound with its constant ache of thoughts, feelings repressed. Sometimes she thought she would like to take off the top of her own head just to see what was really in it. All she was certain of was her own trained reactions.

"Everything all right, then," Lou said, with the faintest doubt in his voice. It was almost, she thought, as if she was expected to ask him the questions that bothered her.

"Oh, quite," she said.

XIII

THE house at Winnetka was really Lou's house more than Mary's. He had spent a great deal of time and money on planning it and furnishing it, and once done, he forgot about it and left it up to Mary to finish. First he wanted a bigger house than Judge Harrod's, where Mary had made her home before. Since the Judge, in spite of his superior fortune, was not a showy spender, it was fairly easy to get a bigger house. Next, he wanted a larger living-room, since the Judge prided himself on his large living-room, so Lou's was two feet longer. The extra floor used for Aunt Felicia's little concerts did not interest Lou so he skipped that. The Judge's fresh-air obsession with sleeping porches all over the back of the house, also did not excite Lou's envy. However, the Judge's bar and game room in the cellar was only half as well equipped as Lou's and had but one ping pong table, whereas Lou had two, both usually ignored for the bar. Lou, through his whole-sale rug connections, had fine Orientals through the house instead of the worn carpeting the Judge deemed sufficient. And if the Harrods prided themselves on the thick stone walls that made their house so cool in summer, Lou countered this with air-conditioning. At least his wife was not going to complain of being deprived of former comforts, nor could she boast of having left a more expensive home. Lou saw to that.

There was a quiet and bare peace about the house that

seemed to Lou, always happy in his connection with the Harrods, the very epitome of class. Mary loved her music room and the baby's sleeping and play quarters and whatever whimsicalities of taste she possessed were expressed here. The rest of the house was as impersonally well-done as any other interior-decorating professional display. Mary bowed to Lou on this as she had bowed to Aunt Felicia before on home decorating. She did like flowers and collected beautiful vases wherever she could and on drives with the nurse and baby through the country she would often stop to gather appleblossoms, pussywillows, or other decorative branches for the house.

Lou was almost prouder of Mary's lack than he was of her virtues. The thing he admired most in her and counted on the most for his own happiness was her reserve. He never had to listen to what went on in her little mind, and she never asked him what went on in his. If she cried about little things now and then, and he supposed she did, he did not know what it was and certainly did not want to find out. If he himself felt sunk he didn't want anybody asking what was the matter with him, and Mary, even if she noticed, did not ask questions. If he suspected she disapproved of something he said or did—he was forever doing something wrong about her aunt and uncle—all she did was to stay in her room with a headache for a couple of days. It couldn't have been a more agreeable relationship.

Another thing that had won Lou, besides her good breeding, her name, and her discreet passivity, a quality he'd never found in any other woman, was her youth. She was twelve years younger than he and it seemed to give an added piquant flavor to the conquest, as if her youth was a rare diamond that he was able to buy and show off. He spoke of her youth oftener than necessary because, to tell the truth, she seemed older than himself with her restraint and dignity, qualities he was still struggling to master. At twenty-one, when he met her, she even looked a good deal older. She was no beauty, even then, unless fragility could be considered a beauty. Whatever was pleasing about her appearance was certainly nothing he had ever admired before as seductive. Hers was no full luscious body, radiating tropic passion or even the natural vitality of youth. Instead her tall frail frame radiated nothing more than an ingrown anemic sickly spirituality. She had grown too fast as a girl, everyone said, but it was fortunate that her motions were sufficiently graceful to give an air to her lanky limbs. Her face was full, however, and her slender bones seemed well-enough covered. She had heavy drooping eyelids, enormous gray eyes, full wide mouth with fine teeth, an appealing quite angelic face, the luminous dead white skin striking against the short coppery curls. Her face and the mat of casual curls was so pure and childish it was always a shock to see her standing, see the long thin body, too long and too thin, the delicate neck, the incredibly thin wrists, the almost papery white fingers. The upper arm was rounded enough as were the hips and thighs, but the ankles again were unbelievably delicate. Up to the time he met Mary, seven years ago, Lou had been attracted by the very opposite of every one of Mary's bodily characteristics, it seemed to him. But then he fell for her and he found something quite devastating in her dreamy sexless charm. One thing he had guessed—was that here was a woman he would never tire of, because there was not enough of her to tire of. Nor would he ever leave a mark on her, so that would make him keep trying. That pale virginal quality would

remain, and even after he had slept with her for six years
—a not too satisfactory business because he was still afraid
of her—he never felt that he had really made the complete conquest. Her eyes had no different glow than before.
He learned something, and that was that while he had
dismissed much more satisfying women from his life, the
challenge of the too cool woman went on forever with him,
as it did with many men, the virgin challenge, and sometimes he reflected that the great courtesans of the ages must
have been like that,—cool, unmoved, perpetually unawak-
ened, giving less than nothing to tease the lover into further
bondage, instead of being the hot babies history assumed
they were.

He came home about six, his brief case full of the material Miss Frye had gotten together for him. Mary was
in the bed-room dressing and he went in and kissed her.
As soon as he saw her sitting in her slip, thin shoulders
bare, brushing her hair before the vanity-table, he realized
with a shock how lost he would be without Mary. He still
wondered how he had ever had the courage to go after
her, how he had ever braved that other world for even
a little while, but here was permanent evidence of his
bravery, he still did not understand just how or why unless
his very effrontery had pleased her. It gave him new confidence in himself just to see her, part of his home, like this.
Whatever had been on her mind these last few weeks he
was determined to override. This was not so difficult for
him, because as soon as he came in the room Mary's doubts
lightened, his vigorous presence threw such a dust of general
confusion in the air that it was hard to remember what
little headaches his absence had caused.

"So you're walking out on me," he said, grinning at her

in the mirror. "Leaving me to shift for myself while you run around with those dude cowboys."

The little reproach showed that he really did mind her going so her face lit up eagerly.

"It's only for Baby, dear," she said, "and even now I wouldn't go if you wanted me badly—I mean——"

"The kid comes first," he said firmly. "You and I don't count. It's the youngster. Wait a minute—I haven't seen her for a month—is it all right to go in?"

This, too, lifted a burden from Mary's soul, for it showed he was interested in the baby, and words of her aunt had insinuated that Lou was an indifferent father. She slipped on her robe and followed him down the hall to the nursery.

Baby was sitting at her small table on the porch eating her supper in the company of her two favorite friends, an enormous Easter rabbit on one small chair, and a black and gold Krazy Kat in the doll high chair. The nurse was straightening the bed in the nursery.

"She's still a little pale," Mary said, though the little girl was like her mother, naturally pale and underweight.

"Well, how's daddy's girl?" Lou asked and lifted her up.

"Please don't disturb her supper, dear," Mary protested, "and it always frightens her to be lifted up."

Lou put her down.

"I don't mind," said the child politely, "if daddy wants to play that way."

Lou laughed, embarrassed. Baby was a Harrod just as Mary was and even though she was only four Lou felt afraid of her quiet, gray eyes, he was uncertain what the Judge and Aunt Felicia may have taught the child, at any rate it was completely theirs, not his. Mary stroked her head, copper-curled like her own.

"Perhaps daddy had better visit you in the morning when it won't make the little head ache," she said tenderly. "Nurse says company at night always gives her a headache."

Lou left the room while Mary gave some instructions to the nurse. That was the way it had been from the time the baby was born, there was no beating that situation, he knew that. Baby was Mary's, just as his business was his. All right, if it made her happy. But he was glad that none of his business friends saw how badly a good mixer came off in his own child's nursery.

"What about dressing?" Mary asked him.

Lou shook his head.

"No, hell, this is just a little home evening, we want Jay and Flo to feel at home, friendly, you know," he said.

Nothing could have alarmed Mary more than the thought of a friendly get-together with Flo Oliver, but she braced herself.

"I thought we'd have mint juleps," Lou said. "It's late for them but there's nothing like them for icebreakers. Have them down in the game room, see."

The new set of silver mint julep mugs was a Christmas gift from the Judge and always made a good anecdote, would show Jay Oliver that the old boy was friendlier to Lou than his attitude on the train would indicate.

"It's all right for me to wear a long dress, isn't it, dear?" Mary asked.

Lou was firm about that, though. It had been an informal invitation, Flo was scared to death of Mary anyway, and the only way to handle that was to show that although the Donovans had a little more dough they were not putting on any dog about it.

"I suppose bridge would be the best thing later," Mary said with resignation.

"No bridge," said Lou. "I've got a little surprise for the evening's entertainment. Leave it to me."

Mary was glad to. It was such a relief to see Lou bustling noisily all over the place again that she began to think perhaps the evening would not be so hopeless after all.

XIV

THE Olivers had started their fight at a brisk tempo at four-thirty—the hour when Flo had summoned Jay to Marshall Field's for ominous reasons—but by six-thirty they were running out of material and on the ride to the Donovans it looked as if there would be no photofinish at all, merely whimpers and "Oh, is that so?"'s, and "That's what *you* think!"'s, and "Oh, for crying out loud!"'s. As the Donovan house hove into view there was one brief moment of complete rapport when both Olivers joined in a vast rage at the Donovans and a mutual silent vow to get stinking as fast as possible. Flo was looking singularly warlike in the brand-new gold-embroidered red evening dress she had bought that very day for the occasion, and had smartened herself up with one of the grimmest permanents her beautyshop had ever turned out, every curl seemingly made of purest iron. She was in the habit of using more rouge than was advisable and had gone to town this evening with a brand new shade, which Jay sorrowfully begged her to wipe off.

"Listen, everyone wears rouge," Flo had snapped back. "You don't like me in red, you don't like me in jewels, listen, I'm not an old lady, yet, I got a right to a little gayety."

The little ermine jacket Flo had purchased at the last minute had started the fight, since the Oliver bill at the store was already steep enough, and Jay didn't see why a little family dinner at the Donovans' should cost him three hundred dollars. Besides Lou had said nothing about dressing. He kept protesting about this point all the while he was putting on his dinner coat.

"Listen, dope, people like Mary Donovan always dress," Flo expostulated. "They don't say anything about it because they take it for granted. Or else maybe they think we're the type that wouldn't know anything about that. They give me a pain."

"Keep your shirt on," Jay said. "Wait till you're insulted, for God's sake."

"What's so special about that house, I'd like to know," Flo sourly observed as they approached the driveway. "I suppose they thought it would be a real treat for us to see their lousy place."

"You asked for it," Jay grumbled. "You've been bellyaching about it from the first time you met them."

"Oh, is that so?" Flo said.

"Oh, for crying out loud," said Jay. "You jump on me every minute I'm home, is it any wonder I hate coming home? I'll betcha there isn't another married man in town that has to put up with what I do every damn minute."

"That's what *you* think," said Flo and permitted herself to be helped out of the car. "You don't know how lucky you are."

The ice was not immediately broken by the homey spectacle of Mary Donovan in a knitted sportdress and Lou in loose collar and sport jacket of vivid green. Lou had spotted the magnificent spectacle of Flo in trailing red taffeta and ermine as she got out of the car and he groaned.

"How nice of you to dress!" Mary said. "You needn't have, of course, but——"

"Well, we did," said Jay. He avoided the lightning look from his wife's eye, for even though it was she who had insisted on dressing he knew that would not save him from blistering reproaches for her own error.

"It's just us, you know," Mary said desperately as she took Flo into the powder room.

"Not really!" Flo said in such frank dismay that Mary was even more confused.

Downstairs in the game room Lou was having no better time of it, for Jay was in a state of profound gloom. If he had ever been a man to admit defeat Lou would have confessed that even a straight heart-to-heart talk alone with Mary about all of his past sins would have been easier than this craftily planned evasion of such privacy.

"What's Flo beefing about?" Lou jovially asked. He was getting out the handsome mint julep service and carefully making his preparations with the help of the fat black maid, Annie, who knew better than to volunteer too much help on this sacred chore of Mr. Donovan's.

"Nothing the matter with Flo," Jay said testily. "What's *your* wife beefing about?"

This was going a little too far, and Lou almost lost his temper. Mentioning his Mary and a battleaxe like Flo in the same breath.

"I was just wondering if anything came up about Ebie," Lou said.

"No, that's all right," Jay said guiltily, wondering just how soon Flo would be tight enough to say something about her own misconception of whose girl Ebie was.

"I was going to get her to do a little mural for the New York office," Lou said. "Not her line but no reason why she shouldn't take a whirl at it. Called her couple of times but Rosenbaum's office says they haven't been able to locate her for two days."

"Can you blame her?" Jay queried indifferently. The wives came in then, Mary looking unusually pale and skeletonic compared with Flo's flamboyant aggressiveness.

Lou hastened his julep ritual, keeping up a genial flow of conversation, all about how the Judge had paid a small fortune for the julep set and had taught him his own special way of making the drink, inverting the glass first over the powdered sugar, and so on, till Flo, said, "Isn't it too bad your uncle couldn't be here to make them personally!"

"That's an idea," said Lou. "We may give him a call on that."

"We were hoping we'd have a chance to meet them tonight," said Flo.

"Do you mind making mine just plain Scotch, old man?" Jay asked. "I started on that and I'm afraid to switch."

"That's a good idea," said Flo. "I always get sick on juleps. They look wonderful, too, but I think it's the Bourbon. I never can take Bourbon."

Silently Lou nodded toward the Scotch decanter on the bar, and Jay happily poured a couple of drinks for himself and Flo. Mary was about to ask for her usual sherry but the collapse of the mint julep experiment was too much for her and to Lou's gratification she took a julep.

"I thought Lou was lying when he said you didn't drink, Mrs. Donovan," laughed Flo. "I guess you're one of those women who just drinks in the home."

"Oh, sure," Lou said. "Mary can carry quite a little package with nobody noticing a thing. You ought to get her to teach you, Flo."

Cooled her off with that one, he thought with satisfaction. He thought no wonder Jay goes for a swell girl like Ebie, anybody would with a hellion like Flo swinging the axe around every minute. He had thought this little friendly dinner would fix up the whole little unpleasantness between himself and Mary and between Flo and Mary, for Flo's wound at being so consistently snubbed by Mary was no secret. Instead it looked as if they were all going to end up in a free-for-all.

Jay and Flo helped themselves to the Scotch again, Jay getting gloomier and gloomier and Flo gayer and gayer. They seemed bent upon outdoing each other and in showing their host and hostess that so far as they were concerned the party, the house and everything in it was no treat to them.

"Go on, show Flo the upstairs," Lou urged. "Show her that mirror we got for the blue Bed-room."

"Is it an antique?" asked Flo.

"Antique, nothing," said Lou. "That antique stuff is nothing but a fad anyway. That's the trouble we had with Castles-in-the-Woods, Jay. Got a man down there, friend of the Major's, wants to load the whole place up with antiques. Bought out the neighborhood, I guess. I put my foot down. Modernistic, I say. Stream-line. Stick to your period."

"I think antiques are such good taste," said Flo, to Mary.

"Yes," said Mary helplessly.

"What's Castles-in-the-Woods?" asked Flo.

"Now you're asking something," said Lou. "After dinner tonight I'm going to show films our Baltimore man took of the whole property, then I've got colored pictures of our plans, the whole proposition. That's what Jay and I have been working over in New York when you girls thought we were playing around."

"I didn't hear anything about it," said Flo.

"I never ask about Lou's business because I know I shouldn't understand it," Mary said apologetically.

"Well, this will give you an idea," Lou said.

Dinner improved Jay's spirits slightly and when the wine came out Jay decided to make amends to Lou for his former rudeness by asking for one of those old mint juleps. Flo decided she would change her mind and try one herself. Lou no longer cared what happened and left the soup course to go downstairs again and throw a few juleps together, not such a delicate operation when performed without an audience, chipped ice, a couple slugs of Bourbon in each glass and some mint poked around in it for a second.

In the dining-room Flo complimented Mary on her china service, her linen, her cook and her complexion and Mary squirmed in her seat unhappily, not having the faintest idea whether Mrs. Oliver was mocking her or flattering her. Flo adjusted each compliment so that it would have a boomerang effect and fly back and hit Jay. All of the things she admired were things she too would have if it were not for Jay's indifference to nice things, his inferior business head which prevented him from making the money Lou did, and his never listening to his wife. If Jay had listened to his wife they would be living in a house bigger and better than the Donovans' and instead of Jay coming to Lou that time for the loan it would be the other way round. But oh, no, Jay was just like his whole family, a good-for-nothing don't-care lot, you couldn't blame them, it ran in the family.

"Oh, is that so?" Jay asked.

"You bet it's so," said Flo.

"That's what *you* think," said Jay.

They were really having a splendid time, but Mary could not know that and looked helplessly from one to the other, smiling politely till the full import of the remark would hit her, then looking with wide grieved bewildered eyes down at her plate. Lou, coming back bearing the mint juleps, saw that Jay and Flo were rattling down to their usual act, no harm in it, and was only annoyed that Mary seemed to be giving them the freeze. He thought resentfully that it wouldn't hurt once in a while for her to loosen up for his friends, God knows he loosened up to her crowd when he saw them; the only thing was he probably loosened up too much with them judging by the way they snubbed him. He was annoyed at her, too, for not mentioning the friends he wanted her to mention, so it left him with the clumsy task of working her contacts into the conversation.

"I read that speech your uncle gave at the college festival," Flo said to Mary. "Believe me I think that old boy knows what he's talking about. These foreigners trying to run this country. I could tell him some things about that."

"Why don't you give him a call, Lou?" Jay asked.

Lou looked him in the eye.

"All right, why not? Go ahead, honey, call up the Judge. He'd be interested in the Castles-in-the-Woods pictures. We're showing the models at the World's Fair next year, Jay."

"No kidding!"

"Why not?" Lou begged to know. "Jay, you old buzzard, you don't seem to realize this Castles-in-the-Woods is the biggest thing since Boulder Dam. For anybody that's getting as nice a cut as your company is out of it——"

"Maybe I'm not getting as big a cut as I should," said Jay, which was not quite cricket, as the little extra cut he turned back to Lou on these deals was strictly confidential.

"There's other firms, my lad," said Lou, dead pan. "There's Cannon. There's Lady Pepperell."

The gentle little threat straightened Jay out and he shrugged.

"When did the World's Fair thing come through?"

"I started it before I left New York," Lou said airily. "Put it up to the Major and Rosenbaum and now it's practically in. The hotel itself, in miniature, serving nothing but Chicken Maryland and coffee. And mint juleps. Then the working models of the whole project with leaflets and photographs. An agent in charge."

"You're a fast worker, all right," said Jay.

"It'll take a few more weeks to get set, of course," Lou said. "I'll have to run back to New York oftener."

"Oh," said Mary involuntarily.

"I guess you don't care much about Lou's work, do you?" Flo laughed. "I was in business myself once in New York, so I understand. I ran a tea-room."

"For six months," said Jay. "Lucky I came along and bailed her out."

"That's all right, I know what business men do in New York," Flo said roguishly.

"For crying out loud, you'd think all we did was chase, from the minute we leave this town," Jay said indignantly.

"That's all right, I can see where Flo might get that impression from some of these fellas," Lou said judiciously. "Take some of these fellas, they get to New York and make fools of themselves."

"It's the high buildings," said Jay. "You got your neck out from the time you leave the station."

"The point is that it's tough on the rest of us," Lou said earnestly. "We got a job to do, we haven't the time to play around."

"Oh, oh," said Flo. "I could tell Mrs. Donovan something about that."

Jay gave her a quick kick under the table.

"Do that, will you?" Lou said. "Give her an angle."

The loud voices, the wrangling, and the new doubts she had of Lou, made every moment seem intolerable to Mary. She had wanted to please Lou but she did not know how, and Lou with these friends was not the Lou she knew. The allusions they made to their common interests made her feel desolately left out and again filled with the odd fears Aunt Felicia had started. She made a desperate try to salvage the evening, when they started in to the huge living-room for their coffee.

"It's Aunt Felicia's night for Chamber Music, Lou," she suggested. "Perhaps the Olivers would like to go over there and listen to some Haydn."

"Say, now, doesn't that sound ducky?" Jay said.

"Shut up, dope," reproved Flo. "A little music wouldn't hurt you. You might learn a little something."

"It's all right with me," said Jay. "I can take it or leave it alone."

It was Flo's turn to give him a nudge.

"If you folks don't appreciate an invitation to one of the most high-class homes in Chicago, then the hell with you," Lou flared up. "If my wife's willing to take you into her Aunt's private musicale, by golly, you ought to be proud to go."

"I thought we were asked here," said Jay. "What's the idea? Trying to brush us off?"

"Now, Jay," Flo complained, "I don't see why we can't drop in the Harrods' for a while. I've never been there. I'd like to see the house even if there is music."

The fat colored maid produced brandy and benedictine, and Lou poured them out.

"Pardon me, just a minute," he said, suddenly. "Is there anything you have against my showing my friends the Castles-in-the-Woods films? That was my original suggestion. Apparently the idea bores you, my dear."

Mary blushed.

"No, no, I—I mean, of course, I'd like to, but——"

"That's all right," he said with elaborate indifference. "We'll go to your uncle's. A little music at your uncle's would be so much finer than your husband's business pictures. Oh, sure."

"It's all right with me," said Jay. "I can take anything."

Mary rose quietly.

"I'll call and tell them we're coming," she said. "I'm sure Mrs. Oliver would enjoy it."

"You bet your life I would," said Flo, loyally. "Personally, I'd rather listen to some good music right now than anything in the world."

"Personally, I'd rather sit around and get cock-eyed," stated her husband. "That's the way it is with me."

Lou was still looking with silent anger after Mary's proud exit when the maid called him to the extension in the hall.

"You didn't call me back," said a charming voice. "I am so cross. You're a naughty boy."

It was Mrs. Kameray. Lou was delighted.

"You don't like me," she pouted. "Here I am, a stranger, and you are too busy to see me."

Lou closed the door and talked to her in a low voice. When he came back he was beaming.

"Hold your hats, kids," he cried. "We're going back to town and fix up the Spinning Top."

"Thank God," said Jay.

Mary came back in.

"Aunt Felicia will expect us in about half an hour," she said. "She says it's always a pleasure to have guests who really enjoy music."

"That's off," said Lou briskly, still angry with her. "The Donovans have to meet some friends at a restaurant downtown. We can drop you at the folks', since that was your suggestion. I'll show the pictures to Jay and Flo at the office sometime where it won't bother you."

"Isn't he mean?" exclaimed Flo, happy always in a little misunderstanding.

"Excuse me while I change," Mary murmured, flushed and head bowed.

"Oho, she changes for the Harrods, then," Flo said triumphantly. "I knew that was how it was."

No one said anything while Mary was gone. Flo tinkered with the piano, playing "Begin the Beguine" with one hand. Jay tossed off a couple of brandies silently. They were sorry for him, Lou thought indignantly. They had stopped kidding him because now they saw how it was about his wife waving her fine family over him all the time, freezing all his business friends and brushing off his business interests, making a cheap tramp out of him by showing off her superior taste. Barely saying ten words during the evening. Making him a laughing stock before Jay and Flo.

"Doesn't Mrs. Donovan care for nightclubs?" Jay asked.

"They give her a headache," said Lou, and then as she came in he thought he'd add for good measure, "just the way my business does. And the way the Harrod family does me."

Everyone laughed.

"Jay, you drop Mary in your car and I'll take Flo on down," said Lou, as they got out to the driveway.

"Oh, but I'm going on down to the Spinning Top with you," Mary said in a low voice. Lou glanced quickly at her but her eyes were staring straight ahead. It suddenly struck him that she had been on the music-room extension when Mrs. Kameray had called and had not hung up.

"That's great," he said. Never let them get you. Ride it through.

XV

"Maybe we'd better go to the Colony," Flo suggested to Lou. "Maybe the Top is too rough for Mary. Maybe the Chez Paris."

"The Top's all right," Lou said easily. Flo was trying to be a pal, show how well she understood a man's problems. The trouble with a "good egg" was that you had to talk to them all the time, you couldn't just drive along, thinking your own thoughts in silence, the way you could with a girl like Mary who wasn't and never could be a pal. Flo squirmed around in the seat to see if Jay's car was following.

"I wonder what Jay's talking to her about," she mused aloud and then chuckled, as if she and Lou and Jay were one kind and Mary another, instead of Lou and Mary being of a piece. Even if they weren't Lou preferred to keep the knowledge to himself.

"I sure feel sorry for her," said Flo sympathetically.

"Just why?" Lou asked, but getting it just the same.

"Oh, I don't know," Flo said. "She doesn't understand you at all. She doesn't get one thing about you."

"Maybe I don't want to be got," Lou said, sore, but trying not to show it. He wished it had been possible to ride with his own wife but of course that was out of the question. Even mad at each other and the slip-up on the Kameray dame's call he was sure they wouldn't have had to talk it out, anyway. Talking things out was what

made people so sore at each other. They were madder
at the things they said talking it out than they were over
the original misunderstanding. He and Mary, thank God,
could misunderstand each other and never have to speak
of it. Right now he was appalled at the idea of Mary
in the Spinning Top, but he certainly was not going to
talk it over with Flo. Flo was the type that fifteen years
ago after a few drinks would have welcomed a pass driving out like this with the other guy. Now that she was
forty and bulging in the wrong places she took it out in a
good heart-to-heart pal talk. Lou stepped on the gas to
shorten this intimate little chat.

"No, seriously, Lou, you've never had a woman who
really understood you," Flo went right to it. "I mean,
you're ambitious, you've got a lot more guts than Jay,
you get an idea and go right to town on it. Jay never has
any ideas. He just does his job and sells Whittleby Cotton."

This was all okay with Lou but it made him mad to
hear it from Flo, especially with the little sideswipe at
Mary.

"I don't blame a man like you—I mean I *wouldn't*
blame you if you had a little hideout in New York," Flo
went on knowingly. "You're too big a man to be tied to
one woman."

"I'm satisfied, never mind about that," Lou cut in.

"I mean your wife doesn't understand you the way
I understand Jay," Flo explained. "There's no excuse for
a man running around when his wife understands him
like I do Jay, but in your case——"

"Why should I want a woman to understand me? Just
to have the b'jesus balled out of me all the time?" Lou

asked. He gave a short laugh. "That's why a fellow runs out; so he won't be understood."

"Well, if you're going to be that way," said Flo. "That's the way I'm going to be," said Lou, and that cooled her off till they got to the Spinning Top.

If Jay and Flo thought there was anything funny in Mary deciding to come along, as indeed there was, Lou was determined not to show it. He wanted to show Flo, damn her hide, just how Mary could be a good egg without making a fool of herself. A woman didn't need to get so fried she had to be carried home in order to be a good egg. She could be a good egg by just keeping her trap shut and letting other people enjoy themselves. She could be a good egg by meeting the husband's girl friends and not throwing a plate at them.

The Spinning Top was not one of Chicago's better spots; its chief charm for its customers was that it was not popular and was no place to take a wife. It was a jolly combination of seedy Hollywood glitter and old-time honkytonk. It was near enough to the station so that a busy man could nip over for a drink and the show between trains, say hello to the girls, maybe, and then, after he missed his train, could even be put up in the little adjoining hotel. The girls were good-natured, not bad-looking graduates of various exclusive burlesque wheels, and they sat around at the bar in little fig-leaf costumes, fluttering their blue-greased eyelids at strangers, and on dull nights at least keeping up a semblance of gayety by their perpetual squeals and chatter. It was said, with authority, that a favored customer could toss his coat to Marie, the hat-check girl, for repairs while he drank, and he could even send her out to do his wife's shopping, if necessary, while he downed a few at the bar. Homey, that was the way a traveller described the Spinning Top, and it was fine dropping in a place where they didn't snub you, a place where the waiters all called you by your first name, and the girls kidded and scolded you and took care of you, and took every nickel you had. All right, it was a clip-joint, but if you passed out the manager himself took all your valuables out of your pocket to look after till you came to, so that at least nobody else would steal them. It was your own fault if you forgot next day where you'd been.

It was a dull evening tonight and the girls had listlessly walked through the dinner-show with little more than the orchestra and waiters for audience. Since their gifts were little more than walking under any circumstances the performance was not too much worse than usual. As soon as the Olivers and Donovans arrived, however, the place sprang into action. Two girls who had been slumping at the bar wrangling with the bartender now rushed to attach a cigarette tray and flower tray respectively to their persons; Tessie, the accordionist, struck up "Give My Regards to Broadway," a roguish reminder that on Mr. Oliver's last appearance at "The Top" he had obliged with a simple timestep to that tune. The head-waiter, a punch-drunk ex-fighter, who was making himself feel like a crowd with a series of short brandies, snapped to his heels, with an almost reverential bow.

"Good evening, Mr. Donovan," he said. "And Mr. Oliver. Well, well!"

He had fortunately learned to take no chances on calling the ladies by name, but men customers sometimes wondered whether the flattery to their ego of the bow and their names remembered was really worth while, since the lady was often not impressed so much with the regard in which her husband or boy-friend was held as by the deduction that he must spend a lot of money here.

Lou saw that Mrs. Kameray had not arrived yet and he had a moment to plan. It was foolish, he thought, to be alarmed at any meeting between Mrs. Kameray and Mary, since there was nothing between him and Mrs. Kameray. That is, nothing as yet. Nothing but a level look exchanged at their last meeting and her eyes dropping, an electric hint that when the time was right would be time enough. It was these little promises without words, not the conquests, that gave zest to a man's life.

"My goodness, those girls don't have much clothes on," whispered Flo.

"Some women get along better without clothes," said her husband.

Lou could tell by the lift of Mary's head and the cool look in her eyes that she was hanging on to herself, she hated the place, the noise, the gaudiness, the company she was in. But he was not sympathetic. She asked for it. When she got that frozen Harrod look he felt either hopelessly inferior or mad as hops. Tonight he was mad. He could do a freeze, too, in his own way. They didn't bicker like the Olivers but they knew how to give it to each other without an unpleasant word. She was continuing to be graciously attentive to the Olivers, with dampening effects on their spirits. When Jay used a bad word or Flo passed out an off-color joke Mary's polite laugh was worse than a rebuke. She had decided now to show Lou that these people were really not her sort and so she was giving an exhibition of correct, thoroughly irreproachable behavior that was more disagreeable than anything that could happen in "The Top." To punish her Lou motioned Jay to come over to the bar. More people were coming in and the girls' voices keyed a little higher with expectation, Tessie started moving around kidding the newcomers and the orchestra took over with a deafening, drum-thumping rendition of "Oh, Mama, please get that man for me," which the leader sang through an amplifier and his own nose.

"The Kameray's coming in later," Lou notified Jay.

Jay whistled.

"Boy, are you in a jam!" he exclaimed with delight.

Lou took a pack of Luckies from the girl, waved away the change for a dollar, offered Jay one.

"What do you mean—jam?" he said. "I got nothing to worry about. Just an extra woman, that's all."

Jay shook his head.

"I wouldn't trust that little baggage," he said. "She's looking for trouble and not for herself, either."

"She's working for me, that's all."

"I hope," said Jay.

"I was just thinking we'll have to look out for her, on Rosenbaum's account," said Lou. "Don't let the women ride her too hard. You know how they go for a new dame."

"Oh, sure," said Jay. "Only hang on to your watch, fella."

"Never let it be said," said Lou, and then he saw Francie and the punk walk in. He might have known that a fourth-rate joint like the Top would be about the punk's speed. He might have known, too, that they'd hang around town till they made trouble. Francie was dolled up to the gills in an olive green fall suit with a pair of supercolossal silver foxes swinging to her knees and a green Robin Hood cap jauntily tilted over the doll-hair. If you hadn't known her of old she wouldn't have looked bad.

"The little floozy's back in," Jay muttered to Lou. "Don't let her speak to me, for God's sake, or Flo will start throwing."

"Is that all?" asked Lou. "I would have said Flo was about ripe for a good hammer murder right now."

"Well, Mr. Thompson," said the bartender and reached in his pocket for some bills. "You're in luck again. She came in third today."

"Better than nothing," said the punk and took it. Thirty bucks.

So he was playing the Pimlico races from here. He glanced up while he was counting it and caught Lou's sardonic eye. Francie followed the quick flush on Thompson's face back to Lou and she gave a little gasp. It was the time to clear up this headache, for good, Lou thought. He would never be in a better position to do it, even with Mary and Flo watching, they could not hear the conversation above the orchestra din. Jay had quietly slipped out to the john.

"Hello, Francie," said Lou quietly. "Glad to see you're in the dough again." He looked over the foxes thoughtfully. "Spend much time at the Top?"

Francie was flustered, looking from Lou's impassive ruddy face to Thompson's pale sullen one.

"Frank won about forty dollars in bar checks here the first night we came here," she explained breathlessly. "We sort of stayed in town to spend them. No good any place else, of course. And then we got a little extra——"

"So I see," sad Lou. "Well, I was glad to be of help."

He nodded to Thompson and started away but Francie grabbed his arm.

"Give me that thirty, Frank," she commanded the punk, and as he reluctantly drew it out of his pocket, she pressed it into Lou's hands. "Here's the thirty you gave me. Thanks."

"Wait a minute——"

"No, no, take it. Take it, Lou, you've got to. Feeling the way you do about it—no, no——"

He managed a laugh, for the sake of the ones watching, and took the money to keep her from yelling any louder. Thompson looked down into his drink and didn't speak to him at all. Lou wasn't jealous of him, how could he be when he hadn't the faintest feeling left for Francie except annoyance, but somehow every time he saw the haggard, weak little blonde face of his successor he wanted to take a poke at it. He did the next best thing.

"What kind of a gambler do you call yourself, Thompson?" he called over to him with an attempt at a grin. "With all your expert information I should think you could play more than two bucks. No use being a piker. Why don't you branch out?"

"I bite," said the punk bitterly. "Why don't I?"

"Lou, please—" Francie pleaded.

Lou brushed her aside and walked over to Thompson.

"Tell you what I'll do," he said. "Here's a hundred. If you can make that pay fifty to one, it's yours. If you can't you owe me a hundred. Of course if you're out of town there's no way I can collect. But——"

"Don't take it, Frank," Francie begged. "Don't take it, honey, he just wants to humiliate you."

"Nuts," said Lou, "he'll take it."

He did, too, slowly, but he took it without a word, Just stuffed the bill in his pocket with a queer look.

Lou started back to his table, with Francie still tugging at his sleeve, and to make it look better he swung her into the dance floor, pretending that was what she had asked him.

"All right, he took it," Francie whispered. "I know you've got that on him just like you wanted, but honest, Lou, the reason he acts so terrible with you is he's so jealous——"

"What for?"

"Oh, Lou, you know. He loves me, don't you see, and it hurts him to know I stay crazy about you, he's not a fool, he knows, I can't hide it, I'm so happy just this minute with your arms——"

Lou stopped.

"Thanks for the dance," he said. "As for the hundred nothing would please me more than to hear I lost it. Night."

He managed a big laugh again, as if they were kidding, but Francie's yearning look after him was no corroboration.

"What a pretty girl!" Mary said when he sat down.

"He can pick 'em," agreed Flo. "If he can't, Jay can. Kinda hard boiled, though, I would say, and certainly no chicken."

"I wouldn't know," said Lou. "Women nowadays can trick themselves out any age at all."

More people were coming in and the orchestra was playing louder, the crooner was going to town on "Tonight We Love" and Flo was blowing the little whistle the waiter left as favors to the ladies. Francie and the boy-friend were doing some fancy steps and whirls that would have finished off a healthy man let alone a guy supposed to have only one lung. Jay came back with an uneasy glance at Francie but she seemed bent on drowning her sorrows in the dance so he got back safely.

"Too bad you can't find a girl-friend like Lou's," Flo shrilly cried. "Then Mary and I can go home and leave you to your fun."

"How do you like the place, Mrs. Donovan?" Jay politely asked.

Mary turned a pale bright face toward him.

"Oh, terribly amusing," she said. "I had no idea there were places like this."

"I knew it, all right," said Flo. "The only thing is try and get your husband to take you to one."

Ha ha ha, laughed everyone, and then the drinks came, and Lou saw that Mary was having plain soda, and to add to this exhibition of good sportsmanship she was taking a couple of aspirin with it to help endure the pain of having a good time. She looked at him apologetically but got no sympathy from his hard smile. It was really the worst thing that could have happened to either of them, this little introduction into his business life, for he could feel not the faintest remnant now of his old-time pride in her. If she had only gone to the Harrods', as he had thought she would, then he could have excused her chilling out the dinner guests by the thought of her later being at ease with much bigger shots. It was the thought of her, that he loved, and how can you have the thought of anyone if they're around your neck at the moment complicating everything? He would have liked to sit here

with the Olivers—yes and maybe even with Mrs. Kameray—and brag about how his wife never went to night-
clubs, never drank, loved music and culture and riding,
that sort of thing, a real lady, and talking he would have
sold himself all over on her. But here she was being a
lady in person, and away from her own background, a
lady was just a dud on a party, a liability, a wet blanket.
He could not feel even the slightest admiration at this
moment for her wide gray eyes and the gray dinner suit,
all he thought was that every aspirin she took was a
martyr's silent but public reproach to her brute husband
for bringing her out with such people to such a place, and
he felt an icy indifference to whatever torment her suspicions of him must be causing her.

"What's the woman's name?" Flo teased. "I mean the
blonde. Jay, do you know?"

"Me? Why should I?" Jay asked.

"I thought she kind of looked at you," Flo said, and
Jay slid further down in his seat.

"I believe it's Kameray, isn't it, dear?" Mary said,
but Lou did not bat an eye.

"No, dear, this is Mrs. Kameray coming in," he said.
"The other lady is Mrs. Thompson. I used to know her
in Dayton."

Mrs. Kameray looked wonderful to him, coming in at
that minute. Her trim little black suit, the simple fur bow
at her neck, the charming calm face, not childishly sweet
like Mary's, no, this was young but dignified. Lou and
Jay got up and brought her to their table. No give-away
here, either, thank God, Lou thought, for her little hand-
clasp to each man was accompanied only by the most
gracious little smile, any watching wife could see it with-

out a flutter. Lou, without looking at her, could see Mary preparing herself.

"My husband has often spoken of you, Mrs. Kameray," she said.

Mrs. Kameray looked in pretty amazement at her.

"But Mrs. Donovan, how could he?" she said. "It is true I work for him, yes, for him and Mr. Rosenbaum, but even though I call up and call up, Mr. Donovan will not let me see him in person until tonight. Isn't he naughty?"

Lou mentally doffed his hat to this superb job of fixing. It was as if she sensed the telephone extension eavesdropping and was covering every angle. Mrs. Kameray looked appealingly from Flo to Mary.

"But it is naughty, isn't it? I have to see the man, I call up, I tease, I flirt, and when Mr. Rosenbaum calls me up long distance to ask, I say, I cannot talk until I have seen Mr. Donovan and that naughty Mr. Donovan will not meet me. Tonight, I caught him, yes?"

Mary, drawing a long breath at this unexpected solution of her fears, looked at Lou, wanting him to forgive her her suspicions, wishing she had never doubted, longing for the old look of admiration, but Lou, cleared, at least momentarily, was arrogant. He must take Mrs. Kameray to another table for a little talk on Castles-in-the-Woods, a matter which had proved so boring to the others at dinner that he was sure they would be glad not to hear it mentioned again. Mrs. Kameray obligingly drew notes and pencil from her bag and gave every indication of being nothing more than a dutiful, attentive secretary, and her little bottle of white wine was further proof that she was only here in the line of duty. Proof, that is, to Mary. To Flo it was a case for exchanging winks behind Mary's back with Jay, and to Francie, watching from the bar, it was cause to down half a dozen drinks quickly and insist on playing the drums with the orchestra, her hat on the saxophonist's head, her husband Mr. Thompson passed out slumping over on a corner table. The spectacle of Francie at the drums was too much for Flo, and in a huff at Jay for not dancing with her, she joined a lone wolf at the bar, a swarthy Spaniard, and cajoled him into doing a tango. Mary looked at Lou, then at these women he knew and it seemed to her her head would split with the din and the strangeness of this side of his life, the effort of understanding him. She knew that to leave was another hideously wrong step, but tonight had been full of wrong steps anyway.

"Mr. Oliver," she said, "I mean Jay—would you mind taking me to a cab? I feel—I've got to have air. I'd like to go home, so much."

"Cab, nothing, I'll drive you home," Jay said. There was nothing here for him. He'd had the good luck to miss the floozy's recognition but the way she was acting up there with the orchestra it wouldn't be long now before she started the stuff on him, and then Flo would take over. Flo came dancing past with the Spaniard, showing off. She could take care of herself all right. Or Lou could. He got Mary's cloak, and piloted her past Lou.

"We're driving out for some air," he said, and Lou nodded. Mary smiled a little too eagerly at Mrs. Kameray and Mrs. Kameray smiled a little too sweetly back. Jay was glad to get out before anything started. At least Flo was busy with the stranger and she wouldn't be jealous of Mary.

But that was just exactly what Flo was. In fact Flo never took a chance on anything. It was no fun showing off her powers with other men without Jay to see it so she snatched her ermine cloak and ran after them.

Lou and Mrs. Kameray were so busy going over their data, scribbling addresses and other inspirations in their little notebooks, that they were remarkably oblivious to this last departure. All the more wonder then that they stopped talking at exactly the minute the door closed on Flo and looked at each other. It was the same look that Lou had remembered with heightened excitement, the slow measuring promise of complete surrender. He quietly signalled for the check and when they got up they did not even bother to collect the valuable data they had been so busily exchanging. They did not speak as they got in Lou's car and they did not even hear the special drum roll from the Spinning Top orchestra as they left.

XVI

"You're sure Mr. Donovan's coming back today?" Jay asked.

He sat at Lou's desk drumming on it till Miss Frye thought she'd go nuts. She looked up from her typing.

"Look," she said. "Would I tell a lie?"

"I don't know, sister," said Jay. "All I know is you said he'd be back last week, then you said Monday, then Tuesday, now today. Where'd he go anyway?"

Miss Frye had only told him that about five times, too.

"He's been making a swing through the West," she said. "The way I told you before. Do you want his itinerary?"

Jay saw his persistence was getting on the busy woman's nerves.

"That puts me in mind of my old man," he said. "He was a regular old-time travelling salesman, quit school in the eighth grade and started canvassing right outside Taylorville here. Got to be head of his own business and put me on the road soon as I got out of school. Called me in one day when I got back and he says, 'What's this here?' and I said, 'Why, dad, that's my itinerary.' 'The hell with this itinerary stuff,' he says, 'after this you send us in your route.' That was the old man for you."

"That's darned interesting," said Miss Frye.

"Do you want me to tell more?" asked Jay. "I got a million of 'em."

"Put 'em in a book," said Miss Frye.

"Hell, money means nothing to me," said Jay. "I'm glad to give you a little family history free of charge. You can mull over it while wrassling with the boy-friend."

"I don't 'wrassle,' " said Miss Frye.

"Fine!" said Jay. "That's the kind I like."

Miss Frye got up and giving her caller a measured look, laid a sheet of paper before him.

"There," she said, "is Mr. Donovan's itinerary."

"What's he doing at the Knickerbocker in Los Angeles?" read off Jay. "I thought he stayed at the Ambassador. And what's this about the Park Plaza in St. Louis? I thought he used the Statler."

"Look, Mr. Oliver," said Miss Frye, patiently. "Would you like to wait in the bar? I'm sure Mr. Donovan would rather you made yourself at home."

"I'm at home anywhere," said Jay. "Any old place I can hang my head is home sweet home to me."

"I know," said Miss Frye. "I heard that one."

"I never promised my script was new," said Jay. "All I said was I'd keep sending."

He looked over a stack of telegrams idly.

"All this on Castles-in-the-Woods?" he inquired but Miss Frye pretended the noise of her typewriter deafened her. "Did he put it through with the Frisco Fair people, too? He did! Well, well. And here it says the station wagons are to be maple with a Dubonnet trim, hospitality lights flood every driveway leading to the Castle Hotel, male help is Filipino—what does he want down there— race riots?—wearing white silk blouses with red sashes, pardon me, Dubonnet sashes."

"I know," said Miss Frye patiently.

Jay picked up another piece of paper.

"What was he doing at the St. Francis in San Francisco?" he inquired. "He's a Mark Hopkins customer."

"Mr. Oliver, I don't think Mr. Donovan wants you going over his mail," said Miss Frye. "There's a lot of stuff there in the bar. You look as if you needed something."

Jay got up with a sigh and strolled over to the bookcases which swung open showing the bar.

"In case Mr. Donovan wants my itinerary," he said, "put down that I'm going from Canadian Club to Ballantine's and will spend a short time in Martel. How come the boss stayed so long?"

"It's a big country," said Miss Frye. "It takes three weeks for that Western trip. I admit he's delayed, though."

"Maybe he's having trouble with Indians," said Jay.

Lou walked in and threw his hat on top of the safe.

"Well, son," he said to Jay, and shook hands. "Let's see your report card."

"Thank God, you're back," cried Miss Frye. "Everybody's calling. Mrs. Donovan has called from Arizona a half dozen times, that Mr. Truesdale has telegraphed for all kinds of information, Mr. Oliver here——"

Lou started leafing over the stack of mail.

"Lou, I got to see you," said Jay. "I got to. Just a minute. It's——"

Lou looked up, surprised at the odd tone in Jay's voice. Jay looked terrible. Hollow-eyed, miserable. Lou, staring, walked into the bar behind Jay and closed the door, leaving Miss Frye to throw up her hands in despair.

"It's Ebie," said Jay. "I can't find her. I put in a couple of calls to her apartment and no answer. I called Rosen-

baum about something else and slipped in a little inquiry
about Miss Vane. No Miss Vane. Severed her contracts.
Can't be located."

"That's ridiculous," said Lou.

"Wait. I flew to New York two days ago. No Ebie. And
not a word anywhere about where she is. God, Lou,—
what am I going to do?"

Lou lit a cigarette.

"Just have to replace her, that's all," he said.

"Lou, this isn't funny, supposing something's happened
to her, maybe she's another Dorothy Arnold———"

"Sure, maybe I'm another Charlie Ross, too. I'll bet I can
locate her in ten minutes."

Jay poured a small brandy. He was torn between genuine
anxiety and his natural desire to believe in Lou's ability to
fix everything.

"Lou, I'm crazy about Ebie. It's been going on for years.
You know, I chase, and I keep Flo going, but it's always
been Ebie with me. And mind you, not a note, not a letter,
not a call. It's not like her." Jay saw he was beginning to
impress Lou. "Ebie tells me everything she's doing. And if
she was mad she'd want to fight, she isn't one to pick up and
walk out, without a fight-talk. I thought of everything. I
thought—well, she was sort of worried last month, maybe
she went to a bad doctor, maybe she passed out and he
stuffed her in a furnace—you know those guys are liable
to twenty years if they're caught———"

"Good God, Jay, pull yourself together!" Lou exclaimed.
"Now, sit down. Let's look this thing over. Last time I saw
Ebie was—well, the time Flo pulled the cute trick and beat
you to New York. All right, Ebie was sore as the devil at
that."

"I know," groaned Jay. "And if I had the guts I would have kicked Flo out as soon as I met Ebie. That's when I should have done it. First time I ever laid eyes on Ebie, I should have broken with Flo. Ebie's worth ten of Flo."

"Check," said Lou. "All right, Ebie isn't the type to walk out, you say. Look. There's the type that walks out and walks out and walks out, know what I mean, round the corner and back, it's a habit. Then there's the type that walks out. That's how I classify Ebie. Just once she walks out."

"But why this time?" said Jay. "She's caught me fussing with other women, and I'm always dropping her as soon as Flo gets in the picture, not because I like Flo better but because Flo raises such hell."

"This was just once too often," said Lou. "You know how it is. You excuse a fellow putting the bee on you a dozen times but all of a sudden it's that one time too often. And you're through. Maybe Ebie's through."

"I got to get her back," said Jay. "I mean I can't get along without Ebie."

"Don't talk like a fool," Lou expostulated. "There's a dozen Ebies in every block. Nobody has to have just one particular dame, you know that. But we'll track her down."

He stepped to the door.

"Get me Truesdale at the Hotel Ellery, New York," he said to Miss Frye, and closed the door. "I'll put my man on her trail."

Jay drew a breath of relief.

"Gee, old boy, you take a load off my mind. It was getting me. Couldn't talk about it, of course."

"We'll find out what there is to know," said Lou. "Now, if you don't mind, I've got a month's stuff to clear up out here."

"What was the idea your changing hotels?" Jay asked.

"Don't you ever change hotels?" Lou growled.

Jay whistled.

"I get it."

Lou scowled.

"Nothing to get. Just trying out different services. I can't be too partial to one place, in my business."

"You put on some weight, too," said Jay, looking him over. "You must have about ten pounds more on you. Must have had a good trip."

"I did," said Lou.

"You old son of a gun," said Jay. "That's one thing I never could get away with—taking a woman along on a business trip."

"I never tried it myself," said Lou, offhanded. "If you want to know I was so damned busy this trip building up the Castles-in-the-Woods I wouldn't have had time for any women."

"I saw Rosenbaum in New York," said Jay. "He said the Kameray was working out all right at the job. I had to laugh. She called him up while I was there."

"Oh, she did?" Lou exclaimed.

"The secretary had given it away, so he couldn't gloss it over much, just said she made a daily report to him from wherever she was, by phone or wire. I got her little phony voice squealing, oh Wosebush, darling——"

"Where was she talking from?" Lou asked.

"St. Louis," said Jay. "Old Rosebush went into his other office to give her the babytalk back. How was she in St. Louis, old boy?"

"Mrs. Kameray is a wonderful person," said Lou sternly.

"If you make any more cracks about her I'll have to poke you right in that mush of yours."

"She's a two-timer, pal," said Jay. "I'm warning you. Old Rosebush has ten times the dough you've got."

Lou was irritated at having betrayed himself.

"Mr. Truesdale can't be located," Miss Frye came in to say. "The Ellery is leaving him a message."

"Go on, now, worry about Ebie," Lou recommended Jay with a nod. "I'll worry about me getting two-timed."

XVII

Your lives, said the analyst to Mary Donovan, are drifting apart, it is up to you to join them again. Make an effort, he said, to draw your husband into your life, above all do not show him you can have a perfectly pleasant life without him; make him feel that your social and musical life is flavorless without him. And in the relations between your family life and your husband do not act as if it was you and your family versus a stranger husband, but you and your husband against even your own family. An egotist like your husband demands this assurance.

So here they were at the Harrods' intimate little dinner party where for two hours Lou had been glancing at his watch and wondering how long it had taken these people to get this way. The ladies were fluttering about the fireplace in the great living-room while the gentlemen dallied over coffee and brandy in the dining-room, chewing at their cigars and their memories. There were Grahame, the big hotel man, Carver, an ex-governor, Sweeney, the old banker, the Judge, and Mr. Donovan, promoter. Mrs. Harrod had sent the butler down four times to get the gentlemen upstairs, but old Mr. Grahame always had one more story to tell, and after he finished that Governor Carter had a now-defunct state secret to reveal, and Mr. Sweeney, a stern gentleman with a trim Vandyke, threw out some secret statistics on world affairs with prophecies on how these figures would affect the war in Spain and the progress of Russia.

"Do you realize," said Mr. Sweeney, turning to Lou on his right, "that in the city of San Francisco there are over two hundred thousand Chinese, a city in itself, with its own telephone exchange? Now what would you say would happen there in the event of the Japanese and Hitler forces combining?"

"I don't bother much with Chinatown there," said Lou. "I usually stay at the Mark Hopkins."

"No prettier spot in the world than the roof of the Mark Hopkins," said Mr. Grahame, sucking at a cigar. "Look right out over the prison across the bay. Top of the Mark, they call it."

"I know," said Lou and thought of Trina Kameray and wondered how long before he could get away. He had assured her he would be out by ten-thirty since he was known to be a busy man and had half a dozen sound alibis at his disposal. Besides, there would be music and Mary knew how he felt about that, she would excuse him and come home later herself in her uncle's car. He nodded to have his brandy glass refilled and looked glumly down the long table to where the Judge was benignly puffing away at a cigar, a large glass of water in front of him with a small vial of his after-dinner medicine beside it. The dinner had been distinguished, as many of the Judge's dinners were, not only by the powerful names of the guests but by the display of medication. Both the Judge and Mrs. Harrod had small medicine bottles beside their plates and Mr. Grahame, before gorging himself on the roast beef, popped two large alka-seltzer tablets in his glass. Mrs. Sweeney, an angry gray woman of sixty, had denied herself every course but the salad which she attacked with the grim determination of a person finishing once and for all a persistent old enemy.

It rather surprised Lou to find himself noticing all these disagreeable features of the occasion. Usually he was so impressed with the magnitude of the combined fortunes and power present in the Judge's house that he noticed little else, and there were always his untiring efforts to show them that he was as good as they were, a conversational effort that took up so much of his time and energy that he had little opportunity to observe anything else. Tonight Mary had told him that if he didn't go, she wouldn't; she had added that her uncle was very eager to hear more about that new project of his on Chesapeake Bay, and that Aunt Felicia particularly had asked for him.

"No kidding," he had said, not really believing it, but half-pleased at the same time. In the veiled arguments he and Mary had been having ever since her return from the Southwest he had for the first time hinted that she had allowed her family to snub him, that they had used his indifference to music as an excuse not to ask him to their most publicized entertainments, and it was very nice, very nice indeed, that in guest lists in the society columns she was referred to as Mary Harrod Donovan, instead of Mrs. Louis Donovan. It was very nice, too, that Mary never had the Harrods to dinner except when Lou was out of town, very much as if he wasn't quite good enough for them. It was odd that at the time these points had mattered most to him he never allowed himself to even think of them, let alone mention them. Now he had it right out, and to tell the truth, it hardly bothered him at all any more. The only thing that had been on his mind lately was what was Trina Kameray doing when out of his sight, and how soon could he get out of whatever he was doing and join her. A woman on your mind did have its advantages that way, he had to admit it, you might not sleep and you might lose your grip on some things because of it, but at least it wiped out a lot of more important worries.

Having made his complaint there wasn't any way of backing out when Mary produced the dinner invitation with personal messages from the Judge and Aunt Felicia. It was something he could mention next week in New York when he saw the Major. He had that to think of. Over the martinis (with tomato juice for the Judge. Aunt Felicia, Mary, and Mrs. Sweeney)—Lou had launched into the Castles-in-the-Woods project, since Mary had told him the Judge wanted to hear.

"The land is right near our place," the Judge explained to the others, "so that the project is of peculiar interest to, hmm, yes, hmm."

"But surely, Mr. Donovan," said Mrs. Sweeney with a menacing smile, "you can't mean you're having neon lights all through that lovely woods and all down the roads!"

"That's just one of the improvements," said Lou. "We're going to put that place on the map as the last word in modernity."

"But I thought the people there had been petitioning the government to make the town into another Williamsburg," said Mrs. Sweeney, looking to Mrs. Harrod for confirmation. "I thought there was an old tavern there with historical relics and a whole group of Revolutionary buildings. It was to be like Williamsburg, wasn't it?"

"Nothing about that in our contract," said Lou.

"Neon lights!" murmured Mrs. Sweeney.

"Same thing happened to us," said Mrs. Sweeney. "Last year I went downstate to visit the old Sweeney homestead. Nephew lives there now. Imagine how I felt when instead of the old rolling acres with cows and horse grazing there were derricks. Oil there now."

"We just wept, literally," said Mrs. Sweeney. "And the young people just sitting around the porch, rocking, watching the oil-drilling."

"How awful!" sympathized Aunt Felicia.

"You mean you didn't have any interest in the property any more?" Lou inquired. "All that oil going to your nephew?"

"Very good," politely laughed Mr. Sweeney. "Incidentally, do you realize that Illinois ranks ninth in petroleum production this year?"

All right, there was something about the Castles business that rubbed these people the wrong way, and as usual they were brushing him off. Lou was about to crash right through again but there was no loophole. Aunt Felicia was giving out an ecstatic description of the gardens at Williamsburg, aided by Mary's memory, and they were getting into the Revolutionary chamber music revivals and how perfectly enchanting they were. Mary actually got excited over this subject, and Lou, rebuffed, watched her with hostile curiosity. He saw how much she looked like Aunt Felicia and it was funny he never noticed that before. Old Felicia was a lean old giraffe, her smiling, smug blonde pinhead stuck on a lean old neck with attached arms and legs. What was she doing with that old diamond dog-collar, when with a neck like that she needed a giraffe collar? Her eyes were still wide and dewy like Mary's and had never seen anything they didn't want to see, you could tell that. Watching them together, Mary's strained eager face a young replica of her aunt's, Lou couldn't understand how the resemblance had not frightened him before, had not, indeed, scared him off when he first met Mary.

It was after Aunt Felicia had assiduously devoted herself to him during the shrimps and soup that the suspicion struck Lou that this evening was all framed up by the Harrod family to make him more tractable. Mary had spent her time in the Southwest confiding in Aunt Felicia all of the little things that had been giving her headaches lately, and Aunt Felicia was doing her best to patch it all up for her little pet niece. Or did those two congenitally cold women confide in each other actually? Probably they had some silent wigwagging signals of distress, understood only by each other and unaccompanied by any indecent revelation of emotion. Whatever it was, old Felicia, instead of the sour reflective smile with which she usually listened to her nephew-in-law's conversation, was giving him the full battery of her graciousness. This obvious resolution to pacify him with undivided attention did not include listening to what he said, so that he had to answer the same question half a dozen times, finally noting the eager glassy old eye shifting around the table during his answers, and noting, also, Mary's anxious gaze on him from time to time as if to see if this attention didn't make him happy.

"I had no idea you were a university man, Louis," said Aunt Felicia. "Princeton, you say?"

"I said Michigan," Lou repeated for the third time, "and just for the football season, if you call four months being a university man. I guess I learned as much as most of them did."

"I had a nephew who went to Princeton," said Aunt

Felicia, with the gusty intensity with which she rode all conversation. "Perhaps you knew him when you were there. Farwell Lease, Junior."

Lou gave up.

"No," he said. "He wasn't there when I was there."

He sank into gloomy silence while Mrs. Carver, the ex-governor's third wife, a little bird-woman with darting head and bright little robin-eyes, twittered about life in Washington and how, really, there was nothing to compare with it in America. Oh the cherry-blossoms, cried Aunt Felicia and Mary in a breath, the wonderful Japanese cherry-blossoms! And Arlington! Perfectly beautiful! Lou looked at Mary's and old Felicia's suddenly animated faces and wondered again at what brought that quick rapture to their eyes—cherry-blossoms, music, a view. His lips curled. That was supposed to be culture, maybe that was supposed to be "sensitivity." Give him the sudden narrowing of the eyes, the intent frown, the suspended breath, that marked Trina Kameray when his hand sought her knee under a table. His glance travelled around the table and he thought of how little they knew of real magic, all this talk of stars over Mexico, fog over the Potomac, tunes from a harpsichord.

Mary must have observed his restlessness for she bent and whispered something to her uncle. Lou shrugged. So now the shoe was on the other foot. Instead of Mary whispering him to please ask uncle this or that, please be nice to Aunt Felicia, please don't monopolize the conversation, here she was urging them all to be nice to her husband. Well, he wasn't sure he liked it any better this way.

"Ah, um, Louis, hmm, I understand the New York office is a great step forward," said the Judge. "I understand you have contracts for the New York Fair and the San Francisco as well. It's not quite clear to me what your particular contribution, hmm, I should say, hmm."

"It's the Castles-in-the-Woods," Lou said. "I've been in business for ten years and I swear this is the most interesting proposition I ever came up against. You take the property itself, now——

"Supposing we ladies go up to the living-room for our coffee," suggested Aunt Felicia, and in the little flurry of exits Mr. Sweeney took charge of the conversation, and Lou gloomily retreated into his own thoughts, emerging only now and then to say, "Yes, sir, that's about right, sir," and "That's about the size of it," and other vague disgruntled little comments. Mr. Grahame, wedging his vast bulk against the table, his watch-chain resting almost horizontally on his bay-window, dozed happily over his cigar; the Judge chewed at his cigar without smoking it, as per health regime, Mr. Sweeney was reminded of a dozen and one anecdotes peppered with statistics and spiced with the great names of banking and international politics. The ex-Governor of the nearby state came in with his war prophecies and went to the trouble of demonstrating on the tablecloth with the handle of his coffee spoon possible military maneuvers for the Spanish warlords. By this time Aunt Felicia upstairs was peremptorily tapping on the floor with some weapon or other, and the Judge signalled the butler.

"Tell Mother we'll be up directly," he said. "Go on, Sweeney."

Mr. Sweeney did not need to be told to go on, having gone on so long now that nothing short of a stroke would stop him. Lou, on whom he turned the full battery of his

well-informed mind, had long since stopped worrying
whether his face looked interested, since the tribute was
not necessary at all.

"Mind you, two hundred thousand Chinese in San
Francisco," repeated Mr. Sweeney, "one third of the
population of Nanking, China. An unassimilated foreign
group, you see."

"Is that a fact?" said Lou, and quietly noted that it was
now ten-ten. It was funny he had made such a fuss all
these years about the privilege of being bored by his wife's
family. What was the matter with him, anyway, boasting
of having been kicked around by these old big shots? Like
saying, "Believe it or not, I had my evening spoiled last
night by a personal friend of J. P. Morgan!" Or "I was
fortunate enough to have a second cousin of the President
bore me to death last night."

There was another message from the ladies. Mrs. Harrod
was impatiently waiting to regale the gentlemen with a
recorded concert beginning with Stravinsky's "Peter and the
Wolf" which Mr. Grahame had never heard. Mr. Grahame,
roused from his spasmodic napping by hearing his name,
pushed the table away from his stomach and extracted his
body from the chair.

"Come on, old boy," he urged Sweeney. "Mustn't inconvenience our hostess. You and Cassidy can have this out
some other time."

On the way upstairs Lou figured what he would say. He
had to get out quick because he could never tell what Trina
Kameray was likely to do. She could be brilliantly discreet
in public, sometimes, but on the other hand she could be
alarmingly high-handed if her little caprices were not given

proper consideration. She called up his house whenever she pleased, she wrote whatever she felt like, often quite naughty little notes, and when Lou tactfully tried to correct this sort of mischief, she shrugged.

"Either you are a man or you are not a man," she said. "Either you are afraid of our friendship or you are unafraid. If it is an inconvenience to you I have many other friends."

She never said it but he knew what she meant. It was that there was always Mr. Rosebush. Such a dear, such a valued friend, and she had been so unkind to him, giving him up for Lou, who wished she would not telephone him or speak to him in public, or show her friendship for him. It made one sad to think of giving up a loyal friend like Mr. Rosebush for a man who found her preference merely an embarrassment. In fact, she really ought to be meeting Mr. Rosebush in Baltimore this very minute instead of loitering around the West this way, within meeting distance of such an unappreciative man as Louis.

That persistent little threat usually brought Lou desperately out in the open, and unable to say more about the danger to his home life. They would have a home together some day, Trina said, so what did it matter how soon his present arrangements were blasted? Lou never answered this, for the immediate urgency of being with her always blinded him to future complications.

"Sorry, but I have to see a party from Rochester at ten thirty," Lou said to Aunt Felicia, upstairs, while Mary looked at him questioningly.

"Yes," said Aunt Felicia graciously, "I believe someone did call a few minutes ago inquiring if you had left."

Can you imagine that? That little Kameray had even had the nerve to call him at his wife's old home. That was the sort of arrogance that left a man breathless.

Lou got into his coat and hat in the hall, trying to act pained at this business intrusion of his social life. In the living-room Mr. Grahame settled in the largest chair with a loud creaking of indignant springs, the Judge adjusted the great phonograph, Mrs. Sweeney and Mrs. Carver arranged their velvet skirts on a small loveseat in reverent silence, the ex-Governor stood gazing gloomily into the fire, and Mr. Sweeney took up a safe position in a corner retreat where he adjusted his reading glasses for a refreshing glance through the *World Almanac,* handily placed in a magazine rack.

"You'll be back for me, dear?" Mary asked in a low voice. She knew he wouldn't. She knew he was meeting a woman at the Evanshire bar in Evanston because the operator had called from the Evanshire first. She only wished she had the courage to say she knew. The psychoanalyst— as she had justly feared—had done nothing to give her the simple everyday courage to make a scene. He had done nothing for her with this suggestion to draw Lou into her family's life. And when she had told him, with bursting temples and trembling hands, about the unmistakable evidence of another woman in her very bed during her Southwest trip, the stupid man had merely given her sedatives, and told her such a tiny catastophe was not the end of the world.

"I'm sure the Carvers can drop you," Lou said to her. "And by the by, there's a chance I may not drive back out tonight. Have to meet an early train downtown in the morning, so I may stay downtown. Night, dear."

He hurried out. Aunt Felicia and the Judge exchanged a look. Every one knew he was going to meet a woman. It would have been better if he had not come at all, Mary realized. She wished she dared rush out and follow him, see the woman, accuse her, flaunt the hairpins and handkerchief (shamelessly left under the pillow) and the hoop earring. She wished she was as bold as this woman, whoever she was, who brazenly visited her house. She stood waving to Lou in the door for a moment, then came back to take her seat on the sofa beside the fire. The music began. Aunt Felicia and the Judge were looking at her, so she kept her own eyes on the leaping fire, her long thin fingers interlaced in her lap, and in the pause while the records changed she mur-murmed "Isn't it charming?" just like anyone else.

It couldn't have been her fault, Mary thought over and over, it couldn't, it couldn't. All the things he had admired when he first saw her, had shown so clearly how much he admired them, were still hers, she had not changed, even her feeling for Lou had not changed, her appearance had not changed, nothing was any different from the moment he met her on the ship coming from Honolulu when the Captain gave her a birthday dance. And Lou had made her uncle and aunt furious by taking her away from the dance out on the rainy deck where they sat not saying much, not even holding hands, but when she rose to go back to the others he said, "Believe it or not, I'm going to marry you or your sister." "I haven't any sister," she said, laughing. "Then it's going to be you," he said. So that was her love affair, her only one, the only one she ever wanted—six years of having someone demand more than she could give, of having him look steadily at her when they were out together until her gaze fluttered to meet his, of having her own happiness consist in curbing his desire, in finding that her protests could control his impetuosity. It was the way she was, it was her own version of passion, denying more than she gave, for the charm of her love was what she withheld, just as the basic force of Lou's love was in demanding what would be denied, wanting more, no matter what, than would be given. It was all part of their own special love that she should want him to make approaches so that she could say, "Oh no, no, Lou, you mustn't, you mustn't," and so keep the process within the strictest bounds, no intimate fumbling over her body, which after all was her own, and no reason why marriage in spite of its implicit obligations should give the lover complete and outright ownership to it. That was the sort of quaint daintiness which Lou had found intriguing from the very first, and nothing had happened since to make her bolder or more adventurous in sex. What made her head spin now with curious indignation was the faint suspicion that other women allowed and even encouraged this worst side of him; there might be dreadful creatures like the naked girls at the Spinning Top, like the woman he must have in New York, like the one he was meeting tonight in Evanston, dreadful women who pretended to like it just to trap him and so betray her, make her refusals seem wrong, his cajoling demands right. Puzzling over these doubts Mary cried all night, and she didn't know which was her greatest woe—his probable unfaithfulness, or the possibility that these other women were right to surrender completely and she was wrong. Even so she knew that what she wanted was for him to go through life wresting love from her, and being perpetually denied full abandonment.

It was frightening to wake up in the morning and know that love did not last, no matter how it was treated. Even a shrew, nagging, ragging, bullying and deprecating the husband out of sheer discontent with her own dream of him, must believe it can go on forever, and must be bewildered when, at a kind glance from some gentler woman, he leaves. People think relationships are made of rubber and stretch and give to every crisis, and it is a shock to find they can snap in two like a glass thermometer. Why should anyone feel that a great truth is hidden from him when it is written all over the sky that nothing is permanent? Mary reasoned it all out, rationalized the way the doctor had told her, but what good is reason when the heart is out of order? Just so many sheep to count till the brain got numb, that was all, and then the old heart could go ahead hurting, even exploding, for all the good reason could do.

The worst part was the half-dream before waking, the half-dream that everything was the same as it used to be. She could see herself and Lou dancing, walking, dining in little lovely corners, the way it was when he told her every day he was going to marry her, whether she liked it or not, and whether Aunt Felicia liked it or not. She thought of the way he kept looking at her until she was forced to look up and see the shock of desire in his eyes, and the way in a little while he would be striving for some excuse to touch her, to put her coat on for her, to help her get into her car. And then when she was home, undressing for bed and thinking of this resolute suitor, the phone would ring and he would say, "Mary? All right? I just wanted to make sure. Sweet dreams." And now Lou was calling up someone else, waiting for someone else to look up and meet his eye, calling up someone else to make sure she was all right. And there was no reason for it, no right to it, but there was nothing to be done.

No, there was nothing to be done, no questions to be asked and answered. She tried to do what the doctor had suggested, to think of the man's side, to realize that it is as sad to stop loving as it is to stop being loved. Sad to look at the back of a neck, the slope of a cheek that once gave quick pleasure, and here was the same curve, the same gesture—no change except that no joy, no love was inspired, object and eye were two unconnected telephones. Poor curve, sad gesture, void of all magic, powerless to convey life to expired love. The way she rumpled the back of her hair, once so dear to him, was just the way she rumpled her hair and no more. Her slender foot squirming around when she was embarrassed was just an annoying habit, not an endearingly childish trick. His looking at the menu to see if her favorite duck was on it, not because he wanted to give her pleasure, but to see if there wasn't something he could find to mollify her outside of a caress. Oh, of course, it was a sad role, the lover no longer loving. But once the perfunctory sympathy was given him the heart went out fully to oneself, the real victim, the unloved.

If she was at fault, and she might be, then the fault had been with her at the very start. If all the things he first loved were still there and he no longer loved, then these must now be all the things he hated. She would have to be different, she would be like Flo Oliver, like the women at that nightclub, she would get up with the orchestra and beat the drums, she would talk to strange men, she would drop in at bars by herself the way that Mrs. Kameray did, and ask other women's escorts to join her at her own table. Those were all the things she was *not* and therefore they must be the things he wanted of women since those other women seemed to know him better than she did.

She knew, of course, that he wouldn't come home that night. She knew that Aunt Felicia thought the same. That was the drawback to confession. After the consolation of confessing, the confessor knows the facts and can offer no blind consolations. Mary slowly undressed, knowing he would not come back and knowing she would not sleep. Knowing that if and when he came home tomorrow she would not ask.

The telephone rang suddenly, unbelievably. Mary picked it up with trembling fingers.

"Hello, Mary? All right?"

It was Aunt Felicia.

"Of course," she said. Aunt Felicia didn't ask if Lou was home but that was what she meant.

"Sweet dreams, child," said Aunt Felicia.

"Bless you," said Mary, but after she got into bed she lay there hating Aunt Felicia for thinking, indeed for knowing, that Lou was not home.

XVIII

Mrs. Kameray lay on her stomach in the hot white sand and shaded her eyes with her hand to squint up at Lou.

"You have a very pretty figure," she said. "I don't know why it is you are always so cross."

Lou would not be flattered.

"What do you mean, a pretty figure?" he said. "I'm getting a pot like that old boy over there in the water."

"I like a pot," said Mrs. Kameray. "I think a pot is very nice for a man. A man at forty should have a pot. How old are you?"

"Forty-one," said Lou.

"Seventeen years older than me?" Mrs. Kameray sighed. "You forty-one and me twenty-four!"

Lou didn't answer. She was twenty-eight, he knew. She had started being twenty-four a week or two ago and he suspected it had something to do with the young Cuban band-leader she had found in Havana. He was still mad about it, mad especially that she had flown to Havana without telling him, so that when he arrived in Miami, and with considerable trouble about arrangements, too, he had to wait two days for her to come back. Two days when you worked on a high pressure basis such as Lou did meant a lot of explaining, to the different clients he was supposed to be seeing in New York and Washington. But he didn't dare scold Trina or she would quietly pack up and leave. He had gotten rooms for them at one of the town hotels, but as

soon as Trina arrived she had announced they must stay at
one of the Beach hotels. So they were at the Roney Plaza,
and, awkwardly enough for Lou, as Mr. and Mrs. Donovan, since Trina declared she was not to be regarded as a
mistress but as a wife. It was not nice, she said, tiptoeing
back and forth across halls in the night. They should have
a nice little suite together like a honeymoon couple, and if
she wanted to scold a waiter or maid she could do so with
perfect freedom and not have them give her that insulting
"mistress" look.

"Besides I am your true wife," she stated. "I am the one
who should be Mrs. Donóvan. What are you doing about
that, Louie? You promised me you would fix it all up."

Lou avoided her earnest inquiring gaze. God knows
what he said in the tantalizing circumstances under which
Trina extorted promises. It was unwise of him not to have
handled the marriage thing better, however, because that
came up all the time and she was getting very insistent
about it.

"Don't let her tie up all your money, Louie," warned
Trina. "You must let me help you with the settlement or
she will want to take it all."

"You can't hurry those things," Lou mumbled.

"No? Not even for me? Not even to keep me from going
back to Europe?" Trina raised her voice and Lou looked
uneasily around them to see who might be listening. "You
mean you would like me to go back into a burning building? That's how much you love me?"

For the first time Lou was glad to see the beautiful young
Cuban lad coming up to them, for Trina at once was all
smiles and demure charm. He was a slight, bronzed young
Latin Apollo with little black moustache and sleek black

hair. Mrs. Kameray swore that she had been instructed by the Major himself to find a suitable band-leader for the Castles-in-the-Woods ballroom orchestra and Tommy Padilla was one of the very first names she had been told to investigate. It was fortunate that, popular as he was in Cuba and Palm Beach, he still was able to spend all the time in the world at Miami getting acquainted with Mr. Donovan and talking things over so they could make a nice start that very summer. As soon as the young man joined them, Lou became acutely conscious of the brazenness of Trina's white bathing suit, the mere figment of a halter over the fine little bosom, a scant frill for a skirt, the pretty little navel all but out. Since she never under any circumstances went in the water she permitted herself quite an elaborate beach get-up, with a garland of red flowers in her flowing long brown hair, and a little red parasol.

"I love that little mole!" said Tommy gazing at the little brown flaw on Trina's bare diaphragm.

"Naughty!" said Trina primly. "Run along now, Tommy, let us see how beautifully you swim."

Tommy sprinted out to the water and flashed into the waves. Lou watched stonily. This was supposed to be the happy life, having your sweetheart on the beach of some tropic paradise, lolling in the sand, idling away the late winter days, not a care in the world but trying to hold on to your houri and watching other younger men exhibit their superior strength and beauty before her far too appreciative eyes.

"I still don't see why you had to stay a week in Havana just to get a bandleader, "Lou said.

Trina reached out a small hand to clasp his. This was another gesture that made him uncomfortable in public, but when he rebuffed it she revenged herself by rebuffing his private advances. So he returned the pressure of her little fingers.

"I like Havana," said Trina dreamily. "It is like a little live heart beating away in the ocean. How it sways and beats with the maraccas and the dancing feet. Like a little live heart."

"No town for a woman, alone," said Lou sternly.

"I have friends," said Trina. "I have a great many friends all over. There are many Russians in Havana. If there were no Russians there would still be the friends from Berlin and Vienna. You have friends I do not know. I have friends you do not know. Why not?"

Trina, pouting, was as irresistible to him as Trina, smiling, and he always felt a wave of frantic love for her when she made him feel guilty. She was reminding him now of the many times they had encountered business friends of his in the West and even these few days in Florida when he was obliged to pretend he was not with her. He knew that it was a scurvy thing to do, especially with a high class girl like Trina, but in every friend's eye he saw the image of Mary and for the life of him he could not ignore that image. It was thoroughly stupid of him, too, since on other occasions with other casual ladies he had arrogantly brazened it through. It was because this was different, that he had to mess it up. He knew Trina would behave with the most exquisite discretion before strangers—that is almost always—but she never failed to reproach him afterwards. He was ashamed of her? He was sorry he had made her love him? Very well, she would go back when the government made her. She was not a citizen, anyway. She would have to go unless some American man married her. No one would. So she would go back and very likely be killed. Certainly she would be killed. In Russia she was not a Communist. In Germany she was not a Gentile. Very well, she would be killed. It did not matter. Her poor little life meant nothing to no one, no one—expect Mr. Rosebush. Dear Mr. Rosebush. How wickedly she had treated him! He had been so good to her, had paid her whole passage back and forth to America two or three times. Such a good friend. Until Louie had made her fall in love with him and forget all her loyalty. For Louie's sake she must give up all her friends and her loyalties and for Louie's sake she must be treated like some bad common woman, someone not to be introduced to one's friends. Of course she could go back to Paris, but then her old husband Kameray would try to get her to come back to him, and then she would starve for he had no money.

"I thought you said he had money in a New York bank," said Lou. He hated to have her talk of other men, other husbands, other friends.

"A few thousand dollars," shrugged Trina. "It was really mine anyway because he had never made any divorce settlement. And if I had sent it to him in Europe Hitler would have taken it away from him. It could do him no good."

"I guess he's not starving," said Lou, uncomfortably. Trina's little allusions to the discomforts of her friends and relatives still in Europe made him bad-humored. Friends in concentration camps, grandfathers chased across Siberia by bloodhounds for all he knew, an ex-husband living like a rat in a Paris cellar, none of these seemed to stir Trina's emotion so much as the fact that European difficulties made her allowance from her grandpa in Geneva so slow in coming. Lou wanted to write out a check to end his pangs of

conscience over the little pictures Trina's occasional remarks evoked in him. Why it should bother him, he didn't
know, since she seemed philosophical about it. It bothered
him, though, that it didn't seem to affect her. Or maybe
it did. She was so mature, not like the American women he
knew, she disguised her feelings since there was nothing to
be gained by showing them. She was really braver than she
seemed. Thinking this made Lou feel better.

"You've seen a lot of trouble, haven't you, Trina?" he
said, moved.

Trina's hand gripped his.

"Some people are born for trouble," she sighed. "All my
mother's people have had trouble in Russia, so why not
me? And a little drop of the wrong blood in my husband
causes us both more suffering! I am not born to be happy,
Louie. Do you blame me I want everything, everything,
quick, before it is too late?"

Her dark brown eyes welling with sudden tears had their
usual effect on Lou. He would, that minute, have made a
fine clean break with Mary, told her in ringing language
that although she could get along beautifully, even better,
without him in her life, there were other women who could
not, women, or rather *a* woman, who had been through
enough hell in her life to appreciate the protection of a
man like Lou Donovan. He had one of his secret tempting
visions of how sweet it would be to possess once and for all
the charming little creature, to have this secret pleasure
permanently instead of spasmodically and uncertainly. The
image of Mary and the pride in the Harrod connection
vanished with his quick longing to take Trina in his arms
and hold her forever. These fleeting resolutions were lost,
usually, in his sound later reflection that with Trina as his

wife, who would there be for the little secret outings that were so much a part of his zest in life? A wife on a business trip, for instance, was just a wife, a poor piece of business, a dangerous exhibition of fatuity, very different indeed from the favorable impression of being independent.

"Tommy is not married," said Trina, sitting up and hugging her knees. The young man was still flashing sinewy brown arms through the sparkling water, occasionally pausing to wave to Trina.

"At twenty-one that shouldn't bother him," said Lou. "What I want to know is how he can spend thirty dollars a day for his room when he hasn't had a regular job for a year? I don't see how he can afford to stay in this hotel."

"He is like me," said Trina. "He likes the peacocks and the flamingoes. And the pretty fish in the dining-room. Everyone is not like you, Louie, seeing only the beefsteaks and the turtle soup."

It was a blonde day on the hotel beach and it may have been a surfeit of blondes in ice-blue bathing suits, or white shorts, that caused eyes to turn to Trina's flowing brown hair and swaggering little figure when she walked down to the water's edge to meet Tommy. Lou's appreciation of her curves was marred by his knowledge that it was shared by many. Trina used very little make-up and her public conduct was elaborately discreet; she never permitted her eyes to roam, and lowered them rebukingly when some crass stranger tried to stare her down. Her modesty and seeming fear of masculine attack gave an added piquancy to her merely average good looks, so that Lou was frequently disturbed by finding that her appeal was so general. For a man like Lou who did not like to be tied in any affair, it was harassing to realize that his little friend could not safely be neglected. Right this minute if he had to leave her Tommy would probably take over, or at least try to. Just as he was savoring this irritating thought a hotel boy came out on the beach and handed him a telegram.

"CAN YOU MEET ME HOTEL MAYFLOWER WASHINGTON TUESDAY CASTLES COMPLICATIONS CONFERENCE NEW YORK THURSDAY STOP ROSENBAUM."

The wire was forwarded from the Lord Baltimore in Baltimore where he was scheduled to be. Trina, coming up with Tommy, looked at him inquiringly.

"Have to fly north right away," Lou said briefly.

Trina's face fell.

"Can't we wait till tomorrow?" she begged. "It's our only really true vacation, Louie, you and me. Like a honeymoon. Don't you like to be on a honeymoon with me, Louie?"

"Yes," Lou said.

Trina took his arm.

"Our real one will be much better, you wait," she said. "We must go talk it over, Tommy. When you are dressed come and have champagne with us."

Back in their room Lou tried to be peremptory with her. Rosenbaum said he should be in Washington at a certain time and it was his duty to be there. He sat on the edge of the bed waggling the telephone receiver to convey that very message, but Trina flung herself down on the bed and wriggling on his lap took away the telephone.

"If you have to see him anyway in New York on Thursday, why must you go to Washington first?" she pouted.

There was something in what she said but in business you cannot point out the customer's mistake, just for your own convenience. However, what the customer doesn't know won't hurt him and Mrs. Kameray persuaded him to spend the hour pleasantly enough, both of them laughing at the idea of the Cuban Apollo patiently waiting for them below.

"Poor Tommy," sighed Mrs. Kameray, her eyes dancing. "He will be so worried about us."

The telephone rang.

"If that's Rosenbaum, I'll say I can't get out till tomorrow," Lou said, but the call was not from Rosenbaum at all. It was from Mrs. Donovan in Chicago. She wanted to speak directly to Mr. Donovan and, said the operator, *not* to Mrs. Donovan. This message, overheard by Trina Kameray, amused her almost as much as the idea of Tommy waiting. It alarmed Lou enough to make him decide to leave at once. For all he knew Mary might pull a 'Flo' on him and descend in Miami to meet this false Mrs. Donovan. He knew Trina was coldly unsympathetic about his alarm over Mary.

"Tell her at once you want a divorce to marry me," she said. "Do you want me to get another husband? If I don't have a husband I must go back to Europe. You want me to be killed, Louie, or is it you want me to make love to another husband?"

"Tell Chicago Mr. Donovan has left," Lou told the operator.

They went downstairs in silence, Lou stony-faced, Trina's cameo skin dewy, and looking fresh and smart in her trim little white flannel suit, her brown eyes sad, the full lips tremulous. The young Cuban did not find his friends very gay even over the champagne. He wanted to know why.

"It is because Louie's wife makes so much trouble for us," Trina explained gravely. "She does not want him to be happy one minute. I'll bet she would be nicer if you took her a present sometime, Louie, eh?"

"Oh, sure," Lou said gloomily. It did not make him happy to hear Trina talk, as she constantly did, about Mary. He had no intention of having anything out with Mary, but on the other hand he had not dared face her for weeks alone. All you could do in complications like this was to mark time. The hint about presents gave him a thought.

"Tell you what, I'll ship you on to New York and I'd better stop off in Washington," he suggested. "You can do a little shopping in New York."

"What kind of presents do you give your sweethearts, Tommy?" Trina gayly asked the young bandman, whose adoring gaze never left her face. He seemed astonished at the question.

"But what would the man give presents for?" he exclaimed. "It should be the lady who gives the presents. The lady always gives the present. It is much better that way."

The waiter brought the timetable and Lou glanced through it. Trina was content, now, to have him plan whatever he wished for them. She could go to New York and report directly to Lou's office on the result of her tour. She might well contact the Major himself, Lou thought. Meantime he, Lou, would see Rosenbaum in Washington and find out what was what; he would even, he graciously told Tommy, discuss the importance of having Tommy Padilla's Band. Tommy was delighted.

"Tell Mr. Rosenbaum it was my band he liked so much at El Dorado last Monday," he said. "Tell Mr. Rosenbaum that."

Lou did not flicker an eyelash.

"I will," he said.

He did not look at Mrs. Kameray, and she went on sipping her champagne unconcernedly.

"So old Rosebush was in Havana last week, too," he muttered.

"Didn't I mention it?" Trina lifted pretty brown eyes frankly. "But then I told you I had so many friends in Havana. In Porto Rico I have friends, too. But I love Cuba best. I like the way the airplanes swoop down flying over the city, like in a circus when the rider swoops down to pick up the handkerchief in his teeth, oh, it is thrilling!"

"Threeling?" Lou mocked her.

"And the cars that go so fast, whiz, whiz, coasting so fast down hill, and guns and masquerades with fighting, always, I love it."

"Life is cheap with Cubans," admitted Tommy, beaming.

"I could leeve forever in Cuba," sighed Trina. "To me it is like a little live heart, you know, beating and dancing like a little heart."

"Exactly!" exclaimed Tommy. "That is Havana to me, too."

To Lou, Havana was a place where Trina Kameray had casually spent a week with Rosenbaum and kept Lou waiting for her in Miami. The only way he could ever keep her away from Rosenbaum was to marry her, and he knew the reason she was not the least disturbed by his finding out was that she knew far too well that this would serve her purpose better than anything else. He wanted to upbraid her, but he had no threats to offer. It was she who held the whip, talking so affectingly with Tommy about the simple joys of swimming at La Playa, and dancing in the peaceful tropic night at Sans Souci. Dancing with Rosebush? Swimming with Rosebush? Lou dared not even ask.

XIX

Lou had dinner in Rosenbaum's suite at the Mayflower with Mrs. Rosenbaum, Rosenbaum, and their little niece, Hilda, and a dark, pinched, intense spinster sister of Mrs. Rosenbaum's, named Liza. In the course of the dinner a thin spectacled student at medical college, the Rosenbaum heir, paid a short visit and at his mother's earnest behest, ate her banana cream pie dessert, then departed. That was Everett. The entire Rosenbaum family seemed to have transported itself to Washington from Park Avenue for the purpose of attending some school function in which Everett was taking a proud part. Mrs. Rosenbaum was a fading Valkyrie, large, blonde, and domineering, with very little conversation, achieving her points by a commanding gesture, or merely by calling out a name as if the duties of each member of her group were so automatic that the sound of his or her name released a set program of action.

"Hilda!" she called out and the plain little ten-year-old with sandy pigtails immediately finished up her vegetables.

"Liza!" she called. "Liza!"

And poor Liza, who was called most often, rushed to pull down the shades, answer the door, pick up Hilda's napkin, answer Mr. Donovan's question, pass the butter, or show Everett the congratulatory telegrams from other relatives. Most of these brief commands seemed to be not for her own satisfaction but to save annoyance to her husband who broodingly sat through the five courses, making very little effort to draw out his guest, and crumbling his rolls into little balls on the tablecloth, an annoying gesture which Mrs. Rosenbaum's attentive blue eye caught.

"My husband is very tired," she said to Lou. "He has no appetite. He gives his life's blood for the Major. He's a family man and it's hard for him to spend so much time away from us."

"He sees more of Everett than he does of us," said Liza. Her thin dried face glowed with worship when she looked at Rosenbaum, as indeed it had glowed for the twenty-five years she had been privileged to assist her brother's wife in making him comfortable.

"Well, an only son, of course," said Rosenbaum.

"Our two daughters are on a cruise for the spring holidays," explained Mrs. Rosenbaum. "They are sixteen and eighteen. To Central America. They wanted to postpone it till summer and go abroad, but Father says Europe is too unsettled."

There was no mention of Castles-in-the-Woods and Lou grew restless. The waiters removed the dinner, Rosenbaum offered him a cigar, Hilda and Liza turned on the radio in the corner of the living-room and listened with somber unsmiling attention to Major Bowes' Amateur Hour. Mrs. Rosenbaum got out her knitting bag and sat down on the sofa beside Lou.

"Everett has to prepare an article tonight, so he couldn't stay with us," she said. "He'll take us to his fraternity house to tea tomorrow and then we won't see him again till he comes home in June."

"We're comfortable here," her husband reminded her. "It's a nice change for you. I wish I could stay over tomorrow night myself."

"If this is your last night," Lou made a stab at escape, "supposing we go downstairs and have a brandy, listen to the orchestra. Or we might drive down and catch part of the show at the National."

Mrs. Rosenbaum shook her head, smiling, her needles flying.

"We don't like public dining-rooms," she said. "We always like to have it seem like home. After all we came down here to see our son, not the city. You go out with him, Father, go ahead."

Lou was relieved to see that this suggestion was approved by the master. He went into his bedroom for a hat.

"Liza! Hilda!" commanded Mrs. Rosenbaum, and the two hurriedly came out to say good night to the guest. The little girl curtsied.

"She can speak English when she wants to," said Liza fondly, "but she is shy. She is so glad to be over here."

Lou didn't know what to say.

"Somebody ought to blast that guy, Hitler," he said. "He's a bad man, eh, girlie?"

Hilda burst into tears and hid her face behind her aunt Liza.

"She can't stand to have anyone say anything bad about anyone," explained Liza, apologetically. "She doesn't want anyone to be unkind to anyone, she says. It makes her cry."

"I'm sorry," said Lou, awkwardly.

Something in the little girl's brown eyes reminded him of Trina and they both seemed sad figures, sad kind figures, for Trina did not like any unkindness either, it seemed to him. Yes, that was what made her different from a fleeting affair, Trina was sad and kind and lonely, just like little

Hilda. Maybe Rosenbaum noticed that, too. It reminded Lou that Trina had other characteristics that did not exactly apply to Hilda and doubtless never would, but now they were mixed up in his mind, and he thought he would make up to Hilda for making her cry by buying Trina a bracelet.

The World's Fair deal was off on Castles, Rosenbaum told Lou in the Occidental, where they went for a highball. The San Francisco contract hinged on the New York one, so that too was off.

"But it was all settled," said Lou. "What went wrong?"

Rosenbaum shrugged.

"The world," he said. "You can't pin down parties to contracts when politics get into it. Besides both ventures were prestige more than profit. We lose nothing."

"We?" Lou laughed mirthlessly. "You mean you and the Major lose nothing. I lose. The firms I contracted for lose. Whittleby Cotton, for instance, loses."

Rosenbaum smoked quietly. The fellow got on Lou's nerves. Getting him to jump to Washington just to let him have the bad news. As easy as that, it was. The World's Fair deal off, he says, and smokes his cigar and looks down at the table, dead-pan, nobody could tell what he was thinking, but you knew he was in the clear all right, the Major's old right-hand man didn't have any worries.

"How does the Major take it?" Lou asked.

He wouldn't give the fellow the satisfaction of showing how much the loss meant to him, personally, the little slices here and there he'd cut for himself that were now shrunk or out of the picture.

"The Major doesn't know, yet," said Rosenbaum gravely. "As a matter of fact the Major is a very sick man. We've kept it out of the papers and it would be bad policy to let it go further—all of his commitments, you see—but the Major suffered a stroke two days ago."

"But he couldn't have—he can't do that!" Lou cried out in frank indignation. "Where are we going to be without the Major?"

That damn cigar of Rosenbaum's. He sucked away on it as if it was piping him the right answers.

"It was wife trouble, mostly," Rosenbaum said, after a proper consultation with his cigar, "The Major's not too self-controlled in the home, and moreover he's a very jealous man. His wife usually leaves him after a row, they divorce or separate, then remarry, then he has a jealous fit again, and the same thing over. Last time was too much for the heart."

"That's too bad," said Lou bitterly. "That's just too damn bad."

All right, what if the World's Fair was out, that wasn't the biggest thing on their programs. It had helped publicize the idea of the Castles, and had been a feather in their cap, but hell, it wasn't everything. What made him sore, though, was that a millionaire, just because he has the world by the tail, could just calmly step out of the picture and say, "Things are getting a little complicated around here, boys, I guess I'll treat myself to a little stroke."

"You have a tan since I last saw you," Rosenbaum said, suddenly looking straight at Lou.

Lou gave it straight back.

"So have you," he said.

"I didn't realize you were spending that much time in the South," Rosenbaum said. "You were lucky to be able to play a little."

"I've always been lucky," said Lou and knocked wood.

"Perhaps opening your New York office is what has brought you luck," said Rosenbaum. "I understand this has been your most successful year."

"I'll make enough to pay my last year's income tax," said Lou, watching him, not knowing what jump was coming next. "That's all I can ask."

"So last year was good, too." Rosenbaum nodded thoughtfully.

"You're damn right last year was good," said Lou. "After all, I do know my business, old fellow."

"You're a clever man, Donovan," Rosenbaum agreed. "You've got a lot on the ball."

But—? Lou waited.

"All right, what's the tag?" he asked, smiling.

Rosenbaum studied the photographs on the wall beside them thoughtfully. Maybe they worked with the cigar to feed him his answers. Lou couldn't figure out what he was getting at, half friendly, half sinister, and so oppressively gloomy, like some big operator waiting for the D. A. to catch up with him.

"You give me the tag," said Rosenbaum. "I mean, where you heading for? What's next? Do you vision a chain of branch offices all over the country, thousands of people working for you, consultants for hotels on a big scale, investigating, even buying and selling instead of just recommending?"

"Not for me," said Lou. "I go faster travelling light. I got to be flexible, change my position at a minute's notice. I'm doing all right handling a half dozen big outfits. You can't delegate my kind of work. Small but personal and selective, that's my angle."

"That's right," Rosenbaum approved. "It's your personality, of course. You're a lucky guy, Donovan."

"I never trust to luck," said Lou. "I work hard and use the bean every minute. You can't go wrong on that formula. It's these fellows that trust to luck that lose out. Me, I'm studying all the time. New angles. New twists. You got to keep at it."

"I wouldn't play down luck," said Rosenbaum. "You can work hard and use the bean and still lose."

"Not the way I work," Lou grinned. "I take no chances."

"Take the war in Spain, the hurricane, the political purges," Rosenbaum went on reflectively. God knows what he was getting at, but Lou kept his eye on the ball. "There must have been plenty of clever business men whose brains didn't help them there. The Major's brains didn't keep him from blowing up over a little wife trouble. No, you need luck. Maybe that's all anybody does need."

A crack in there somewhere, all right, but Lou didn't pick it up. If Rosenbaum wanted to insinuate that his success in business was pure luck, no brains, okay, there were other times for a comeback. You have to wait for a really good comeback. Keep 'em wondering when it's coming.

"I don't know, I don't know," Rosenbaum shook his head wearily. Liver, thought Lou, it must be a bad liver that made a man as glum as Rosenbaum. "For instance, supposing the Major should die. It turns out the entire Maryland estate goes to the Government for retired army men and their families. The Major was sentimental about the army."

"If the Major dies—what?"

Lou stared at him in blank consternation.

Rosenbaum nodded.

"That's the will. I didn't know it myself till I talked to his lawyers yesterday."

Lou drummed on the table, thinking.

"Then the Castles work would all be scrapped the minute he conks out?"

"If he conks out," assented Rosenbaum. "He probably won't. But we might as well know where we stand. It's all luck now."

"You're a cheerful bastard," Lou said. "After all the work we've put in on that job. You've seen my reports. You've seen the plans."

"I know. You get your fee just the same," Rosenbaum said. "The estate will have to settle the contracts broken as best it can."

Lou smiled wryly. Rosenbaum must know perfectly well that the fee was the least part of the Donovan profits. It was the side bets that made him the dough.

"It's going to help me a lot on new business with a lot of litigation about broken contracts hanging over," he said. "That's going to be just great."

"Adjustments can be made," Rosenbaum said. "You won't lose."

You bet he wouldn't. He'd stick a price on wasted services that would make them wince, all right.

"Did Mrs. Kameray's work seem satisfactory?" Rosenbaum asked. He didn't look at Lou, just kept his eyes on the tablecloth.

"Perfectly. Mrs. Kameray is a very intelligent woman, and made a very good impression. So far as her work went, it couldn't have been improved upon. Made some excellent contacts and did some very good field work."

All right, how do you like that? If you want to find out

something, Lou thought, go ahead, you won't get anywhere beating around the bush. The same thought must have struck Rosenbaum for he suddenly clasped his hands together and looked at Lou directly for a minute in silence.

"I know all about you and Mrs. Kameray," he said. "I knew she was probably going to meet you in Miami, just as she met you in St. Louis and on the coast. I don't know you, but I do know Trina. Trina's out to get married. Trina's out for safety and security, and she's going to get an American husband. You can't blame her. A person that's been kicked around, one country to another, through revolution, politics, war—that kind of thing makes a person determined to save his own hide at any cost. Security, that's all. You can't blame Trina."

It was Lou, now, who looked down at the table and then at the photographs on the wall hunting for answers.

"No one could blame her," was all he could get out.

Rosenbaum didn't care about answers, anyway. He seemed to know them.

"I've known Trina off and on for five years. In London, Paris. Her visits here. I've done more for her than anyone else. I can always do more for her than anyone else. All right, the one thing I can't do is marry her."

Lou busied himself with his drink. It was the last kind of conversation he liked. If Rosenbaum wanted to show his cards, go ahead, but he'd be damned if he, Donovan, would. He wasn't sure what they were himself, anyway. He was marking time, that was all.

"You saw my situation, tonight. I'm a family man. I have feelings. I love my wife and my girls, my son. Even if I didn't— . . . You don't have my feelings. You can walk out of your marriage and take Trina without a pang. I can't stop you."

229

"There's nothing the matter with my marriage, either," Lou said slowly. "It's not as easy as that."

Rosenbaum threw out his hands.

"Talk about happy marriages! It's the man with wife troubles that is the luckiest. He can walk out, with justice. But what about the rest of us with the wives that stood by us when we got started, and then we change, we grow, and they don't, they just go along, bewildered, watching us change, get rich, get smart, and they're hurt and puzzled and even angry that they can no longer name our favorite dishes, even, we don't eat the jelly rolls they make, but they can't see why our taste should have changed. And we feel sorry because we loved them once so we must go on. We don't like to cut off our own memories, and our habits, the habits we don't know we have till they're disturbed."

It was not especially pleasant to know that Mrs. Kameray had been heckling Rosenbaum to marry her, too, all these years. Somehow Lou had gathered from her that he had offered to do this himself, but that she had thrown away this opportunity for Lou Donovan. She had indeed given up everyone for him because, she said, her little tiny love affairs had been so unsatisfactory up till the moment she met him. There was no doubt about her double-crossing, maybe, a little bit with Rosenbaum, but it was not really double-crossing, it was a little show of power, to make him do what she wanted. Well, it worked.

"But you are getting a divorce, I understand," said Rosenbaum. "I can't. You saw that I couldn't. I wanted you to see my situation, so you would see that it wasn't just that I didn't care enough about Trina. It's—well, you saw."

So that was what was weighing him down all this time, trying to make up his mind to meet Trina's terms. And she had given him the "or else." The "or else" was Lou. Well, it must have given the old boy a kick to knock the bottom out of his business while he was handing over his former love. That must have been a compensation to him. No wonder he wasn't worried about the Major dying and leaving Castles up in the air.

"You'll marry her, I can't meet that," Rosenbaum mused. "Maybe you don't want to cut up your home, either, but you will to keep hold of Trina."

"Maybe," said Lou. "I'm not sure."

Rosenbaum signalled the waiter for the check.

"If you're catching that plane we'd better leave," he suggested. They got their hats, both of them somber-faced, unsure of each other. Lou got a cab but Rosenbaum decided to walk a while before he went back to his hotel.

"I might as well tell you that marrying Trina won't settle your future," Rosenbaum said quietly. "Trina never gives up anything. And even married to you, she won't be able to do without me. Good night."

XX

WHAT a lousy town, what a two-timing, ungrateful, ugly, crooked, stinking town New York was, Lou thought, on his way to meet Jay Oliver at the Biltmore. You spend your life, the best years, working to help New York get richer, yes, that's what it amounts to, and as soon as you decide to put your stakes in and stay, then it turns on you. You could almost say that as soon as he got his name in the New York phone book with that good address and the Fifth Avenue office the city put the Indian sign on him. The contacts that he had worked so easily from the Chicago office melted away as soon as he was right around the corner, or at least his office was. It made no sense. The big hotel chain that he had been consultant for these ten years got cagey and talked about paying out too many commissions, their new general manager could handle everything, thank you. The New York receptionist was no Miss Frye, she kept her own hours and if the office was instituted just for the prestige of a New York address the whole point was worse than lost when occasional callers found nobody in, implying vaguely that Louis Donovan Service was out of business. What made Lou sore was that he was working as hard as he ever was, he knew his job even better, he was trimming for the shifts in European affairs, working ahead on propositions for railroad lines and continental air lines to build American playgrounds to take the place of the now problematical foreign resorts, places like Sun Valley to keep the traveller's

232

dough at home instead of Mexico and South America where the trend now was. It made him boil, now that the Major had deliberately gone and died, to think of the winter wasted on Castles-in-the-Woods. He had his fee, all right, but that was only a drop in the bucket to what he had expected to make. And these New York business men. Fine fellows, till it came to a little need for co-operation, and then it was them against the out-of-town fellows, like himself. Rosenbaum, for instance. Nothing hostile, nothing you could object to, all on the level, but just a calm cool brush-off. No chance of even a show-down. "You have your fee," he says. "Your contracts will be settled by the estate with the firms involved. Present your statements. Too bad. Regrets."

He had not run into Jay Oliver recently and he didn't know what had happened since Truesdale had located Ebie for him. There was some talk of Whittleby Cotton merging with a Delaware firm and that might leave Jay out on a limb. All right, they'd have a hard times session. That was one thing about a pal like Jay, you didn't have to put up a front with him.

Jay was in the bar working on a Scotch and soda.

"When did you start?" Lou asked, taking the seat beside him.

"Did I ever stop?" Jay countered. "Hi ya, Lou."

"God, how I hate this town," said Lou and signalled the bartender for the same.

"What about coming out to Ebie's with me on the two ten?" Jay suggested. "Do you good to get out in the country."

"I'd like to see Ebie," said Lou, "even in the country, but I got to see Bill Massey up at Florabella at three. Every god dam thing has gone wrong since I landed in this lousy town."

"What you needed is to relax," Jay counselled. "I been meaning to speak to you, Lou. You act as if everything stops when you stop and it just doesn't. Why, they tell me you been jumping all over the country like a Mexican bean this last year, and look where it gets you."

"That's right," said Lou. "Where?"

"Still you look good, Lou." Jay looked him over approvingly. "That suit must have set you back some."

It was a brown worsted with a faintly shaded darker stripe. Mrs. Kameray liked him in stripes. He wore a mahoghany tie with it, a beauty, that Jay eyed enviously.

"I got a new tailor," said Lou. "I'll send you there."

"The hell with it," said Jay. "What good is a suit when you've lost your shirt? What a fellow needs then is a drink."

It was as good an idea as any and they had a lot of things to talk over. The cancellation of the Castles order, Jay thought, was too bad, but only too bad. The merging of his company with the Delaware firm was ominous, sure, but there were other firms. He was thinking of getting in the hat business. He'd had some propositions. He'd rather make less money and live in the East. Anyway he wasn't going to worry now about anything but catching the two-ten to Danbury.

"I got to take a dog out to Ebie," he said. "I bought her a pup."

"Where is it?" Lou asked, looking around.

"I got a Western Union boy walking him around," Jay said, "I got him at eleven o'clock and I can't get in anywhere with him, so I got this lad to walk him. He'll be back."

"See Rosenbaum?"

"Sure I saw him," said Jay candidly. "He was playing footy-footy with little Kameray in the Versailles last night. The Major checking out didn't seem to upset his plans any."

Lou thought of Mrs. Kameray's tremulous voice on the phone yesterday, saying that such a nice man as the Major dying made her feel too too bad, Louie, she must cry and cry, her nose was red, she could not let him see her. It must have been just the right color for old Rosebush. Lou had suspected something but dared not accuse, instead he took out one of the Florabella show-room girls, but he was blue, it wasn't any fun. He knew Rosenbaum hated to go out to night places, so the price Mrs. Kameray was demanding of him was that, if he didn't marry her, at least he must take her out to nice places, he must not act so ashamed of her that it made her feel bad. And she was a stranger, she wanted to get acquainted with her new country, it was her own dear country, yes it was, even if she did have to go back quick because no American man would marry her and the nasty government wanted her to go back to burning Europe. Lou could hear her coaxing Rosenbaum, and it didn't make him feel any better. It was no comfort to think Rosenbaum being out celebrating the night his boss died wouldn't look good to people. Rosenbaum could look after that part all right. Nobody needed to worry about Rosebush.

He ordered a double Scotch and knew that he was on his way to pinning one on, but Jay was right, there were complications that only a drink could straighten out.

"Tell you what, Lou," said Jay, "I'd like to have you look over this pup of Ebie's. I don't know. I may be wrong."

They had a couple for the road and then went out to

look for the pup. The Western Union boy was returning him from Central Park and Jay waved to him. It was an English shepherd dog, enormous and unwieldy.

"You call that a dog?" Lou demanded. It looked as if two men were working it, like a vaudeville act. That was the pup Jay was taking out to Ebie. It struck Lou as funny and the two of them went down to Grand Central Station, laughing, the dog pulling them along. There was difficulty getting the dog on the train but with a drawing room it was arranged and they sneaked him in. The dog sat with an enormous mournful gray face looking from one to the other. It was the best time they'd had since they'd gotten into the Castles' big money, and they slapped each other on the back and shouted with laughter.

Lou took his coat off and carefully hung it in the closet and Jay kicked his shoes off and they ordered three rounds of highballs so they wouldn't have to wait. It was like old times. When the train started Jay rang for the porter.

"Who's the engineer on this train?" he demanded.

The porter shook his head.

"Tell him I'd like to drive the engine from Stamford on," said Jay. "Here's my card."

The porter took it doubtfully.

"You tell him," urged Jay. "Tell him I'll call the General Passenger Agent if he doesn't. It's Mr. Oliver."

The porter was still doubtful.

"Before you put Mr. Oliver in the engine will you send back a pair of medium sized blondes from Car Number 856?" Lou asked seriously. "Here's my card."

The porter, for another dollar, was willing to be amazed and after he left Lou and Jay laughed again. The dog looked anxiously from one to the other. It was funny thinking of Ebie's face when she saw the pony-sized puppy that Jay was bringing her.

"No kidding, how did Truesdale find Ebie?" Lou asked.

"He sold her a farm," said Jay. "It was easy. Then she got sick and was stuck there. Ebie's all right. Ebie doesn't give a damn where she is so long as I get there once in a while."

"Where's Flo?" asked Lou and then chuckled. "Or do you know?"

"Sure I know," said Jay. "When Whittleby got shaky so did Flo. Seemed to think it was my fault. Christ, nothing I could do. So she kept reminding me everything was in her name, God knows she had me there, and I'd better not count on her, so by the time Whittleby went under there were no surprises. She threw a fit and I walked out."

"Jesus, Jay, she's got everything sewed up," Lou exclaimed.

"That's the nice part," Jay chuckled. "She can't complain. She was so scared of being left out that she hung herself. Told me she'd been putting everything away in her own name for years. Her mother told her. Her mother says, on her wedding day, 'Looky, Flo, you're very happily married, but you must learn to put all the savings in your name against the day he runs out on you, the bastard.' Something like that. So she did. So I says, 'Okay, then you're all right,' and then I says, 'Could you loan me fifty thousand to get back on my feet?' and she says, 'You don't get any of my savings, don't kid yourself, they're mine' so I says, 'All right, then, I'm a bum, I'd only be using up your money' and I walked out. It's a wonderful thing, having a smart wife."

"You mean you're living with Ebie?"

"Sure, I'm living with Ebie," said Jay. "Ebie doesn't care whether we eat or not so long as I'm there. Those two play right into each other's hands."

Lou thought of Mary and of Mrs. Kameray and how they would never play into each other's hands. He was irritated at Jay for thinking that the answer to everything was just throwing the pot of gold to the injured party and walking out. All right with Flo, but what did you do with a wife like Mary? And what did you do when you didn't want to leave her, when she was the kind of wife you knew you wanted, the kind you should have, and you didn't know what to do about it?

"What'll you bet you're in the same old noose?" he said. Jay didn't get mad.

"Listen," he said. "A noose is what everybody goes for. Soon as they get out of one they look around. 'Where's my new noose,' they say, and nobody's happy till they got the new one, love, business, it's all the same; everybody's got to have the neck in the old noose, it's better than nothing. They call it a place to rest their neck. Everybody's got to have a place to rest their neck, so long as it's always out, anyway."

The dog knocked over two of the waiting highballs lined up on the the windowsill, so they rang again for the porter.

"How big is Danbury when we get there?" asked Lou.

"It's a hat town," said Jay. "They make hats."

"I don't give a damn what they make," said Lou, "I'm just getting information. How big is the place?"

"All right," said Jay. "It's about seven and three-quarters."

"I'm sorry, sir," said the porter, "but the conductor says you got to wire New York for permission to run the engine."

"Did you tell him it was Mr. Oliver?" asked Jay.

"Did you tell him he was with Mr. Donovan?" asked Lou.

"Are you the Lou Donovan that used to manage the Olympia Motion Picture Theatre in Rahway?" asked the porter.

He was. He was indeed. And the porter was the very same porter.

"How's Mrs. Donovan?" asked the porter. "She sure used to play the organ nice. I certainly enjoyed Mrs. Donovan playing that there organ. The only high class feature we had."

"That's right," said Lou, and suddenly it all came back, the old days in the afternoon, the run through of the film of the evening, Francie playing the organ to feel out what pieces to play, the colored porter pausing in his scrubbing to say how good it was, and Francie afterward in the beer place remembering that the porter had said he liked 'I Loved You Truly' particularly. And it made him feel very old to suddenly think of Francie with kindness, it made him feel old to want to remind her of those days, days she was always reminding him of, it was queer being in the other position. He thought, maybe that's all Francie wants, not to sleep with me, just to talk over the same things, on the other hand he never had wanted to even talk over the same memories before this very instant.

"You sure put that movie house on the map," said the porter fondly. "Don't you remember how you used to always be yelling out for William, Mr. Lou?"

"I certainly do," said Lou and slipped him a bill, feeling queer. It was the first and only time he had ever thought of any part of his past before Chicago as if it was a normal pleasant past, and a wave of surprise came over him that it hadn't been a bad past at all. He'd had fun there in little towns with Francie, they hadn't made a lot of dough, but when they did they enjoyed it. He couldn't, at this moment, figure out just when he stepped out of his past and became a different man, despising his past and everything connected with it, but he would remember this moment as the time he went back and looked at his past freely, and saw it was as good as anybody else's. Sure it was. Maybe it was in this present insecure period he was trying to catch on to anything that was solid, and if your past wasn't solid, what was? Maybe that was all it was, but suddenly he felt that it was nothing to be ashamed of, years of scramming in and out of boarding houses, bills half-paid, jobs not paid for, no, it was part of something. And there was old Francie, sticking by like mad. Now that he thought of it he'd never had anybody stick to him like that. When he got going good that was what threw him, it made him feel as if he *needed* someone sticking to him. Well. . . .

"Tell the conductor to go ahead with the same engineer," he said to the porter. "Act like nothing has happened."

Jay looked at him.

"So the fluzy was your wife," he said.

"Any objection?" said Lou.

Jay whistled.

"I'm just beginning to get you, pal," he said. "You're smarter than I thought. You know when I saw you going under for that Kameray phony I began thinking you were not so bright. I see now it was a gag to get Rosenbaum."

Lou lit a cigarete. The big dog came over and put his feet on Lou's lap. He had to laugh.

"I was going to give you a piece of advice," said Jay. "I

was going to tell you to stick to the gals at the Spinning Top or the hostesses there on Fifty-fourth Street. Same as you told me. The Kameray is a phoney. She even gets a per cent on the suit you just bought. She calls up the store every time you buy anything and gets her per cent. Ebie told me."

Lou drank the second drink from the end. The dog watched him anxiously.

"Ebie's a great girl," said Lou, sore.

"Ebie's crazy about you, too," said Jay, pleased. "I used to wonder if you pulled anything on me when I was away, but I guess I was too suspicious."

"I hope, I hope," said Lou.

That was the way to look at it. Everybody was phoney, it made it better that way. The unbearable ache at the things he kept hearing about Trina was nothing but growing pains. You had to be a phoney to get anywhere in this world. Trina had to step faster than some because she'd had it tougher, that was all. You had to feel sorry for somebody like that, somebody that had to keep playing a game every minute just to get along.

"William," Jay opened the door and yelled out, "bring me the funnies, will you, Mr. Donovan wants to see where Lil Abner is today."

Ebie's pup looked worriedly from one man to the other. It had a naturally woebegone face, its drooping whiskers adding to the funereal effect. Jay sprawled out on the seat and chuckled.

"Look at Handsome, will you? No kidding, Lou, did you ever see a dog with as much on his mind as old Handsome, here? Listen, Handsome, while you're on your feet, hand me that last drink over there, will you? Might as well train you while I got this time on my hands."

The porter came in with the papers which Jay decided to read aloud. Every time the porter came in Lou was reminded of some long forgotten remnant of his past. Come to think of it he and Francie had had a hell of a good time bumming around the country in those days. If anybody had any better time they hadn't known about it. Tiptoeing out of that rooming house in Albany at two A.M. wearing all the belongings they could get on since the installment people had taken the wardrobe trunk back that day anyway; having to take the car going north instead of the one going south because they were afraid to wait. Breakfasting in the next town, worn out and punch drunk from all night riding and no sleep, and reading the ad in the paper that landed them his best job, the management of a Newark hotel. Then the fire that wiped out that job, then the free rent somebody gave them way out in the Jersey wilds and Francie got a job in some roadhouse, and some guy, maybe it was the manager, kept trying to make her, and one night Lou was waiting for her out in the dump where they lived, miles from nowhere, and when she was late, he got jealous, imagine that, jealous over old Francie, yes, jealous as all get-out, and what does he do but start walking the ten miles to the roadhouse just to see if that guy is keeping her there, and all of a sudden he remembers some kid down the road with a bicycle and he steals it and rides to the roadhouse, pedalling away against a wind for an hour and a half, his calves hurt still just remembering it, and when he got there he saw Francie playing for a big crowd of customers and like a fool he'd forgotten it was the night of some firemen's banquet and the place was keeping open all night, and he felt like such a fool he didn't even let her know he was there, but turned around and wheeled back home. She was there when he got home, the boss' bus took all the help home, and she was worried sick not finding him, and they had a fight because he wouldn't tell her where he'd been, and by God he never did, either.

"William," Jay called the porter, "will you step up to the engine again and say Mr. Oliver will take over as soon as we pass South Norwalk?"

"William," said Lou," will you furbish up these glasses? There are four of us here."

"Sure is good to see you again, Mr. Lou," said William.

"I got held up here last fall in the hurricane," said Jay. "Train from Boston got stuck just ahead of Providence and by golly we sat there for hours. Ferry boat sailed right up past the window. A couple of old bags and I got out and hired a brokendown taxi to drive us to South Norwalk. Fifty bucks. Took all day, what with roads washed up, trees floating around."

"I was in the Biltmore in Providence afterward," said Lou. "They showed me where the water came up in the Falstaff Room there."

The porter brought the fresh supply of drinks and lined them up on the windowsill. The dog immediately knocked one over, and this set Jay off into roars of laughter.

"Look at that face, Lou. Won't Ebie die when she sees him? Looks like my old man, I mean that. By God the old man used to come home from the road on four legs, too, just the same as Handsome here. Used to hear him coming up the steps on his hands and knees, fried to the gills, and the old lady right behind him giving it to him. 'So that's what you do with your expense account? So that's where the money goes? So that's how you wear out your new clothes!' and 'Where'd you get that carnation in your buttonhole, you old bastard?" I used to lie in bed, scared stiff, sorry for the old boy, you know. I was just a kid."

"My old man was in insurance," said Lou. "We used to move every spring. Akron, Erie, Buffalo, Evansville, Lansing—big houses, little houses, boarding houses, mansions—we never knew how we'd land."

Lou looked at his watch. It was four o'clock.

"Say, what am I doing on this train?" he wanted to know. "I had a date with Florabella an hour ago. Where we going?"

"Take it easy, Lou," Jay soothed him, "you got to relax, now, I mean that. We're just running out to say hello to Ebie. You like Ebie. Ebie likes you. Then there's Handsome. I couldn't very well take an animal that size out there alone, could I?"

"Why me?" Lou asked. "Why didn't you get Frank Buck?"

Jay yawned and pulled a newspaper over his face.

"Do me a favor, Handsome," he instructed the dog, with a weary sigh, "entertain Donovan while I catch a nap."

"How'm I going to get back?" Lou asked. "I can't take time out like this with things the way they are."

"Relax, Lou, for Christ's sake. You got nothing to worry about but money and that'll be gone in no time. Relax, old man."

Resigned, Lou stretched out on his seat. He pulled the funnies over his eyes, and the old days, the old hard luck days came dancing past like an old flicker, and for some reason they didn't seem bad at all, they seemed real, even fun, the panics and the triumphs seemed realer now than anything else, he couldn't understand why that was unless it was age, with all its sentimental fog, creeping up on him,

Or maybe it was just his brain trying to keep from thinking about Trina and Rosenbaum and Mary and the kid back in Chicago, and a winter's work gone to pieces. Maybe that was it. Anyway, the whirring of the wheels was soothing. The dog, Handsome, looked anxiously from one paper-covered face to the other, then back to the remaining high-balls poised on the window-sill and moaned lugubriously.

XXI

EBIE was in her studio over the garage, having such breakfast as Buck Kinley, her colored handy man, was in the mood to serve. There was only warmed-over biscuits, bacon and coffee, so Ebie judged that neither Buck nor his wife Minelda was feeling very well this morning after their night in town.

"Where's the cream?" she asked, not caring much.

"Minelda used it up this mawning," Buck said, yawning. "She say she jes' felt like drinkin' some cream this mawning."

Nothing to be done about that. Minelda was boss of this place. If something didn't suit Minelda she was likely to take Buck and march right back to Asheville, leaving Ebie all alone on this godforsaken farm. Serve her right, too. You ought to be satisfied to let little-gray-home-down-by-the-old-millstream-and-so-on be a tenor solo, your own fault if you bought the property. Your own fault, too, if you were fool enough to try to live in it and prove something or other about yourself that didn't matter to anyone but you, and besides you got sick proving it. She couldn't complain, really, about the getting sick part, because that was where Jay had suddenly showed up as the big protector. You'd think that finding her in bed with pneumonia was all he'd ever been waiting for. Now she was well and sick of the place, but it was Jay's dream home, now, and she had to stay and be part of the song, me-and-you-in-the-little-home-down-by-the-old-millstream. That was what she always wanted, all right, then, what was she kicking about?

"Mis' Vane, where'd you put that gin?" Buck asked.

"Buck, you're not going to have gin before breakfast?" Ebie protested.

"Yessum," said Buck, "that's what I'm gonna have. Where is it?"

Ebie, resigned, motioned to the cupboard beside the stove and Buck hastened to help himself. He poured out a tumblerful and started downstairs with it.

"I better take some to Minelda, she don't feel so hot," he explained. "The way she's feelin' this mawning she's ready to pick up and go. Say she's got on her travellin' shoes, heels afore and heels behind."

"What's the trouble now?" Ebie asked.

"Minelda's settin' to retire," Buck said, "She say she's gonna get outa the washin' and ironin' racket."

"Better hustle over with that gin," Ebie advised.

After he went she sat by the stove with her coffee, her back to the work-in-progress on the easel, said work being a "Haunted House" item that after three weeks fussing still looked like an ad for a new residental section, just as the "Old White Church" canvas in the corner looked like a bride's silverware ad, and the "Old Village Character" portrait would be well set-off by a caption "What This Fellow Needs is a Knox Hat." They didn't look so much worse than anyone's else, if she weren't so darned realistic she could believe they were even better than average. That was what you needed to be a genuine artist, vanity, and vanity on a terrific scale. You could talk all you wanted about the virtues of stick-to-it-iveness, faith-in-yourself, but nobody but an egotistical dumb-bell would have such blind faith in himself that he'd stick to it for years, not noticing he was no better than anybody else. Well, she was good in her own line. She could get an odd job now and then if she went back to town. Rosenbaum had called her on a couple. But Jay liked her better out here, waiting for him to show up. He had called her up last night from some tavern around town, she couldn't make out where, and she didn't ask or demand that he come right out, because you can't do that when you're trying to show how much more understanding you are than the other woman. You're on a spot, there. It's no wonder a man takes advantage of it. On the other hand, Jay wasn't required to understand or forgive anything. He'd walked out on a wife for her sake, so now he had permanent privileges to do as he liked and be forgiven.

"Never mind where I am," he kidded her over the phone, "the point is, where are you?" So he was on a bender. All right, then, he was on a bender. "I want you to tell me and tell me right, what the hell are you doing?"

"I'm listening to the radio, darling," Ebie said. "I've listened to Fibber and Molly and I'm almost ready for Raymond Gram Swing. Any objections?"

"I get it, you're in no condition to see Lou and me, then," Jay said. She could tell he must have spent the day on this one, and she could hear dance music behind him so he was still having fun. If Lou was with him they had some girls, too, those two never wasted their time running around alone. Jay would tell her all about it, they would laugh together about it later, and he would say how well she understood him. Well, she had to. "Sure, I run around," he'd tell her, "it's my nature, but you know you're the one I always come back to, you're the one I have to have, you understand that, Ebie."

"I know, darling," she would say.

The trouble was she had too much time to think out here in the country, waiting for him to pop in and out. It was a little scary getting your heart's desire after getting used to a life of just wishing for it. Here was Jay, all set to marry her as soon as he got his divorce, and also all set for her to forgive him legally the rest of his life. Any fool could see that was no improvement over their old situation, so far as she was concerned. She'd just have to sit home waiting to hear his confessions and forgive him. That was the trap she had been begging for. That was all everybody fought for, worked for, demanded as their right—traps. There was Lou Donovan, getting along fine, free, arrogant, sitting pretty, when he notices he has no trap so he hunts around for a super-duper-trap, little Trina Kameray. And here was she, Ebie, smart girl, for ten years chasing after a man who was pure poison to her career, to any career, made her business success seem silly because *he* was all she wanted, made this whim of hers for a farm a permanent cage for herself because it suddenly struck *him* just right. Talk about learning through your own mistakes, all you ever learned was, "This thing I'm after, this thing I'm going to do is a mistake and I'll always regret it, but that isn't going to stop me now." That was the value of experience. Experience told you not to lose your temper when the man you'd been wanting for ten years called up for the third time long after midnight and cordially invited you to hop in a car and bring Fibber and Molly and Swing over to Billy's Back Room somewhere on the road between Danbury and Brewster. Experience told you that was where the other woman lost out, nagging him to death, accusing, raising Cain, so it was up to you to be sweet, so what do you do? You lose your temper.

249

"But I tell you we can't leave now, Ebie," Jay patiently explained. "Listen, honey, will you just keep your trousers on while I explain? I'm in a game, I tell you, I just got a dream hand, I can't leave. I——"

So she hung up. Sweet, that was what she was. Now she was sorry, because there it was, she'd rather have Jay driving her crazy the rest of her life, than anything else. She put on the sweater hanging on the hook under the eaves and went downstairs, through the dark garage into the bright April sun. There was the old red barn where her mother was always storing her auction treasures, there was the elegant chicken house, the only modern, well-heated, well-roofed building on the place, now made available to Buck and Minelda by the fortuitous demise of the last chicken. Ebie crossed the road and opened the little white gate to the house proper, a jolly enough little house except that the roof leaked and it was cold as Greenland in every room but the kitchen. Minelda was in the kitchen, large, black and bossy, whipping up a cake, and plainly benefitted by the potion Buck had brought her.

"Mr. Oliver coming out today, Miss Vane?" she asked. "I thought he was bringing you a dawg this week."

Ebie was just explaining that Mr. Oliver must have forgotten about the dog when there was a loud honk-honking out in front from a yellow taxicab, an unfamiliar sight on these deserted roads. Ebie went out, with Buck running behind her, and saw a large gray doleful face peering out the window. It was Handsome, unhappy beneath a pink paper hat. The driver leaned out to ask if this was Miss Vane.

"The gentlemen kept me waiting all night there and then

they thought the dog had better come home," he explained. "Get out, there, Handsome."

It was such an unhappy, dignified beast, that Ebie began to laugh, as she patted him. It was plain to see that being sent home from a bar at this hour in the morning was a mortifying experience for him. A Scottie was what she'd asked for.

"Would you mind telling me what happened to the gentlemen?" she inquired.

The driver was willing to tell anything he knew. The two gentlemen had asked him to summon two other cabs, one to take one of the gentlemen out here later on presumably, the other to drive the other gentleman to New York. Personally he had no idea when they were leaving Bill's Back Room, but maybe they had started right after he left.

"Tell Minelda to feed him, will you, Buck?" Ebie ordered.

She was sick with disappointment. That was the way it would be, she'd be stuck out here waiting for him, and he'd be some place else having a good time, forgetting to let her know, just being sure that anything was all right with old Ebie. She'd just like to show him. She thought she had when she came out here but it hadn't worked out that way. It would be just like him to go back to New York with Lou, without even coming out to the farm. She ought to be braced for anything after all these years. Well, she had her work. She'd just put him out of her mind, forget about him till he walked in, paint like mad, bad or good, and just show that women could forget the same as men. She started back to the studio, while Handsome loped into the kitchen with Buck. At the bottom of the studio stairs she turned and came back. She looked down the road after the vanishing taxi, and after a moment's hesitation started walking rapidly in that direction. If Jay *had* started—and the taxi man said he might have—he'd come this way. She'd walk along to meet him and—if he *did* come, if he *hadn't* gone on to New York with Lou, she could ride back with him.

That was the kind of sap she was.

XXII

MR. LOWRY paused on the way to the bar to cast a furtive look of admiration at himself in the mirror, observing once again how exquisitely his beige shirt set off the rich chestnut waves of his toupée. Two young ladies, emerging from the elevator, bowed to him with what he felt was more than their customary warmth and he thought that next time he saw them having a drink in the bar it would do no harm, as manager, to suggest their having a drink on the house. He smiled gently picturing their astonished, happy faces, their grateful cries of joy, and he was mentally offering them a second round and what-about-dashing down to Barney's for a third (the dark one decided to go home here and he was left with the red-haired one, who made no bones about the terrific physical pull he had for her) when he actually did get to the bar and had to readjust to the somewhat drab reality of old Mrs. Vane.

"Well, well, my dear child," he said in the fatherly tone he used with the old ladies, "you're looking fifteen years younger today."

Mrs. Vane, who was going over some pink slips at the bar, and lecturing Albert, the bartender, on the outrageous indifference of America to the poetry of Emily Dickinson, looked sharply at Mr. Lowry through her lorgnette.

"Nonsense," she stated, "that toupée seems to have gone to your head, Mr. Lowry. Here's a message from Four A.

Says the butterfly sofa I brought her from Pittsfield was filled with baby mice. Ridiculous on the face of it."

"Must have been a mother mouse there somewhere," agreed Albert.

"Sit down, Mr. Lowry," commanded Mrs. Vane. "I was just telling Albert that Emily Dickinson used to carry a little scrap of poem in her apron pocket for days, days, mind you."

"Absent-minded, I guess," Albert said understandingly, and swiped up the bar before placing Mrs. Vane's brandy before her.

Mrs. Vane leafed over her pink telephone slips, studied them through her lorgnette, finally straightened them out fondly and with a deep sigh of responsibility tucked them away in a special corner of her large plaid handbag. Since the maw of the bag revealed a delirious tangle of goggles, cough-drops, aspirin, bank-books, post-cards, timetables, road-maps, memorandum pads, and spirits of ammonia, the careful consideration Mrs. Vane gave to the correct filing of her telephone slip seemed, even to the amiable Albert, a perfectly unreasonable waste of time.

"How's the antique business?" inquired Mr. Lowry, now studying his image in the mirror behind the bar. "Our little manicurist tells me you're branching out wonderfully."

Mrs. Vane nodded with a preoccupied air, then fixed the eagle eye intently on Mr. Lowry.

"Mr. Lowry," she asked. "How would you like a gun?"

Mr. Lowry blinked, and stammered that it was not his heart's desire that moment, but——

"We have a beautiful piece," she interrupted, "a Revolutionary musket that was used by General Washington. The thing for you to do is to put it on the wall in the lobby, with a photograph of Washington."

"Ah, yes," said Mr. Lowry, looking vague, "That might be a good suggestion. Still——"

"Listen to this, Albert," said Mrs. Vane, and held a small volume close to her nose, "this is the stanza I was telling you about yesterday——"

Albert, drawing a beer for the glum man in the derby at the end of the bar, hastily delivered same and leaned on his elbows respectfully, but Mr. Lowry escaped to the doorway, where suddenly a smile of visible ecstasy came over his face. He opened the door and held it open with something approaching a salaam, while a sharp draft whizzed in and enlivened the customers at the bar, indeed obliging Mrs. Vane's camphorated velvet drapes to flutter about her shoulders. The cause of Mr. Lowry's pleasure was soon evident. A shining new station wagon with a slight dusting of snow on the roof to testify to its voyaging had stopped in front of the Ellery, and from this emerged a middle-aged figure in checked brown trousers and swaggering polo coat, brief-case in hand. He was about to pull another bit of luggage from the car, but Mr. Lowry anticipated this by snapping his fingers at the venerable porter now delivering a fresh pink slip to Mrs. Vane.

"Get that luggage, there, boy," ordered Mr. Lowry, and then called out the door, "The boy will take it in, don't trouble about it, Mr. Truesdale."

Mr. Truesdale nodded briefly, acknowledging this, and came in the bar pulling off great woolen mittens so busily he ignored the manager's outstretched hand.

"Howja do, Lowry," he murmured, glancing around the bar.

"Well, well, well, Mr. Truesdale," boomed Lowry, beaming. "Hope your trip was successful."

"Get that front suite for me, Lowry?" Truesdale demanded. "I'm too exhausted to put up with that noisy hole you gave me last month."

"Everything's arranged, Mr. Truesdale," said Lowry, happily. "We moved the Peppers out of the corner suite and it's yours. That back suite was a mistake, very regrettable, I had no idea those people in the next room were so undesirable."

"Hope you put 'em out," said Truesdale. "Can't have that sort of thing in here."

"Exactly," agreed Lowry, tiptoeing behind Truesdale to the bar. "I said to them, 'See here,' I said, 'Mr. Truesdale is one of our oldest and most valued guests. Anyone he complains of in this hotel must go,' so—they went. I said, 'The Prince George or the Seville are up the street or the Lafayette further down,' I said——"

Truesdale waved his hand, frowning.

"Never mind, never mind, Lowry," he said. "I have to talk to Mrs. Vane here, no time for horseplay."

Mrs. Vane tucked away her reading glass and book in her bag at sight of Truesdale.

"We'd better take the booth," she said significantly. "Did you look at the choir-pew?"

Truesdale nodded.

"Beautiful piece," he informed Mr. Lowry. "Victorian pew, you see. Found it in an old barn outside Pawtucket. Ideal piece for the bar here, as a matter of fact, unique doncha know, especially with the stained glass window."

"He wouldn't take the gun," Mrs. Vane accused.

"I have to consider," Mr. Lowry protested, "I'm only the manager."

Mr. Truesdale took out a pencil and envelope and scribbled something.

"I'll speak to one of the better places, if you like, Mrs. Vane," he said patronizingly. "Of coss, only a rally fust claws place would be interested in a choir-pew bar corner."

Mr. Lowry looked unhappily down at his nails. He was not comforted by the appearance of the two pretty girls in the bar-room who this time definitely gave him the eye.

"I'm sorry you don't consider the Ellery a first class hotel, Mr. Truesdale," he said. "We're not big, we're not the newest hotel in the world, but we try to keep up our own little standard."

"I dassay, I dassay," impatiently retorted Truesdale. "Come, Mrs. Vane, let's take the booth where we won't be annoyed."

Mr. Lowry hastened ahead to the corner booth and flicked his handkerchief over the table, lifted the ashtray and set it down again, stepped aside with a bow after these preparations to allow the seating of the couple. Mr. Truesdale looked over the manager, frowning. The manager smiled, waiting for the comment, and finally ventured it himself.

"I know what you mean," he giggled, "It's the toupée. Do you notice it? It does take a little off the age, doesn't it?"

"Maybe so," conceded Truesdale, and added reminiscently to Mrs. Vane, "I recall the same remark was made to me at one time by the late Lord Hawkins, personal friend, of coss, we'd been to India together, Tanganyka, too, for that matter, great hunter, of coss, but bald as an owl. 'Truesdale,' he said, 'do you think a toupée of some sort would make me look a bit younger?' and I said, 'Hawkins, does a baby need a toupée to look younger?' "

"Ha, ha," guffawed Mr. Lowry. "That's good, that's damn good. Ha ha ha!"

He went away, wiping tears of laughter from his eyes, and was still shaking his head at the irresponsible wit of Mr. Truesdale as he passed the two young ladies smiling at him from the bar. He was not too overcome to note their eager eyes and reflected that if they thought their youth and looks entitled them to any extra favors from the manager they had another guess coming. If he looked as good as that to them he must look good enough to get younger and prettier women than they, by Gad, no use fussing around your own territory, getting into trouble, getting the other guests talking. In the hotel lobby, behind the desk, he adjusted his face into its normal gravity, picked up some letters for Mr. Truesdale in the "To Be Held" compartment of the mailbox, weighed them thoughtfully, and muttered, "The bastard! Wouldn't you know a little pipsqueak like that would come out on top while hardworking people like me are always in the hole?"

The ancient bellboy shuffled up to the desk.

"Now, what?" snapped Mr. Lowry.

"Everybody keeps asking me when the new management starts," apologetically explained the fellow. "They keeps sending me down to find out. I don't know what to tell them."

"Everything will go on as usual," said Mr. Lowry with restrained annoyance. "The raise in rates is effective next week. Guests will be notified of further changes as they take place."

"Some of them wants to know if the rates will go down after the World's Fair closes," the fellow went on inquiringly.

"How do I know?" barked Mr. Lowry. "Everything possible will be done to keep our standard the same as always, even if we have to double our prices to accomplish this. Everything!"

The sale of the Ellery Hotel had been a shock to Mr. Lowry, but nothing like the shock it had been to discover that Mr. Vernon Truesdale had been the guiding spirit in this transaction. In pointing out the possibilities of the Hotel Ellery to Lou Donovan as a quick profit-maker, Mr. Truesdale had noted the convenience of the hotel to World's Fair bus and subway facilities, the cheapness with which the place was run, and the ease with which a Guest Shopping Service could modestly capitalize on the needs of guests, even to World's Fair escort facilities. Mr. Donovan had, with no trouble at all, persuaded Mr. Grahame, head of the midwestern hotel chain, that this modest little New York hotel could be utilized as an adjunct to his more elaborate western establishments, be exploited, as a club, for the New York use of all of these western hotel customers. Vernon Truesdale was now Mr. Grahame's direct representative at the Ellery Hotel (through the Louis Donovan Service) and it was only a matter of days before he recommended that Mr. Lowry be thrown out on his ear as too snobbishly eastern and—as he expressed it in his last report to the Chicago office— "a genuine Midwestern type of man be placed in charge here with a staff of same types, in order to inspire feeling of homeyness and trust."

Mr. Truesdale, thinking of this surprise in store for Mr. Lowry, permitted himself a slight wry smile as he seated himself in the corner booth opposite Mrs. Vane. Mrs. Vane, with an air of tremendous importance, adjusted her flowing drapes, recaptured from the floor the decayed morsel of imitation leopard which she wore as ornament more than protection against drafts, and after a sharp glance around for possible spies, leaned toward Mr. Truesdale and hissed, "Must have some advice, that's why I sent word to you. It's about my property."

"My advice is to sell it," said Mr. Truesdale with conviction. "Run down neighborhood, repairs required, money in the bank a much better proposition right now, my dear woman."

Mrs. Vane's eyes glistened with approval at this advice which fortunately coincided with the action she had just taken. She opened her bag, a dreamy expression playing about her otherwise ferocious old face, and produced a folded paper which she put in front of Mr. Truesdale. She looked around cautiously again and then spoke in the reverent, loving murmur with which young mothers speak of their new-born and old women speak of money.

"The money's already in the bank," she confided. "Plus the deed stock and collateral. What do you think of Eastman Kodak as my next buy?"

It is amazing how those three little words, "money in bank" can bring the dewy sparkle of first love to old ladies' eyes. Little voices crying "grandma" do not tug at the old heart-strings as do those sweet words "collateral," "stocks and bonds," "piece of property" and dearest of all "money in the bank," and no one who has seen a woman over sixty dress up to whisper these soft words to her banker or broker can doubt that woman's final love must be negotiable. Mrs.

Vane, having passed through her affairs with woman suffrage, poetry, social work and current events, had arrived at the usual triangle, her passion for food and her true love for the Guarantee Trust. It did not matter how small the sums were that passed through her hands, the point was that sums were passing, the little things piled up in the cunningest way imaginable, and what could be more heartwarming than talking about them in rapt murmurs over a glass of brandy? Mrs. Vane had flirted with "property" and "profits" for years without ever being sure whether she was ahead or behind, the main thing was the sense of power, but in the last winter her resolute forays into the old barns and chickenhouses of the Eastern seaboard had unearthed unexpected little profits. Tenants in her "property" were bullied into buying these treasures, and if these deals were merely spasmodic adventures there was a healthy honest satisfaction in getting paid even a modest sum for something quite worthless. It had thoroughly revitalized Mrs. Vane, and while her literary prejudices were as vigorous as ever she was not blind to the even fresher thrills Mr. Truesdale had brought into her life in assisting her "antique" business. Mr. Truesdale had sold Ebie the house in Connecticut which had set off Mrs. Vane, he had tipped her on how to get the customer first before the object, if possible. Mr. Truesdale would long since have wriggled out of Mrs. Vane's clutches except for an exaggerated conception of the old lady's finances, and a pride in her resorting to him for final judgments on matters her bank and broker had already advised her. It was astounding to Mr. Truesdale to find his authoritative words to Mrs. Vane often turn out perfectly sound, and thinking of the profit some word of his had brought her he would mutter to himself, "Well, I'll be damned, what do you know? It really worked, by Gad, it really did. Well, I'll be damned."

"Have you consulted your daughter?" he now remembered to ask.

Mrs. Vane looked pained.

"Vernon, you know perfectly well I never consult any one but you. Ebie doesn't have a brain in her head, and besides I never see her."

"She's still on the farm, of coss," Mr. Truesdale said tentatively.

"I haven't the faintest idea," said Mrs. Vane with candid indifference. "Very likely so. Ebie's just like her father, no spirit of adventure at all. Wanted me to stay out there in that godforsaken place. Ridiculous. I have to be in touch with affairs. Let the young people stay out in the country and rot their brains, if that's all they ask. Personally, a woman of my intelligence has to be right here in the center of things, looking after my affairs. You know that, Vernon."

"The art work," said Mr. Truesdale, "does she continue with it?"

The subject plainly bored Mrs. Vane for she tapped the table nervously, impatient to get back to her romance with property.

"Ebie's throwing herself away," she said. "She doesn't make a cent—just paints around the place. Then she cries. Absolutely ridiculous. I can't be around people crying, I told her. No go. I have my own life to live."

"I understand she was sick quite a while," ventured Mr. Truesdale.

"Is that so?" Mrs. Vane rattled the paper in front of him.

"See if that sounds legal to you, Vernon. I don't trust any one but you."

"Hmm, let's see," Mr. Truesdale stroked his chin. "Hmmm. Yes. Hmm. I see."

He was about ready to make a stab in the dark, having no knowledge of deeds or mortgages, and okay the paper, when he was relieved to be called to the telephone by the bellboy. It was a call from Lou Donovan, asking if he could locate Mrs. Kameray for him, who should be at the office that afternoon. Mr. Truesdale had not been keeping his eyes and ears open for fifty years for nothing and he could have given a fairly sound guess on Mrs. Kameray's whereabouts, if not the exact place at least the company in which she could be found most any time she was not with Mr. Donovan; it seemed more professional, however, to merely accept the duty and say nothing. It was a good way to clear himself of an evening listening to Mrs. Vane so he went back to the bar with a lighter heart. She was frowning over her volume of Emily Dickinson when he got back with his excuses.

"I'm sorry you have to go, Vernon," she said. "You're the only intelligent person I know, the only person I can discuss poetry with."

XXIII

"Do you want me to call the house?" Miss Frye asked.

She stood in the door of the office bar, looking at him curiously. Her hat was on, ready to go.

"I know, I heard you before," Lou muttered, just sitting there staring out the window at the summer sun glittering on the blue lake beyond. His bag was on the chromium-trimmed bar chair just he had left it, half-opened, the new dull rose shirt on top. He knew Miss Frye was giving him those funny looks just as she had ever since he came in, and it got on his nerves. You can't keep up a front every minute, and Frye ought to be smart enough by this time not to show surprise when things seemed a little unusual.

"I checked over the liquor supply last week," said Miss Frye, finally getting the idea that routine details of the business were all the boss cared to hear at this minute. "We're low on Ballantines and Black and White and I re-ordered. Short on brandy, too, but I didn't know what kind you wanted. What's that stuff on the end there?"

"Sloe gin," said Lou. "It's the old honkytonk dish."

"You'd know," said Miss Frye, and he grinned. That was a little more like it, she thought, but she still hated to leave him there without doing something for him.

"How many you got coming in?" she asked.

"There's two or three hundred of them over at the Blackstone," he said. "The Western hotel men. They're all looking for something for tonight and without wanting to

brag about my city I think, by God, they'll find it. So probably only a dozen or so will turn up here."

"I guess there's plenty for that many, then," she said.
"They couldn't have used up that six thousand dollars
worth of liquor here in just a year. Look, Mr. Donovan, do
you want me to say anything to Mrs. Donovan? Tell her
you're not back yet or something like that?"

Lou whirled around at her.

"Miss Frye, for God's sake what do you want to know?
I'm here. You got your salary. It's six o'clock. Why don't
you go home?"

Miss Frye's mouth opened.

"All right, all right," Lou shouted, "if you want to know,
I've already been home. I saw my wife. I saw my wife's
room, too, with some guy's fifty-cent necktie hanging up
over the dresser, and a bottle of ten-cent-store hair grease
in the bathroom, a lousy bottle of hair grease in my bathroom! Carnation Hair Oil! That was the kind of guy my
wife picked to put her to bed! A five- and ten-cent store
gigolo!"

"I know," Miss Frye murmured, "it was that Spaniard
she picked up the night she showed up at the Spinning Top!
It was awful."

"You know so much, what do you hang around asking
questions for?" Lou snarled. "I suppose you know all about
her showing up there that night, plastered, all alone, playing the drums with the orchestra, asking this lousy foreigner
to dance with her, taking him home——"

"Listen, Mr. Donovan, she wasn't herself, she was just
getting even," Miss Frye cried out, "honestly, Mr. Donovan, you can't blame a woman, when you never are home
any more and you do have somebody else——"

See p 185. Home with the Spaniard, not his wife.

"Shut up!"

Miss Frye shut up. Lou was ashamed.

"All right, I was a bastard, myself. All right. But when a man's wife, the woman he has a right to expect something from, maybe not faithfulness but at least good taste, breeding, for Christ's sake, when she takes on a phoney with a fifty-cent tie and Carnation Hair Oil—even the pajamas, mind you, were there—imitation black silk pajamas, this sheik, this phoney Valentino——"

"Maybe you left some imitation lace panties around her room yourself once," Miss Frye, nettled, rose to defend her sex. "I don't notice you men always picking your social equals for bed, either."

It was ridiculous taking it out on Miss Frye. Old Frye, the only woman he could ever really count on, so far as that went. She would do anything for him, he knew that. Loyal. Still, there was nothing like loyalty to get on a person's nerves. Funny, but there it was.

"Frankly, Miss Frye, if you want to know the truth, I think my wife is going nuts," Lou said, more calmly. "That's all I can figure out. Takes this guy out to the black and tan every night, flaunts him in front of my business friends——"

"I know," said Miss Frye, "I didn't want to tell you before. That's why the Harrods kept trying to find you. The idea is it's all your fault starting her off with your divorce talk."

"Oh, sure," said Lou. "Everything's my fault. Oh, sure."

"Well, if you wanted to get out, now's your chance," Miss Frye said hopefully. "At least everybody knows now you got a reason. Everybody's seen her tooting around town with that heel."

"Oh, sure, it's all simple as that," Lou said bitterly. "I can walk out and leave a wife that's going nuts, sure, that's easy. What kind of piker would that look like? How long do you think I would be in business when that little news got around?"

"Lots of women doing what she's doing," Miss Frye said. "They're not nuts, either."

Lou didn't answer. He wasn't going to tell about Mary taking her clothes off the minute he got in the house and imitating the Spinning Top hootch dancer, yelling out, "This is what you like, isn't it? This is why you always leave me. This is what you're crazy about, all right, give me time, I'll be the kind of woman you like. Why don't you kiss me? Make love to me, go on, show me how the other woman does, I'll learn—" Lou had backed out of the room, his blood congealing, he had run down the hall to get the baby's nurse. The nurse only looked at him with cold hostile eyes.

"Mrs. Donovan's perfectly all right. She drinks by herself now, that's all," said the nurse. "It's your fault, Mr. Donovan. I don't need to tell you that."

"Well, go look after her, anyway," Lou had ordered. "Call her aunt. Call a doctor."

"Mrs. Donovan doesn't need a doctor," the nurse said harshly. "I'll give her a sedative myself. A doctor can't do anything about a woman being so unhappy she don't know what she's doing."

Lou had quietly picked up his bag and driven back to town. No point in telling these things to Miss Frye. No point in even thinking about them. No point in remembering that cheap perfume smell, that lousy hair-oil—that sheik, that dime-a-dancer——

"I'll stay at the Stevens till things settle," he said to Miss Frye. "Stock up the cognac tomorrow. And don't say anything."

Jay Oliver stuck his head in the door.

"What—no dames?" he exclaimed. "I was told you'd ordered a fresh lot from the Spinning Top for six o'clock maneuvers."

"What are you doing in town?" Lou demanded. "You old son-of-a-gun, they told me you never gave us a tumble since you switched to the Eastern office."

It was fine seeing Jay again. You got so used to getting Jay out of hot water that you missed him more than anybody else when he wasn't around needing help.

Jay threw an arm over Lou's shoulder.

"I sneak in," he whispered in his ear, mysteriously. "I creep in in the middle of the night and creep out. But I heard the gang was coming in over here so I thought I'd drop around."

"Flo still raising Cain?" Lou asked.

Jay nodded sorrowfully.

"When I don't catch it from Flo I get it from Ebie," he confided. "I just choose which hell I want to take. I usually take Ebie's but I get Flo's long distance, then."

"Why don't you hang up?"

Jay looked grieved.

"Listen, can't I catch hell if I want to? Anyway, with Ebie I like it because then we make up. Make a note of that, will you, Miss Frye? You got to fight to make-up."

"Tell our friend here about Mrs. Oliver," Lou urged Miss Frye. "It's a panic."

"She calls up here all the time," Miss Frye obediently revealed. "She says 'You can just tell Lou Donovan I hope he's good and satisfied now that he's ruined a home.' "

"Can you beat it?" Lou exclaimed. "Can you beat that, no kidding? A woman spends a lifetime ruining her own home and then blames it on somebody else. Me. Old Lou Donovan."

"She blames everything on you, Mr. Donovan," Miss Frye giggled. "You're the boy that taught Mr. Oliver to drink, you forced his first drop down his throat, you're the one that made him gamble and chase skirts and be a bum."

"That's right," Lou admitted. "I remember the trouble I had teaching Jay to like women. We had to tie him, he was that wild, but by God, we drove the lesson home."

"I'll leave you to give him another lesson," said Miss Frye. "I'll leave the door open for those little tramps."

"Tessie and Marie and Bobby tramps?" Lou reproached her indignantly. "Hell, they all live with their mothers."

"Then I'll leave it wide open," said Miss Frye, "in case they bring the mothers."

After she went Jay pulled a chair up beside Lou.

"What burns Flo up is that she can't get me back to give me hell to my face," he explained. "That's all a wife wants a guy to come back for. Either that or she wants to remind him all the rest of his life of how she forgave him that time. Flo's got everything sewed up in her name and it makes her boil that Ebie doesn't give a whoop. It makes her sore that she can't say the other woman is after my money."

"She got me on the phone once," Lou said. "She says, 'If you happen to see that so-and-so husband of mine you can just tell him I'm suing for plenty alimony, and what's more I'm taking a trip to Hawaii after I leave Reno. You can just tell him I'm the one that's got the pocketbook, and don't he wish he could take that woman of his some place.' " I said, 'O.K., Flo, if I see him I'll tell him.' "

"That mother of hers!" Jay shook his head in gloomy recollection. " 'That's right, Florence,' she'd say to Flo, 'go ahead and make him give it to you. If you don't get it, Number Two will.' Not much left for Number Two when those two harpies get through with a fellow. Not that Flo hasn't got some good qualities."

"Doesn't Ebie get sore at all you got to pay out to Flo?"

"Ebie don't care about anything but having me around," Jay said complacently. "She says, 'Go ahead, give her everything, we'll get along. I can always go back to work. Give her all the alimony she wants. All I want is you.' That's the way Ebie feels."

Give her time, Lou thought, give her five, ten years and then ask her how she feels about Number One getting all the money, while Number Two has to do her own housework. Give her time.

"I hope marrying Ebie won't spoil things," Jay meditated, frowning. "I kinda hate to get hooked again. This way suits me, but you know women."

Maybe, Lou granted.

"Jesus, Lou, you're too damn smart, that's what makes me mad," Jay said. "You chase but you never get caught. I thought for a while you were letting the Kameray dame play you against Rosenbaum but I guess you didn't let yourself get in as deep there as I thought."

"That's how much you know," Lou commented silently.

"I used to see that little devil putting the screws on you, flashing Rosenbaum's bracelet around, asking your advice in that little phoney shy way she had about going back to her husband or marrying some band leader since she couldn't get any extension on her passport, and I'd think, well, look at old Lou squirming around in the old trap, old Wise Guy Donovan right on the old hook." Jay smiled at the idea of his own mistake. "I might have known you'd get out of that one if any man could. Stringing her along, letting her give you a little more line, and then getting away. Old son of a gun, I wish I had your technic."

Technic. That must be what it was to lie awake nights wondering how soon you could see her again, wondering how to keep from killing the men you knew she slept with, wondering how to give her more than Rosenbaum could give her, Rosenbaum who was so crazy about her he'd give her anything but marriage, but that was the thing she wanted most, and if Lou could only manage it— Now his back was to the wall. How much longer he could mark time with her he didn't know, the game had been getting sharper and sharper lately. Then just as he was giving in, this thing about Mary throws everything out. He couldn't tell that to Trina. Trina had had enough excuses. You couldn't blame Trina.

"I don't know whether it's brains or just fool luck that you never run into trouble," Jay sighed. "I sure envy you, though, old boy."

"I'll change spots with you any day you say," Lou offered.

There was the sound of voices in the adjoining office. It was no treat, in his present mood, for Lou to recognize old man Grahame coming in, and in a condition that his great friend Judge Harrod would not approve. The old boy was tacking in the wind like an old sailboat and a smile of vast good will illuminated his moon face. It was the first time he'd ever done Lou the honor of a social call, but it took more than that to cheer up Lou this day. Pritchard was with him and to add the last touch to a fine day who should be hanging on his arm but old Francie, all dressed up in white with a big straw hat that gave her more than she was entitled to in the way of looks.

"I brought my friend," Pritchard said. "This is Mrs. Thompson, Lou. Have you met?"

"Oh, sure," Lou said. Francie kept looking at him warily as if she thought he was going to bawl her out for coming along, but that was all right. She hadn't bothered him since the night at the Spinning Top months ago, and even though Mary had found out about the first marriage it wasn't Francie but Flo that had told her. You had to be fair, even if it didn't get you anywhere.

"How long do we wait for a drink in this joint?" Jay complained. He got behind the bar with Lou and they fixed up a round. Some more of the men came in and Lou was busy filling glasses. Keep busy, that was the trick, keep doing something, if it was only drinking, till the old brain quieted down. Noise was good, too, noise was wonderful, and there was so much noise in the place suddenly that Lou didn't hear Francie call him, just saw the hundred dollar bill she slid across the bar to him.

"That's the lucky hundred, Lou," she said. "It brought us luck. Frank never had such a run of luck. He's in Saratoga now, waiting for the track to open there. He told me to give you this and gee, Lou, he's so grateful."

"Ah, keep it, Francie," Lou said, but she shook her head and pushed it toward him. If it made her feel better, okay. Nothing could make him feel better, one way or the other.

"I understand you been doing a lot of running around, Francie," he said, in an undertone. "What's the idea? You got a good guy now, why don't you stick to him? You liked him well enough to marry him."

Francie's eyes filled.

"You're the only person for me, Lou," she whispered. "You know that's the only reason I'm running around. Just so damned miserable that's all, ever since you left. It's always you, Lou. I just happen to stay crazy about you."

It was too bad. You can't go around making a fellow feel like hell for not loving you any more. It isn't right. It isn't fair. When Lou didn't say anything Francie dashed a handkerchief across her eyes and turned abruptly to old Grahame who was hanging on to the bar to keep from tipping over like a leaded inkstand.

"Can a fellow get a little drinkie here?" Grahame asked with a little difficulty, then he rather adventurely let go of the bar and thrust his hand across it at Lou. "Great seeing you, old man. Shake hands. Always glad to see you, Donovan, my boy."

Now wasn't that a break for you!

"Thanks," said Lou, "but Cassidy's the name."

ABOUT THE AUTHOR

Dawn Powell was born on November 28, 1897, in Mount Gilead, Ohio. When she was six her mother died, and Powell later wrote that she was "dispatched from one relative to another, from a year of farm life with this or that aunt to rougher life in the middle of little factory towns." She made her way to New York in 1918, and over the next forty years she wrote more than fifteen novels, two dozen short stories, three plays, and articles for such magazines as *Life, Harper's Bazaar, Mademoiselle* (where she was a book critic for a year), and *The New Yorker.* She married in 1920 and lived in Greenwich Village in New York City, where her literary group included Malcolm Cowley, Edmund Wilson, and occasionally Ernest Hemingway. She was the toast of bohemia's smart set and continued writing until her death in 1965. "True wit," Powell once wrote, "should break a wise man's heart. It should strike at the exact point of weakness and it should scar. It should rest on a pillar of truth and not on a gelatine base, and the truth is not so shameful it cannot be recorded."

The Wicked Pavilion and *The Golden Spur* are also available from Vintage Books.

Also by

Dawn Powell

The Golden Spur

Introduction by Gore Vidal

In *The Golden Spur,* the charming Midwestern protagonist
is romantically convinced of his illegitimacy and
comes to Greenwich Village in the 1950s in search of a
suitably famous father.

"Among the most amusing [novels] being written...quite on
the level with those of Anthony Powell, Evelyn Waugh and Muriel
Spark."—Edmund Wilson

The Wicked Pavilion

Introduction by Gore Vidal

The site of *The Wicked Pavilion* is a musty but oddly
fashionable café, where everybody who is anybody has always gone —
to get over failed love affairs and pursue new ones, to cadge money,
hatch plots, and puncture one another's reputations. The result is a
mercilessly funny, view of New York high — and low—life.

VINTAGE BOOKS